He'd joined the Undead because of his eternal love for her, and she didn't recognize him...

He sank back into the shadows, watching her confusion as she scanned the sidewalks for him. He stayed out of sight with an anguished purpose. He hadn't meant to reveal himself to her, not so soon, not so spontaneously without planning the result.

But he had, and he had his answer.

He passed his hand across his eyes, covering the tender torment that came with beholding her image. The sound that escaped him was half strangled sob, half moan of longing.

She didn't know him.

No recognition sparked her gaze. No awareness leapt at the sound of his name.

He meant nothing to her.

How could that be when she was the very breath in his body, the very reason for his heart to continue beating in its unnatural rhythm somewhere between heaven and hell?

The scent of her lingered. The perfume she wore had passed from her tender skin to his hand, and he inhaled deeply until intoxicated by fragrant memory. Violets. Her favorite. The delicate bouquet had teased him through centuries, quickening his hopes, his desires, his dreams.

She was here. And she would be his at last.

And he would never, ever let her go again.

Other "Midnight" Books by Nancy Gideon

Available from ImaJinn Books

Midnight Enchantment
Midnight Gamble
Midnight Redeemer
Midnight Shadows
Midnight Masquerade

From Pinnacle (Out of Print)

Midnight Kiss
Midnight Temptation
Midnight Surrender

Also available from ImaJinn Books

In the Woods
(Novelization of the horror movie In the Woods)

Midnight Crusader

***

Nancy Gideon

For Loralee—
Hope it keeps
you up all
night.

Nancy
Gideon

MIDNIGHT CRUSADER
Published by ImaJinn Books, a division of ImaJinn

Copyright ©2002 by Nancy Gideon
Printed and bound in the United States of America. All rights reserved. No part of this book may be reproduced in any form or by any means (electronic, mechanical, photocopying, recording, or otherwise) without prior written permission of both the copyright holder and the above publisher of this book, except by a reviewer, who may quote brief passages in a review. For information, address: ImaJinn Books, a division of ImaJinn, P.O. Box 162, Hickory Corners, MI 49060-0162; or call toll free 1-877-625-3592.

ISBN: 1-893896-87-0

10 9 8 7 6 5 4 3 2 1

PUBLISHER'S NOTE:
This book is a work of fiction. Names, characters, places and incidents are products of the author's imagination or are used fictitiously. Any resemblance to actual events or locales or persons, living or dead, is entirely coincidental.

Books are available at quantity discounts when used to promote products or services. For information please write to: Marketing Division, ImaJinn Books, P.O. Box 162, Hickory Corners, MI 49060-0162, or call toll free 1-877-625-3592.

Cover design by Patricia Lazarus

ImaJinn Books, a division of ImaJinn
P.O. Box 162, Hickory Corners, MI 49060-0162
Toll Free: 1-877-625-3592
http://www.imajinnbooks.com

Prologue

Jungles of Peru, two years ago

At last.

He'd almost given up hope. With the dawn chopping through the tangled jungle in its approach toward the ancient temple, he knew he only had moments before it would be too dangerous to remain.

And then he heard it, the soft snuffling sound of his scent being tested, tasted and weighed for its level of threat. Or potential.

He waited, wishing the daylight away for just a few more precious minutes, but there was only silence lying as heavy and as thick as the humidity upon the fetid air.

He had hoped this would be the night when promises would be kept.

"Damn."

Regret sank like the echo of his curse, without a ripple. There was always tomorrow night. After all, he had nothing but time, and his benefactor wasn't going anywhere.

"Do you have it?"

The words rasped against the stillness of the tomb, as unsettling as the dragging footsteps of the undead from an old B movie. He started. Not because the voice, with its gravelly timbre like the pulling of coffin nails, came from right behind him but because with all his newly returned superior senses, he had failed to detect the approach.

But urgency quickly overcame Quinton Alexander's fear.

"Yes, of course. Now, what about what you promised to give me?"

"Patience, my greedy friend. When you have waited centuries, what is a few more minutes?"

"For you perhaps, but I didn't choose to be shut in here by those who betrayed me." His bitterness and fury still simmered, cooking up the suitable revenge he'd seek once this bargain was fulfilled. He'd been outsmarted by his enemies. They'd found a way to make him mortal and had shut him away in this tomb, thinking to seal his fate. Wouldn't they be surprised to see him again. For he hadn't found death in the dank temple. He'd found renewal. And a new alliance, one so surprisingly powerful that even the most clever and capable of his nemeses wouldn't be able to defeat him. But with this new partnership came an annoying allegiance to the other being's agenda. He'd done his part. His obligations were now satisfied, and as soon as he received his reward, he could get on about his business under some new name, some new identity. And this time, he'd make them all sorry. He hadn't been a merciful man when he was alive a century before. His twisted mind would have provided a field day for modern psychoanalysis. Time had taught him a reluctant patience. He was willing to wait for what he wanted. But not forever.

"What do you know of betrayal?" came the harsh response to his whining. "Your own avarice brought you to this place."

Daring to be bolder with the knowledge he held still unspoken, he challenged, "And you were any different?

A taloned hand caught him by the throat, shutting off his insolent suggestion, lifting him off the tomb floor and drawing him close to the pant of stale breath.

"You know nothing of me. We are not alike. I did not come for riches. I came for knowledge, for power."

Forcing a swallow, the dangling man whimpered, "And doesn't one beget the other?"

A hoarse chuckle. "Yes, of course. What good does knowledge do me, or riches, if I cannot escape this prison?"

"I could open the door."

A regretful sigh. "No. What I am is held here by legend and by the curse of superstition. I can only be unleashed by the chosen. And I fear with your bungling, that chance has escaped me. I will never leave this prison of rock. Now I have only you through which to implement my plans. You will have to do. The first drink of you has awakened me to a higher level. I had almost forgotten over the years what it was like to think as a man, to speak as a man. For that, I suppose I should be grateful."

He didn't sound grateful. Feeling a nudge of panic, his

greedy visitor asked, "If you can't get out, then how is our bargain going to be fulfilled? You said you would give me riches in exchange for your freedom."

"And I will, impatient one. You will have all you desire. But first, tell me what you have learned."

Realizing there was no way to postpone the moment, he said, "She's in Las Vegas, as you requested. I made all the arrangements."

"You're sure it's she?"

"Yes." Restlessness edged his tone. Dawn was close, and he was no closer to his reward. "Who is this woman who's worth so much trouble to you and to me?"

"She is the past . . . and the future."

Growing tired of the word games, he grumbled, "But what good does it do for her to be there and you to be here?"

"Oh, I don't plan to remain here for long. At least, not all of me."

Quinton Alexander sighed in frustration. "Everything with you is a puzzle."

"I thought you liked puzzles."

"Ones I can eventually solve."

"Oh, believe me, you will figure it out soon. You are an important piece in this one. You are my link to this century. I could not do what I plan without the knowledge you possess. You are the doorway through which I will pass."

"Yeah, right," Quinn mumbled, not even pretending to understand or to care. "Now, what about your promise?"

"Oh, I always keep my promises. You will be wealthy beyond your wildest dreams. You will have power unlike anything you can imagine."

"I can imagine a lot, and I have very vivid dreams." He smiled, his eyes glittering with anticipation. "Give them to me."

"But there is a catch."

Cautiously, he took a step back. "Oh? What catch?"

"You will have to enjoy them through me. Or rather, I will enjoy them within you."

And the beast sprang, delivering his promise with the slashing of claws and fangs.

One

Death, why must you elude me?
The wail of inward pain echoed through a mind still roiling with drink and despair.

Gabriel de Magnor wanted to die. His conscience demanded it. His broken heart begged for it. And he was doing his best to accommodate both.

He'd charged recklessly down the lists after that evasive goal throughout the week, hoping that a fateful blow might end his misery. Too much of a Christian to seek that longed for demise overtly, he sought it through carelessness and a disdain for his own safety. Refusing to meet his opponent's lance with even a meager attempt at defense, he was bruised but not yet broken. Not yet. But then the day was young, and the man he faced had much to prove.

Unlike Gabriel, Sir Evingrade hadn't gone to embrace danger and glory on a foreign field. No, he'd continued courtly pursuits and competed successfully and safely on this mock-battle ground. Mock heroism was all he could claim, while Gabriel earned accolades in blood and hardship. Defeating a recognized warrior would go far toward erasing the stain of cowardice from his name. Evingrade would give no quarter, even when he could plainly see that the young noble was too intoxicated to sit his saddle straight. Nor had Gabriel yet completely healed from the wound that should have but didn't end the tragedy of his existence. That wouldn't matter when weighed against a win.

And that's what Gabriel counted on as he spurred his big horse forward without securing his helmet or lowering its protective visor.

He felt no fear, only a wild exhilaration. There was salvation to be found in an honorable death. Not like the lingering shame of living with his failure to protect the one he'd loved.

Just one mercifully well-placed blow and all will be over.

He watched it approach—the end of his misery in the blunted tip of his challenger's lance. He smiled in welcome. *Let it come.*

But at the last moment, perhaps upon seeing the death wish in his opponents eyes, Sir Evingrade lowered his lance tip. Impact shattered through Gabriel's chest, and the world went spinning. The fall took forever from saddle to sand. He hit with a world-blacking force. Then waited, praying for it to be over.

Let me die. Let me die.

"Enough."

He heard the low, insistent voice above the ringing in his ears.

"No more, Gabriel. None will put you out of your suffering today."

Hoisted to his unsteady feet between his best friend Rollie and his anxious squire, Gabriel would have decried the unfairness of it, but the words wouldn't form over the swells of darkness engulfing him.

Perhaps not today, was his last coherent thought.

But there was always tomorrow.

***

"Is this what she would have wanted?"

Gabriel glanced up from his mug of bitter ale. Little emotion showing in his own, he met the concern in his friend's expression. Even though the question had him cringing inside.

"If she had not meant for me suffer, she would still be alive to chastise me herself."

He took another deep swallow, letting the brew curl dark and destructive within a belly that had held no food for…how many days? He'd lost track. The name of the day, whether day, or indeed night, it no longer mattered. Nothing mattered beyond putting an end to the pain howling and raging against his shattered heart. For what difference was the day or the time when he had nothing with which to fill it? Nothing to propel him toward the next morning or even the next hour with any degree of anticipation. The moon and the stars had stopped the moment he heard the news.

She was dead. And as soon as he could manage it, he would

join her.

How awful her fear, how tremendous her pain to have pressured her into making such a soul-damning gesture. How, at the end of her regrettably short life, she must have hated him to have wished such an agony of guilt upon him. Her unhappiness was over, gone the instant she hit jagged rock then icy water. But his. Oh, his went on and on, beating within the aching recesses of his mind where her memory yet taunted and tantalized with what would never be. Dear God, he'd loved her, wanted her, needed her. Still. Always. Hadn't she understood that? Hadn't that been enough to sustain her even when she feared the worst? His hand clutched reflexively about the token he wore at his neck. Its sentiment now lay as cold and unreachable as his beloved.

Hadn't she believed his promise that their lives would forever be entwined? Her lack of faith wounded as piercingly as the sword tip that had slipped between layers of supposedly impervious armor to cut him to the quick. Each had laid him out with a near-mortal injury. He'd recovered from the latter. But the first, he would never survive. He'd fallen on the field in the name of her honor and now had forever damned her in the name of his pride.

He glanced at his friend. Solid, steady Rolland watched him through anxious eyes, recognizing his sorrow yet unable to help heal it. Not the way the surgeons had hurriedly closed the wound in his shoulder. That ache would soon leave him, for his body was strong in defiance of his spirit, but the agony of loss would throb forever. Having never lost someone he loved, Rollie would never understand the sharp teeth of Gabriel's demon. His scholarly friend was blameless of the sin of self-importance. *Pride goeth before a fall.* How far must he fall before he reached a merciful end at the bottom of his well of grief? He took another long swallow, shuddering at its recriminating bite.

"Tell your fortune, sir?"

A withered hand seized his, turning it palm up. It wasn't the hideousness of the old woman's features or the punch of her overpowering stench that had him reeling back on his stool.

It was the strength with which she grasped his hand and the sudden shock of cold seeping right to bone. Alarm quickly became annoyance. He had no time for this childish folly. He wanted no interference in his self-destruction.

"Be gone, hag. I have no future beyond the next few nights, and I'll not waste my coin to see what they might hold."

He tried to shake her off, but as tenacious as a terrier, she refused to release him.

"You are mistaken, sir. I see years beyond imagining."

Aware now that the chill crept from palm to wrist to forearm, he began to pull more vigorously. "Unhand me, woman. I'll have none of your witchery."

She leaned nearer, bringing her unwashed stink and the feverish brightness of her stare uncomfortably close. "I see a lady."

Gabriel froze. His breathing trembled. "What lady?"

Rolland stood, his mild temperament now darkening with displeasure and disgust. "Be gone, crone, before I have you beaten."

Gabriel stayed his raised hand, though his attention never left the old woman. "What lady?"

"One you believe lost to you, but this be as false as your sorrow. She calls out to you for justice. What would you risk to answer that cry?"

He replied without hesitation.

"Anything."

"Then come with me, young sir, and we will hear what she has to say."

"Gabriel, 'tis just some rouse to lure you away and rob you blind," Rolland cautioned, but Gabriel would have none of it. Too drunk for restraint, too intoxicated even by the meagerest hint of hope to show due care, he flung off his friend's warning.

"Stay here if you like. I would not heed her wishes when she was alive, and I'll be doubly damned if I ignore them now."

"'Tis not Naomi."

He fixed his friend with an impassioned stare. "I do not know that, and until I do, I cannot ignore this last chance to set things right with her soul. And mine." He searched the other's gaze intently, needing to find understanding. Or at least, support. And Rolland Tearlach didn't disappoint him.

Rolland sighed and swallowed down the rest of his ale. "If you are intent upon this folly, I will watch your back. Lead on, crone."

Once they were outside the noisy tavern, the ancient hag moved through a maze of narrow streets with amazing quickness. The two knights hurried to keep her in sight. They dodged between the poor huddled against the weeping stone walls and the refuse thrown down from rooms above. Focused on the bent figure ahead, Gabriel paid no mind to their destination until Rolland gripped his elbow to once again advise care.

"Gabriel, she leads us on a dangerous hunt. We should break off lest we never find our way out of this rabbit warren."

Gabriel shook him off. "You go."

Uttering a curse, Rolland kept step with him.

They turned a sharp corner, and Gabriel drew up in dismay. "Where did she go?"

"Through there."

A faded, threadbare tapestry hung across a doorway. It swayed slightly, though there was no breeze. Impatiently, Gabriel pushed it aside. And the two of them entered a room steeped in a darkness so complete they couldn't see one another while yet standing shoulder to shoulder.

"What game be this?" Rollie growled to disguise his unease. His hand went to his sword.

Slowly, a light crept into that solid blackness, spreading outward from the room's center. The hag crouched before that light that sprang from no discernable source. Her eyes gleamed with the same strange iridescence. Suddenly, she appeared more sinister than pitiful.

"Come, Sir Knight. Sit by me and I will tell you what your heart needs to know."

Moving with a bit more hesitation, Gabriel crossed the rush-strewn floor and knelt across from the old woman. "Before I give you any coin, I want a sign that you speak for Naomi."

A rusty chuckle rattled up. "'Tis not your coin that interests me, lad. And as for proof...be this your lady?"

A trick of the unusual light. It had to be. For as he stared through its odd glow, the crone's features began to run together and reform...into the image of his lost love. He heard Rollie's cry. Gabriel gasped as well, too swamped with emotion to feel fear. The dank space suddenly filled with a crisp floral scent.

Violets.

"Naomi." Hope quivered in his tone, overcoming doubt and disbelief.

"Help me, Gabriel," said the illusion in Naomi's sweet voice. "My spirit knows no rest."

Thinking of her eternal being wandering in the world of the damned, Gabriel pleaded, "Tell me how I can help you find peace."

"Find me, Gabriel. Search me out. Hear my last confession, so I might know justice and sleep."

"Where are you, my love? Where can I find you? You have no grave upon which I might kneel." He swallowed down that awful truth. Her broken body had been taken by an angry sea. There had been nothing to bury, no form over which to mourn. That only deepened his anguish, a sorrow plunged into further darkness by the apparition's next words.

"My restless soul will drift forever unless you absolve it. If not in this lifetime, then in the next."

"I don't understand. Tell me more. What would you have me do?" Was there a means to escape his pain and atone for his sin?

But her image was fading. The scent of violets was all but gone.

"Naomi, where are you?"

"She waits, young knight," the old woman told him. The same lips once plumped for his kisses were again withered and seamed. "Have you the courage and the patience to pursue her?"

"Yes. Through this lifetime and through eternity. But how? I have the will but not the way."

The old hag leaned forward across the light that now seemed to pulse like a heartbeat. The tempo echoed within his head, a fierce, insistent cadence. Beckoning. Her gaze burned. "It will not be an easy quest. Your honor, your bravery, your devotion will be tested at every turn. You will see the life you knew become no more."

"I am not afraid." The only thing he feared was life without love in it.

"You should be. You will be."

"Gabriel, we should go."

He'd forgotten about Rolland and spared him no attention now. Rollie was always the soul of caution, the first to cry "Have a care!" Gabriel had never heeded that cry before. Perhaps he should have on this evening of strange enchantment and dangerous whisperings from beyond. But he plunged ahead without prudence.

"Tell me what I must do."

"Do? You need only survive, young sir. Survive to conquer the years, the centuries, however long it takes for you to seek out her tortured soul."

"However long it takes," Gabriel affirmed, not truly understanding the magnitude of his pledge.

"Then you will be transformed this very night so you might begin your search in an existence where time holds no meaning."

He never saw her physically move.

One instant, she was staring at him with an almost hypnotic intensity, distracting him from the fact that the three of them were no longer alone in the room. Shadows shifted from within the unnatural stillness to become figures looming just out of the light.

He heard Rolland's briefly uttered warning and the rasp of his sword. But Gabriel had no time to react with alarm or instinct. The crone was upon him, knocking him flat upon his back. His hands were gripped before they could find sword and dagger in his own defense. And then came the pain, swift and sharp, at his throat, at his wrists and elbows. He tried to cry out, but no sound of protest came neither to mouth nor eventually to mind.

So this was death, this slow, chill sinking into dark oblivion.

He surrendered to the sapping weakness of body even as a part of him clung to the strength of his resolve.

For Naomi.

He floated for a time, adrift in a daze of unreality where he saw dark shapes hunched over the form of his friend, feeding upon him like huge, greedy rats. Still no sense of horror or objection formed. It didn't matter than Rolland was probably dead, just as he was surely dying. All that mattered was…was…what?

Then he remembered. He forced himself to say the words as the crone who somehow seemed younger, sleeker and no longer gaunt, leaned back to wipe his blood from her chin.

"Tell me," he whispered in a breath that might be his last. "Tell me you did not steal my life with a lie."

She smiled, touching his cheek with a newly warmed hand. "Why would I lie, sweet boy? You and your young friend have just begun to live. And as I promised, you will see your love again."

And that was all that mattered.

That was what he needed to hear to sustain him through the centuries.

Two

Las Vegas, Nevada, Present Day

The roar rose, rushing at him like an ocean swell. When it hit, the force knocked the breath from him. He rode it aloft for one long suspenseful moment before the crest broke, dropping him hard to the packed sand.

Gabriel McGraw looked up from the flat of his back. His eyes managed to focus as his challenger rode past, tipping his lance in a mock salute. Turning his head away from the grit churned up by passing hooves, his gaze touched upon the surround of revelers. Many were on their feet, clapping, waving turkey legs and tankards, caught up in the spectacle of his abuse. Enjoying his fall. He was the villain, after all.

As he waited for his wind to return, he scanned the sea of tourists' faces, searching then finding the one he sought.

She sat alone, silent, still and pale. She didn't celebrate his defeat. Instead, she seemed stricken.

And the impossibility of seeing her stole away his breath more effectively than the fall.

"Going to lie there all night milking the applause?"

He glanced up at the knight who'd unhorsed him. The visor went up to reveal his friend's gloating features. Rolland Tearlach, Knight of the Realm, now Rollie Lackley, the Green Knight at the Excaliber Hotel and Casino, enjoyed his new role. Too much, sometimes.

Flushed with a combatant fervor and a renewal of the life he'd put on hold for centuries, Gabriel scrambled to his feet. His sword sang free of its scabbard. Though that time was long past, his blood surged with the same vigor and vitality of a young man just home from war, a young man besought with his vision of the future. For a moment, he was Gabriel de Magnor once again. And he had a woman to impress.

"Let's give them something to see, shall we?"

As Rolland dismounted to meet his challenge, the crowd shouted its approval in a bloodthirsty howl. Gabriel grinned.

Not much had changed over the centuries.

They had always been evenly matched, having been raised together as close as brothers and trained by the same fostering masters. As sparks sizzled from the friction of their broad blades, they were again that pair of young combatants filled with the need to establish manhood on this most private and primitive of proving grounds. Rolland's movements had always been pure art and precision, while Gabriel's were spiced with a touch of recklessness, often giving him the upper hand. That, and the fact that Rolland lacked the warrior's heart to go after the follow through. But in this scripted combat, it was fated for the Black Knight to lose, so Gabriel obligingly lowered his guard, taking a hard blow beneath his raised arm. He dropped to one knee and let a vicious cut catch him between shoulder and neck. A killing blow had the swing not been checked at the last moment. Still, the force of it rattled down his spine, numbing his arm and causing his sword to fall from a useless hand. Dramatically, he pitched face first onto the dusty ring while the onlookers cheered his defeat.

Just before the lights dimmed upon their portion of the show, he snatched a glimpse of her. With a flutter of the scarf at her neck, she slipped out of her seat and fled, head bowed as if in tears.

For Gabriel, time stopped.

Did she weep over his pretended death?

Even as every long-denied instinct urged him to race after her, he held himself still, knowing she would return. Patience. He would find out what he'd waited dozens of natural lifetimes to learn. Some night soon, he would discover the truth.

Was this woman who haunted the stands of the Excaliber wearing the features of his lost love somehow Naomi Beorhthilde?

***

"An elegant death. Pure beauty to behold."

Gabriel grinned at the compliment as he removed his dented helm, but it was Rolland who responded to the Red Knight's praise.

"He's made it his life's work losing gracefully to me."

The camaradic slap of Rolland's hand came down upon his shoulder, causing Gabriel's involuntary wince. Pushing back his mail coif, he unbuckled the chin strap of his arming-cap and eased it off, followed by his colorful surcoat. A huge discoloration blotched the area of his collarbone where Rolland's overzealous blow had hammered into him. Such an impact would have shattered a normal man. But nothing about Gabriel McGraw was normal.

"Ouch." Rolland pursed his lips at the sight of the bruising, but he didn't apologize. "You should keep your guard up."

"You should pull your swings."

"You whine like a girl. It's not like you won't recover."

"True enough. Still, I remember a time when you preferred the challenge of rhyming verse to the vigors of combat."

"Things change, Gabriel. Some do, anyway." And suddenly, the bold Sir Rolland was once again his brooding, intellectual friend who sought out books rather than battles. Then that ancient poet was gone, replaced by this new ultra-confident champion. "But I do enjoy seeing you on your back."

"Don't get used to it."

He easily forgave his comrade's over-eagerness. There were too few challenges in this modern world not to take advantage of the opportunity to inhale that age-old rush of victory. Even if it was for the benefit of paying customers. And though he might ache now, Rolland was right. Within hours no sign would remain of the crippling blow.

They put away their gear, exchanging jibes and laughter with the other members of the show. Though he'd been there less than two weeks, Gabriel was already included in the close-knit group of performers with Rollie as his patron. And it was almost like being part of a brotherhood, as if the chivalrous past was alive again.

As if they were truly alive again.

But once they left the atmosphere of the Excaliber behind, reality intruded. This was a new and different world, and Rolland was his only link to the past. They might stand among others and appear like them, but they were not the same. There was more truth to the roles they played in the arena than the one they adopted here in the midst of the living.

"Come out and walk the Strip with me tonight, Gabe. It will be like old times."

Old times best forgotten. Those times when they were adjusting to what they'd become. Savage, fierce times, when they felt like gods and basked in the hot blood of those they took unaware. Surprisingly, it was Rollie who adapted first and with the greatest aplomb. A part of Gabriel never embraced the fact that he was no longer human. He clung to the pretense as if it were his only claim to civility.

There was little civility in what they did to survive.

Which was probably why they had gone their separate ways, Gabriel to pursue the past and Rolland to chase the future. So Gabriel's reply to his friend's urging was predictable.

"I can't."

"You won't. We've had little time together since you came out here. I'd almost think you were avoiding me."

Gabriel's surprise registered in genuine dismay. "Never that." His voice lowered. "I'm not out here on a holiday."

"Then let me help you with your work."

"I can't, Rollie, it's—"

"It's undercover," his friend supplied. "Ah, yes. Your important human profession. Gabriel, why do you feel the need to be like them? You could be so much...more."

"It's personal."

"It's dangerous, Gabe. What if you're recognized for what you do...or for what you are? Have some regard for your safety. This is foolhardy to attempt on your own. Once, you trusted me to watch your back."

Gabriel surveyed the crowd of tourists with a practiced caution, seeming a part of them in a dazzlingly bright Hawaiian shirt, but a world apart. An unnatural world where he and Rolland were the predators and those who milled about them in blissful ignorance, the prey. He brushed aside his friend's observation with a laugh. "Now who whines like a girl?"

He placed a hand upon the other's shoulder, pressing hard. "You know there is no one I trust more. If I find myself in need of assistance, you will be the first I turn to. As always, my friend."

Placated by the strongly spoken sentiment, Rolland nodded then grumbled, "You used to be more fun."

"We used to consider tipping carts and breaking wind as amusements. Some things change for the better. Now, I must go."

"You act so nervous, one would think you're going to meet a woman."

The jest fell flat. Gabriel's response was wooden. "You know better."

"Gabe, it's been…a long time."

His smile was bittersweet. "Since when is time a concern of ours."

"Gabriel, life goes on. You're chasing the wind. You don't even know that it's Naomi."

"If you didn't think so, you wouldn't have called me here."

"I thought I saw the woman we once knew, but now I'm not sure. Gabe, Naomi died centuries ago. Only your stubbornness keeps her alive in your heart. If you truly believe this woman is your lost love, why haven't you confronted her? Is it because you fear she'll disappoint you?"

Gabriel had no answer. He couldn't deny his friend's claim. Yes, he was afraid. Afraid that the woman he'd traced to D.C. and now followed to Las Vegas was just a woman, not the incarnation he sought.

But if that was true, why did she look at the world through Naomi Beorhthilde's innocent eyes? Why was she in the audience night after night to watch the replaying of an ancient tableaux?

If she was not his Naomi, why did his long immobile heart beat so frantically when he was within sight of her?

He could explain none of those things to Rollie. The irony of their reversed roles—of him the poetic lover and Rolland the brusque purveyor of facts - made him smile a faint, sad smile.

Things had changed, just as his friend had changed. There was a new edge, a new boldness to Rolland Tearlach, now Rollie Lackley. After centuries, why had that change been such a bittersweet surprise? Time passed and nothing remained constant. Nothing except his love and his quest for the future denied him.

"Perhaps I made a mistake," Rollie was saying. "Perhaps encouraging you to cling to the past was wrong on my part. Gabriel, you need to move on. I have."

"If that's what you call it." He glanced over his shoulder at the mock castle facade and raised a pointed brow.

"What I mean is I'm not the same man I once was. All that changed for me in a fortune teller's hovel, and I took advantage of the situation to become more than I ever was before. But you, you are content to remain Gabriel de Magnor, knight and defender of the weak and pursuer of lost causes."

Though the summary stabbed with the quicksilver pain of an unexpected thrust, Gabriel refused to wince. Instead, he said softly, "You've become a cynic, my friend."

"And you're still a dreamer." Rolland sighed. "Always the dreamer. Why don't I give up on you?"

"Because you are my best friend. I'll see you tomorrow night."

Rolland watched him go, this best friend of centuries past, and he frowned to himself as he wondered what secrets were being kept from him.

***

She escaped the glare and noise of the arena upon trembling legs. The now-familiar flush of icy heat left her weak and reeling. She sagged against the supporting wall of the escalator, praying the sensation would pass. Before she could grasp at a saving calm, a garishly made up jester bobbed up close, intending to hawk his wares. She reared back, heart jack-hammering. Alarmed himself by her apparent fright and out of proportion response, the jester chose to abandon her as an unlikely sale and quickly moved on to another potential customer along the crowded Medieval mall.

What is wrong with me? If it upsets me so to be here, why can't I stay away?

"Are you all right, ma'am?"

She stared up blankly at the strolling troubadour. Time and place blurred into a nightmarish confusion as she pushed past him to stumble toward the bottom of the escalator. Keeping her palms pressed to the wall so as not to lose her way, she refused to acknowledge the surroundings—the jugglers, the damsels, the shop-fronts, all decked out in thirteenth century style.

This is not real.

She concentrated on her breathing, on putting one foot before the other to get her to her goal. Clinging to the rubber hand rail, she let its momentum pull her onto a wide step and carry her away from the scene of her inexplicable obsession.

As she rode higher and farther away from the mock village, her strength began to return. The bing-bing-bing of the casino replaced the merry Medieval tunes from below as one century blended into another. She took a deeper breath and straightened. Her hands still shook, but her control began to return. Again, as she did every night, she made a vow not to go back. And again, she cringed beneath the truth. She couldn't stay away. Not until she found…what? Would she know it if she found it? If not, how could this compulsion ever end?

In madness, she feared. In madness.

The cool touch of night air eased the fever from her face. If only it could work the same miracle on her troubled thoughts. She walked across the drawbridge as if in a dream, weaving more by instinct than design through the throng of impatient onlookers who waited eagerly for the automated confrontation between the fire breathing dragon and Merlin the Magician in the moat below. Once, she might have elbowed in to see the delightful spectacle for herself, but now she had no more time for fairytales. She was going to be late for work. And in her mind, even sinking into insanity wasn't an excuse for tardiness.

When she reached the street, she stopped, overcome with the recurring sense of being watched. Not just watched, but devoured by the intensity of some unseen gaze. Looking back toward the clump of tourists she'd passed through, she saw nothing out of the ordinary, no one expressing any undo interest in her. But the feeling remained, growing stronger, almost as palpable as a caress upon her skin. The fact that her shiver was not borne of dread was as upsetting as being the object of someone's observation. Instead of feeling violated, the attention lent an odd aura of comfort, not threat. Perhaps a guardian angel watched over her. She smiled at the thought and continued on with greater purpose.

She loved walking along the Strip at night. The energy, the brilliant lights bursting like stars against the blackness of the night created a world like no other. A pretend world where she might belong as she never did during the daylight hours. A world where magic was possible and knights still rescued damsels in distress.

Lost in her musings, she didn't notice her steps were echoed. She always felt safe on the streets of Las Vegas, just another anonymous figure in an ever-shifting crowd. Too insignificant to draw the attention of anyone bent on harm. Why would they bother? In her plain, wholesale store office clothing, she didn't suggest untold wealth was hidden in her bulky purse. So she was completely surprised when a bump from behind was followed by a sharp yank on her shoulder strap.

Common sense told her to let go. But from somewhere deep inside came an angry bellow that said "No!" No, she was not surrendering the few meager tokens of identity she could claim to some street punk out for quick cash.

The kid looked up in alarm when she pulled back and began battling for possession of the handbag instead of doing the sensible, expected thing. His gaunt face was a pin cushion of metal piercings. A tatoo crawled up from beneath the neckband of his dirty tee shirt. He couldn't have been more than sixteen or seventeen. Just a child. Then his expression grew old and ugly.

"Let go, bitch, before you get hurt."

And a small blade appeared in his hand as if to prove that point.

Tenaciously, she dug in her heels and looped the cheap imitation leather strap around her wrist. When he jerked her purse, she was pulled forward to fall hard upon her knees. Pain burned from that rough contact. Still, she wouldn't let go.

The knife slashed in a motion too quick to follow, and she gasped as it severed the strap and her last hold upon her belongings.

None of the passersby who glanced down at the woman on hands and knees offered assistance. They quickly walked on. As if she wasn't worth the involvement of a simple gesture. Until one hand extended down to her, palm up in expectation.

Her gaze lifted. Through the shimmer of anguish, his blond head was haloed by an ethereal light, making her think for just a moment, *Could this be my angel?*

He could have been. Easily, his was one of the most striking faces she'd ever seen, with its dramatic bone structure, strong jaw and sensitive mouth that played intriguingly against that fierce setting. And his eyes...Set beneath the tousle of fair hair and unyielding horizontal slash of his brows, they were dark, piercing her with a brooding intensity. The kind of penetrating gaze one would feel in a crowd.

Was he...? Was his the gaze following her each night?

She should have been afraid once that thought surfaced. But there was no fear in the timid way her hand slipped across his palm.

Rough and cool.

His fingers closed about hers with a protective strength both confident and comforting. She rose to her feet with his firm guidance. Her knees wouldn't stop trembling.

"Are you all right?"

Such quiet power in his voice made his words resonate with a concern far outweighing the interest of one stranger in another's plight. The depth of emotion in that simple phrase brought a dampening of gratitude to her uplifted gaze. She tried to speak. Her lips moved but no sound issued. She was very aware that he hadn't released her hand. His thumb moved across her knuckles in slow, searching revolutions. She fought the need to tighten her grip, instead letting her fingers rest casually in his palm. As if they belonged there. Her whole body felt relaxed and comfortable in its familiarity with this man, this stranger, and she marveled at that, she who never experienced a lessening of her guard with a member of the opposite sex no matter how well she knew him.

"You should not have resisted. You might have been hurt."

His scolding was like his voice—gentle, persuasive and

driven by regard for her safety.

"I know." Her own response quivered, not with apology but with acceptance of consequence. She gasped slightly when he extended her purse. Taking it in her free hand, she crushed it to her rapidly beating heart.

"There is nothing in there worth the risk. Just things."

Her chin came up a notch. Her tone firmed. "My things."

He smiled then, just a small curve of his mouth that managed to convey his amused admiration as well as exasperation. "Nothing worth the risk," he repeated softly.

"Thank you…?" She let that linger, waiting for him to finish it.

"Gabriel."

Like the angel.

He studied her with that consuming intensity. An urgent expectation steeped in his dark gaze as if he hoped to receive something in return. Was he waiting for some sort of reward? She had a five-dollar bill in her change purse. That seemed woefully inadequate.

Slowly anticipation dimmed to disappointment. She'd failed him somehow, without intention or understanding, and she wished she knew how to make amends.

"I will see you again, Gabriel." Not a question for she felt it with a certainty.

His expression lightened. His gaze dazzled with promise. However, his response was carefully tempered with restraint.

"If you wish."

And he brought her hand up, carrying it like something cherished to meet the soft, sweet touch of his lips. Her insides liquified with heat and a giddy delight at that surprising, courtly gesture. He could have had her then with a word. She would have gone with him anywhere, walking away from her shell of a life without an instant of regret to chase the fleeting beauty of that moment. As if following him were the most natural thing in the world.

But he stepped back, releasing her hand to break the spell.

Someone jostled her arm. She glanced away for only an instant. But it took only that instant for him to disappear, leaving her oddly bereft and so alone on that crowded walk.

He hadn't asked her name.

He knew it, she was sure, believing the moment their gazes met for an acquainting union that he knew everything about her. But how was that possible? How could she feel such kinship, such a compelling closeness, to a man she'd never seen before?

But would see again.

***

He sank back into the shadows, watching her confusion as she scanned the sidewalks for him. He stayed out of sight with an anguished purpose. He hadn't meant to reveal himself to her, not so soon, not so spontaneously without planning the result.

But he had, and he had his answer.

He passed his hand across his eyes, covering the tender torment that came with beholding her image. The sound that escaped him was half strangled sob, half moan of longing.

She didn't know him.

No recognition sparked her gaze. No awareness leapt at the sound of his name.

He meant nothing to her.

How could that be when she was the very breath in his body, the very reason for his heart to continue beating in its unnatural rhythm somewhere between heaven and hell?

The scent of her lingered. The perfume she wore had passed from her tender skin to his hand, and he inhaled deeply until intoxicated by fragrant memory. Violets. Her favorite. The delicate bouquet had teased him through centuries, quickening his hopes, his desires, his dreams.

She was here. And she would be his at last.

And he would never, ever let her go again.

***

The elevator doors closed upon the construction noise from the game floor. Silence rode up with her to the very top of the sprawling hotel, opening upon a brilliant vista of the city at play that never failed to steal away her breath.

Quickly, she went to her desk, shutting her damaged handbag in the bottom drawer before flicking on her computer screen to the serene field of aquarium fish.

"It's not like you to be late."

She jumped slightly even though she should be used to not hearing his approach.

"I'm sorry. I had a bit of an adventure on the Strip."

"Oh?" A question with real interest in her answer.

"Someone tried to steal my purse."

"How alarming. Are you all right?"

Again, sincerity rang in his response, warming the chill that seeped through her.

"Yes, of course."

"Good. Step into my office, Miss Bright. You've made me late for my appointment."

Again, she murmured her apology. She rose from her work space and went briskly, efficiently into his massive office, where the chill of the air conditioner woke gooseflesh upon her arms once more.

Or maybe it was the way he moved up so silently behind her after closing the door.

Automatically, she removed the decorative scarf she wore about her neck, baring her throat to the sudden cool brush of his lips.

To the sudden sharp sting of his teeth.

She closed her eyes and let herself drift and dream.

Dreaming of the Angel Gabriel while caught in a demon's embrace.

Three

"I've found her."

"Gabriel, that's wonderful," gushed the voice on the other end of the connection. Then a pause. "Isn't it?"

"She doesn't know me, Rae."

He didn't have to say more than that. His friend and former partner read between the lines even with the width of the continent separating them. That's why he'd called. Words weren't necessary.

"After what she's been through, it's to be expected. Gabriel, she suffered a tremendous trauma." Another pause then a quiet, "Is Zanlos with her?"

Right to business. That was Rae Borden, too. "I haven't seen him, but I know he's here. I know he still controls her, even more so now than before."

Rae's voice toughened. "Are you in over your head out there? Do you need me to watch your back?"

He laughed, and much of his tension drained away with that simple act of lightness. It was good to have friends. "And just when is that baby due, Sugar Rae? Your husband would never forgive me if you dropped it on the plane flying out here."

"Well then you'd have the both of us there to support you." She sighed in frustration. "I feel like I'm letting you down when you need me."

"I'm fine, Rae. Really. It's Naomi I'm worried about. I can't be there to protect her during the daylight hours. I can't get close enough to be a confidant to learn what I need to know about Zanlos."

Rae was silent for a long moment. He could almost hear the gears turning. Affection for the street smart former Detroit cop warmed him like an embrace across the miles and states between them.

"I know someone who might help. Let me call in a favor and get back to you. Until then, you be careful. I don't have that many friends that I can afford to lose them, especially when I plan to name them godfather to my son."

Emotion crowded thick and achy in his chest, preventing a reply.

"Unless you'd rather not."

He flushed the clogging sentiment with a rough clearing of his throat, but his words still rumbled. "I'd be honored."

"Then don't underestimate Zanlos. You're not expendable, Gabriel, no matter what allegiance you feel toward Marchand. You owe it to Naomi and to me and your godson to practice caution."

He laughed again. "This, coming from you?"

"Voice of experience."

He put his cell phone away along with many of his worries, having no doubt that ex-detective Borden would come through for him. Naomi would be protected, and he could concentrate on his other reason for coming to Las Vegas.

That meant getting into the personal and private business of one Kazmir Zanlos without him knowing it. Without the Vegas police knowing it. Without Naomi Bright knowing it.

Marchand LaValois, who controlled the elite group he worked for, would call it justice.

Gabriel called it revenge.

A punch to the shoulder snapped his musings.

"Ready to meet your match on the field of honor?"

He looked up at Rolland with a cocky grin. "Have you seen one?"

Slow to respond to his humor, Rolland finally allowed a thin smile. "Were this a contest in truth, we would see."

"And perhaps I would not be the one on my back."

The passage of time had lessened Rolland's insecurities. What Gabriel saw in his friend was no longer a lover but a fighter. How could their kind not be, considering what was necessary for them to survive? That had been Gabriel's gift to his best friend, and he felt a sharp gnawing of guilt because this change had been his fault, his responsibility. Like Naomi.

He missed and mourned the loss of the gentle, poetic soul Rolland had been. He didn't know this narrow-eyed warrior, but he knew the events that had shaped him. The hunger. The stalking. The occasional killing. It hardened the heart. It took a savage toll on the spirit. And for Rolland, who had never known the horrors of war, it had been a tremendous shock. It forever changed the man he had been into the like creature who stood before him.

And for that reason Gabriel had purposefully avoided him. It was just too hard being with him the way he was now when Gabriel remembered so clearly, so wistfully, who he had been. They'd lost touch with one another, going in different directions to make sense of what they'd become. Rolland's phone call had come as a complete surprise. But it hadn't been a misty-eyed homecoming of two old, dear friends. Rolland met him as an equal, as a comrade in arms. As a challenge. And though he could still see the old Rollie shadowed behind this new tough-edged being, Gabriel guessed that the gentle poet was more memory than habit.

And so Gabriel should have known better than to bait him, but he wasn't without his own share of arrogance. Since they'd last jousted to sharpen their skills lifetimes ago, Gabriel had been honing his in both mind and body. He'd mastered disciplines of self-defense and martial arts from all around the globe. He'd studied self-control and inner harmony in mountaintop temples. He'd experienced war firsthand upon bloody fields both foreign and domestic with everything from flintlock to grenade launchers. But he'd never surrendered his love for the primitive one-on-one that came with the clashing of metal upon metal, with bone and muscle. He'd been bred to be a knight, a bold warrior soldier who believed in honor above all things. Even winning.

A concept Rolland had obviously set aside.

For the next three nights, Rolland proved what mattered most. It was the cheer of the crowd. After he bore down upon Gabriel in increasingly aggressive attacks until Gabriel was left bruised beyond necessity, Rolland was taken aside by the show's director for a talk on self-restraint. It was just a game, after all. Just pretend.

But that's where Jonathon, their meticulous scriptor, was wrong. It wasn't a game, not to men who'd for centuries played to win.

Gabriel should have suspected the problem. His friend coveted the favor of the audience, the flutter of pennants, the swooning glances of the ladies. Rollie the Poet hadn't had the heart for focused competition. But Rolland, the preternatural being, who was beyond the reach of harm and so far above the normal skills and abilities of the others in the ring, needed a challenge, an equal upon whom to test himself. And to him, victory was all. At any cost, by any means.

As Gabriel ruefully discovered in the arena when an unscripted and forbidden strike to his head sent his helm flying and him tumbling to the dirt.

From his back, he saw Rolland's jaunty salute.

And with his keen senses, he heard above the cheers, above the roaring thunder in his ears, one frail voice, taut with fear and anguish.

"Gabriel!"

Naomi!

He tried to sit up, but the world spun for long disorienting seconds. *She was here.* Her absence for the past three nights had had him in a fever of anxiety. But she was back. And she was calling to him by name. Not to the stranger who'd rescued her handbag but to the knight who still wore her token beneath his shirt, close to his heart. Calling as if she knew him. As if she feared for him.

By the time his head cleared enough to distinguish faces in the crowd, hers was not among them.

Had he imagined it, then?

Had his own desperate longing placed the sound of her voice, the call of his name, within his frantic mind?

Unable to walk away from the show with one more "contest of strength and skill" remaining, he dragged himself up from the arena floor as the spotlights sought the next challenger.

Real or imagined?

The momentary doubt joined centuries of unanswered questions. But he would have them settled to his satisfaction. And soon.

***

For three days, she'd fought the compulsion. She could beat this addiction. But after three days of restless, near feverish agitation, after three nights of next to no sleep and shadowed dreams, she couldn't continue the battle.

She didn't know why she couldn't stay away. All Naomi Bright knew was when she approached the gaudy white castle with its colorful spires, her heart beat with life and expectation. When she heard the music and breathed in the scent of horse and man and excitement, the huge, frightening void within her soul began to fill.

She felt as though she was coming home. And that was more than enough reason for someone who couldn't remember where home was. Or even who she was. Within the impersonal tiers of revelers, with her finger food served up in faux Medieval style, she indulged in a sense of déjà vu as comforting as it was confusing. And like her restless dreams, as tantalizing as it was terrifying.

How normal is that, Naomi-girl? Isn't that more than just a little nuts?

She sat in her reserved seat, in the Green Knight's section, her fingers clutching the edge of her chair, her pulse pounding like mad as a crazy thrill of anticipation swirled through her. As she looked down upon the arena, she couldn't be certain the images she saw were part of the evening's entertainment or an extension of the persistent nightmare through which she walked alone.

It was coming.

Asleep or awake, madness or make believe, it swept up and over her. A chill wave she couldn't escape, its undertow pulled her quickly down beneath the surface of sanity. She was drowning right there in her seat, surrounded by strangers. Couldn't they tell something was wrong? And as hard as she tried to grasp for a sense of place and time, it eluded her on the turbulent sea of uncertainty.

Sensations swelled up inside her, so much more intense, so much bigger than the scene she witnessed. Where this combat was a sanitized version of days of old, she could see—transposed like a double exposure—another field of battle, another crowd of onlookers, these clad in gowns and garters instead of denim and tee shirts. Even the smells heightened as she drew in quick little breaths. The greasy odor of poorly cooked fowl, the sour stench of unwashed bodies pressed close, not in a climate-controlled hotel but beneath the chill drizzle of an overcast sky. The sounds became a cacophony of noise and music and voices, layering one atop the other into a discordant mix heard by her ears alone, as if she was watching one event while listening to another on a stereo headset. Trumpets blared, yet she knew there were no horns. Armor clanked and rattled while voices all around her spoke with an accent not native to either clime or country.

She sat still and trembling in her seat, caught between two worlds, two lives, not knowing which was real or where she fit within them. Perhaps it was all a dream, none of it real, not her job at the Amazon, not this strange stirring of familiarity beating within her breast, not the specter of her angel Gabriel who haunted her every moment. Or perhaps they were all entwined in some obscure purpose that continued to draw her, like a puzzle laid out on a table with all of its pieces scrambled. The urge to make them fit into a recognizable pattern overwhelmed her.

That's what she was, a jumble of segmented memories searching for someone to put them togther.

Was that why she was here?

Was that why, night after night, she couldn't tear her gaze from the knight in black and silver? Because he was a piece of the puzzle, or the one who knew how the finished product was supposed to look?

The way she knew him.

Instinctively, without ever having seen his face, she knew him by the way he sat his horse, by the way he coaxed his mount into a powerful knot of controlled energy ready to unleash at his signal. The way he tilted his lance, the way he held his head in a bold, dead-on stare as he propelled toward his opponent. She knew these mannerisms as intimately as she was continuously surprised by her own.

They were both equal parts mystery and innate understanding. Enigmas for real, or just in the tangle of her mind?

The minute he rode onto the field, he consumed her with his air of nobility and ambition. And passion. Yes, passion for the confrontation to come and the rewards that would follow.

What would it be like to be that reward?

The question quivered through her heart in a shudder of dread and expectation. Why both things? Why dread at all? Why would she believe becoming the token of such a man's quest would be linked to any kind of unpleasantness? But men in this age no longer believed in quests. That was just the fantasy they played out beneath the spotlights to earn the cheers of a crowd more used to rooting for the home football team than any demonstration of noble intent. They didn't understand the holy mystique of this place and what it once represented. To them, it was just another amusement.

Why should it be more than that to her?

But it was. She knew it was as she watched her hero surge forward in a blur of ebony and quicksilver. Her hopes and fears rode as hard into her throat as he across the arena. And when the challenger's lance shattered against his helmeted head with a force that sent the protective gear flying, Naomi clutched her temples as she, too, felt the exquisite agony of it. The world spun in sickening swoops as she watched him fall as if in slow motion from his horse. Time suspended as he struck the ground and for a moment, for an instant, the field ran red. And she knew, even before she saw his face at last, who it was struck down there within the clouds of dirt and defeat. His name tore from her throat, from a soul releasing its pain in an expunging exorcism of grief and anguish as her vision went from crimson-splashed to the black of death.

And the next thing she remembered was a firm hand forcing her head between her knees, and the chill relief of a cold cloth against the back of her neck.

"Better now?"

She didn't know the woman's voice. Naomi attempted to straighten in alarm but, guessing at her response, suppressing hands restrained her shoulders.

"It's all right. You fainted is all. I can't have that kind of behavior in my section, or I won't get tips."

Through her yet-bleary eyes, Naomi recognized the flat slippers and ankle-length skirts worn by the hotel's waitress wenches.

"Where am I?" she muttered like a drunk coming around in the morning.

"In the ladies' room. I felt such events deserved a little privacy. Unless you'd like a doctor. Please don't tell me it was your dinner."

"No. No." It wasn't what she'd eaten. It was what she'd felt with the intensity of an emotional collapse. But how could she explain that? "Just felt a little sick, is all."

"You're not expecting, are you?"

It took a moment for Naomi to catch her meaning, then she shook her head, stilling it with a wince as pressure and darkness welled once more. She heard water run in the sink and then the blessed relief of fresh cloth to her neck, forehead and either flushed cheek. Finally, the room stopped its teeter tottering.

"I think I can sit up now."

"All right but take it slow."

Gentle, capable hands controlled the movement, bringing her up carefully so that the world steadied around her and the nausea eased to a quiet rumble. She got her first look at her rescuer. The serving costume was familiar but not the Amazonian who wore it. The other woman towered above her, probably close to six foot tall even in the flat slippers. With her height came no model thinness. She was broad shouldered and buxom with strong, handsome features and a slightly amused smile.

"You've made my first night here one to remember."
She put out her hand. "I'm Rita Davies."

"Naomi Bright."

They shook hands as if introductions were not being
made in the washroom over the harsh scent of sickness.

"Think you can stand up, Naomi? Are you ready to go
back to your seat for the rest of the show?"

The thought of the crowd and the heat and the noise
brought the faint buzzing back to her head.

"I think I've had enough for tonight."

"Can I get someone for you? I kind of got the impression
that you were alone."

"There's no one," she admitted with a flat intonation.

"Are you in the hotel? Can I have someone see you to
your room?"

"No. Actually I have to get to work. I'm going to be late
and…" She tried to stand, and only Rita's quick catch saved
her from going straight to the floor.

"I don't think you're ready to go anywhere, but this isn't
exactly a great place to recuperate, if you know what I mean.
Tell you what, I've got a room here just until I find an
apartment. You're welcome to sack out there until I finish
out my shift."

"You don't have to—"

"I know I don't have to. You can call in sick from there
and take a little nap if you like. I won't bother you for a
couple more hours, and you can make yourself at home."

The thought of weaving through the crush of people in
her weakened state lessened her usual work ethic. "I am tired.
Maybe a little rest…"

"There you go. Now I can say I have my first friend out
here. I just got off the plane this morning, you know. I had
a friend of mine set up the job for me. Do you know him?"

"Who?" Naomi blinked, feeling the conversation slip
away from her as they moved toward the service elevator
and away from the noisy arena.

After calling out to a co-worker that she'd be right back,

Rita pushed the button for her floor. "Gabriel. You were yelling out his name just before you keeled over. That fall didn't scare you did it? It's all pretend, you know. Just show business."

Gabriel...

Then it came back with a tidal surge of remembrance.

"You're not going to pass out again, are you? You look like you've seen a ghost."

Not a ghost. Not exactly.

"Gabriel," Naomi began, startled by how smoothly his name glided off her tongue. "He's a friend?"

"Friend of a friend, really. Someone I used to work with in Detroit knows him and hooked me up for the job. I've never met him, at least not yet. Not until a couple of hours from now. He's coming up to my room to introduce himself."

Naomi didn't hear the rest. The background chatter faded away before one certainty. If she was still in Rita Davies' room, she would be face to face with her guardian angel once again.

And perhaps, face to face with some elusive answers as well.

Four

"Gabriel, my friend, this is not like you."

"Perhaps nearly having my head cleaved from my shoulders has soured my mood."

Rolland chuckled. "I don't think that's the problem. What are you hiding from me? Is it the woman or the work you refuse to tell me about?"

Rolland had followed Gabriel outside where he'd hoped to get a glimpse of Naomi in the crowd. No luck, either in spotting his love or in ridding himself of his friend's suddenly smothering presence. Since he had no intention of telling Rollie what had his nerves twisted in as many loops and curves as the roller coaster swooping about the replicated skyline of New York across the street, he searched for a quick excuse. They stood in the center of a large mill of tourists where the heat and scent of humanity tantalized. The adrenalin of the joust still pumped through them, and with that heightened energy came a sharper, more insistent thirst. And the need to act upon what they were.

"I haven't fed in two days."

Since it was unlike Gabriel to ever discuss his appetite especially in such blatant terms, Rolland's surprise was the perfect foil. But he could see the truth in the tight pull of flesh over bone in his friend's face, in the red-tinged glint of his gaze. Could feel it in the sudden restlessness of a beast stalking prey to satisfy instinct rather than for preservation. They were alike in that which they could not control.

"Well, then by all means, see to yourself, since you prefer to do such things on your own."

Not taking the time to sooth over the obvious hint of hurt in Rolland's claim, Gabriel clasped his shoulder. "Thank you for understanding. I'll see you tomorrow night and then, perhaps, I can explain more about why I'm here."

That seemed to satisfy his friend. "*Bon appetite,*" he spoke to the now empty spot beside him. Gabriel had already flown. He smirked and shook his head. "How like you to go for take out when we're standing in a buffet line."

But then Gabriel was forgotten as he turned his attention toward finding his own entrée of choice.

Just outside the sprawl of the Strip, within sight and almost reach of its glitter and excess, lay another community, one not geared toward the plundering of visiting riches but rather toward the simple struggle to survive day to day.

It started with one tent, one lost soul on a forgotten back street or open lot. Then another sprang up beside it and another, spreading like weeds the authorities grumbled, until an entire patch of the displaced had taken root so quickly, so voraciously, that they were almost impossible to yank out.

So they squatted in the shadows of the bright neon totems that beckoned the foolish to come play. A forgotten civilization like that found in any city, created around desperate necessity and fear instead of the search for reckless fun. In their tents and cardboard lean-tos, they broiled in the midday heat and huddled close against the chill of the night, unable to escape either with any success. Except for a fortunate few.

Charmaine Johnson drew a thin hotel towel up over the sleeping forms of her two youngest children. They didn't complain about going to bed hungry or cry at the discomfort of trying to find rest on a discarded bus seat amid the broken springs and sharp ridges of torn vinyl. They were too tired, too listless, too young to know any different kind of life. And that acceptance brought tears to Charmaine's eyes because this wasn't the life she'd wanted for her children. She kissed both their curly heads and blinked so they wouldn't see the sheen of her despair. Her oldest daughter noticed but wisely said nothing. Her oldest was a too mature fourteen and already a promising beauty much like her mother had once been before the business used her up and threw her away. And that was another cause for worry. Things of beauty didn't last long untouched or untried in such a place.

"Go to sleep, baby. Stay with the young ones while I go try to find us something to eat."

The restless teen Roxanne nodded somberly, knowing her proud mother hated for her to watch as she rummaged through the dumpsters in hopes of their next meal. Roxanne was old enough to remember another life where she had her own room and her mother wore pretty clothes, smelled good and laughed often. But that was before the accident. Roxanne never talked about it because it made her mother cry. And her mother cried way too much as it was.

"I'll stay right here, Mama, and I won't let anyone take off with our stuff."

Their stuff. Charmaine glanced at the paper sacks holding what was left of what they'd once had. The stuff they couldn't sell for a loaf of bread or quart of milk for the little ones. Junk of value to no one but them. All she had in the world of the life she'd lived before. Who'd want to steal it? She would have wept but had no energy left for tears. Stoically, she kissed her daughter's brow and readied to make the journey into town to scurry with the others like rats in search of sustenance.

No, not exactly the life she'd envisioned for her family.

She was straightening as her daughter snuggled down into the ratty surplus sleeping bag when she heard the soft rumble of a car engine. Curiously, she glanced around, not noticing Roxanne's suddenly alert posture. Not many vehicles came down to this part of town, especially not a sleek classic car with its bulky profile, dim running lights and roof chopped to the point that the narrowed windows were squinting slits against the ink blue paint job.

And though she'd never seen the vehicle before, she recognized it from the rumors whispered over the steeping stew pots of spoiled meat and rotting vegetables.

It was him. The uptown Angel of Mercy.

She held her ground as the big car crept closer, its lights winking off so all she could see was a crouching shadow. But what if she was wrong and it wasn't him? What if it was one of the other kind that preyed upon those who couldn't protect themselves or expect any intervention from the law? The law didn't care what happened in their little shanty town, as long as it didn't interfere with the tourist trade. And one less homeless person was never missed.

As she assumed an aggressive pose before her children,

ready to do whatever she could to keep them safe, the hulking vehicle eased to a stop. Slowly, one of the heavy doors opened. The car's interior loomed dark and sinister.

"Get in."

The voice, a man's voice, was low, soft and not in the least bit threatening. But still, the tiny hairs on Charmaine's forearms stirred in a ripple of warning.

"What do you want?"

"I won't harm you. You have my word you'll be back with your children by daybreak."

Charmaine's breath expelled in a shiver as she continued to hesitate.

"Go on, Mama. Don't be afraid. You know who he is."

She glanced back at Roxanne who was sitting up in the cocoon of the sleeping bag, her eyes dreamy, a knowing half-smile on her face.

"Listen to your daughter," coaxed the unseen driver. "This is for them, as well as you."

Reluctance pulling at every move like restraining hands, Charmaine edged toward the vehicle. For the girls. For her babies. Anything to make their lives better.

The wide leather seat was cool on the backs of her legs. Before she had time to rethink what she was doing or to look back for perhaps what might be one last look at her children, the large door shut as if of its own accord and the vehicle glided into the night.

She couldn't see him behind the wheel but she could feel his presence.

"Where are we going?"

"To a hotel just off the Strip."

Charmaine took a deep breath. For the children, she reminded herself, as she folded trembling hands upon her lap and made herself stare straight ahead. They didn't speak again until the big Mercury slipped into a parking spot outside room Three at a secluded but not sleazy hotel. *I'll take Door Number 3, Monty.* She wondered what kind of prize lay behind it—the kind that brought reward or regret? She recognized the name of the hotel chain and knew they didn't reserve by the hour. So why was he willing to pay so much for a minute or two of her time?

She got a brief glimpse of him as he got out of the car, an impression of long, lean legs clad in denim and of a hip-length black leather coat. And pale hands.

She waited, trepidation jittering through her as he crossed in front of the car to her side of the vehicle. He opened the door so she could exit but stayed in the glare of the neon *Vacancy* sign so she had no clear impression of his features. She followed on rubbery knees to Room Three, and when he motioned, preceded him into the chill embrace of the room.

There was a light on in the bathroom. It cast a weak illumination just shy of where they stood next to the two queen-sized beds.

"I've never done this before," Charmaine felt honor bound to tell him, so he'd know what he was getting for his buck. "I was a dancer, not a hooker."

"I didn't bring you here for that."

"Oh." Did she sound too relieved? Her apprehension tickled back up her spine. Why then? She could think of worse things then a quick Wham Bam Thank You Ma'am. Before she could ask particulars, he gestured toward the bathroom.

"Perhaps you'd like to shower first. There's shampoo and lotion in there and something for you to put on."

Kinky stuff. Great.

But the temptation of a real shower, soap and shampoo overcame her worries. Whatever might come, she might as well be clean.

The shower was heaven. Such a routine occurrence was now a luxury to be savored for each sudsy moment. Finally, when the small room was heavily blanketed in steam, she stepped out and into a plush towel. She wiped a circle in the foggy glass so she could observe her face. She still held to passable good looks, though she knew they wouldn't last long in her current situation. Her café-colored skin was still taut, and wavy hair, lightened by the white blood of the father she didn't know, was still free of gray. But she felt old. Old and now scared of what was expected of her.

A garment was folded on the edge of the sink. She reached for it gingerly. But instead of some fantasy-inducing costume, she was surprised to find it was a two piece jogging suit. It was soft, loose and hardly seductive. She slipped into it, grateful to discard the shorts and tank top she had worn for the past week. A clean change of clothes was rarer than the change for the Laundromat.

Feeling fresh and somewhat optimistic, she stepped back into the outer room.

The first thing she noticed was the aroma of food. Her stomach roared in response. On the space next to the portable television was a tray of fruits, bread and cheeses, but it was the large bowl of creamy soup that tantalized her empty belly.

"I thought you might be hungry."

Starved was more accurate.

But looking from the unidentifiable figure standing near the closed drapes, still nothing more than a silhouette, to the bounty spread before her, all she could think of was the tiny little bellies of her children going to bed with nothing in them.

"Go ahead," he urged, as if hearing her internal conflict. "There'll be more for you to take back with you."

She stood next to the dresser, popping squares of cheese and plump ripe strawberries while keeping a cautious eye on her host. He didn't move. Slowly, she relaxed enough to carry the bowl of soup to the edge of the bed where she spooned it up eagerly.

"What happened to you, Charmaine?"

She didn't think to wonder how he knew her name, nor did she need him to clarify his question.

"I used to sing and dance in one of the big downtown casino shows. I married one of the pit managers, and he was a daddy to my little girls. Things was real good for a while." Her voice took on a husky resonance as she stared into the bottom of the empty bowl. "Then one night when we was coming home from a trip to the canyon, just the two of us, some eighty-year-old man crossed the centerline of the highway. My Josh was killed and my hip was broken. I'll never dance again. I sort of forgot what was important and took to drinking to numb all the pain I was feeling. I didn't have no money, no insurance, no nothing. Me and my babies found ourselves out on the streets." She hitched in a ragged breath then toughened up once more. "I not asking for no sympathy or charity. I don't want my girls to see me beg to the government for help."

"That would be worse than what they see every day?"

She faced the shadowed figure, trembling with indignation and angry guilt. "Who are you to judge me and what I do?"

A quiet chuckle. "A friend. Would you refuse the offer of a friend?"

He placed the key to the room on the air conditioner beside him. She eyed it suspiciously.

"The room's yours, paid through the week. A cab will take you to pick up your children in the morning and bring them back here. Three meals will be delivered every day for the four of you. The owner could use an attractive singer for the lounge. He'll audition you if you're interested."

The sweep of a car's headlights arrowed through a slight part in the drapes. It wasn't much light, just enough to illuminate his face for the first time. For a long moment, Charmaine stared, mesmerized. He was beautiful…young, pale, blond and, with his gaunt cheeks and soulful dark eyes, also somewhat sad. The Angel of Mercy, they called him, because those who stepped into his big, midnight-colored car never returned to the squalor of their existence. It was rumored he gave them the chance at a better life. Was this her chance? Perhaps her only one?

Her heart pounded emotion up into her throat. She could hardly speak and struggled not to weep. But experience was a bitter teacher. She held her outpouring of relief in check. Turning to stare at her own reflection, she demanded, "What's the catch? What do you get out of all of this?"

She was looking right into the mirror. That's why she was suddenly so surprised to hear his voice next to her ear where the image showed only empty space.

"Nothing you'll miss."

***

She had no intention of sleeping when she lay back on the big bed and closed her eyes but when she opened them again,

Naomi discovered that three hours had passed since her new friend convinced her to rest.

Amazingly, her first thought wasn't of work and the fact that she'd never made a call in.

Had she missed Gabriel's visit?

Alarmed, she scrambled out from under the comforter that someone had placed over her. Her sensible beige skirt and jacket were wrinkled beyond redemption, and a quick glance at the mirror showed her upswept hair-do hopelessly warped out of shape on one side. As she tried to pat it back into place, sounds from the other room reached her, the toneless humming of a Beatles' tune and the cheerful drone of the hotel's in-house channel discussing its various amenities. She smelled coffee, strong and dark. That's what finally drew her out.

"Have a nice nap?"

Rita Davies smiled at her as she poured out two mugs of the rich, black brew. The wenching costume had been replaced by an aerodynamically designed bra top and baggy harem-style work out pants in a startling fuchsia.

"Coffee?"

"Please."

As Rita moved across the room toward the couch where Naomi had taken a seat, Naomi couldn't help marveling at the fabric in the top that could hold such an overwhelming bounty in place without a single, eye-blackening bounce. She admitted to a moment of bosom envy when she, herself, wore a bra more for propriety's sake than from necessity.

"Careful, it's hot."

Heat was what she needed. A sudden, seeping chill began to spread through her bones, a cold more like death than over-zealous air conditioning.

What time was it? It was late. Very late. She shouldn't have come. She shouldn't have strayed from her routine.

Wrapping her hands about the steaming mug, Naomi fought to still their trembling. Her sense of ease all but gone, she nervously sipped at the drink as pins and needles prickled over her skin. It grew more and more difficult for her to sit on the sofa pretending to enjoy a cup of coffee with a new friend when her insides were winding up tight as her internal clock told her it was time to go and go fast. *Go. Go now. You can't be late. You must hurry.* She took a big, purposeful gulp of the hot liquid to quiet that insistent voice, but she didn't think she could silence it for long. Gabriel…She wanted to wait for Gabriel. She could resist a moment longer. For how ever long it took.

But she knew that wasn't true. Already, anxiety quaked through her muscles in cramping restlessness. The coffee roiled in warning, pitching in her stomach as if in the midst of a storm. A dangerous storm once it started brewing. One she didn't care to be caught in.

"I have to go."

She put the cup down on the end table, sloshing the remaining contents over the sides and all over the faux wood finish. She gasped in dismay, but Rita brushed off her attempt to control the flow with the efficient blot of a wad of tissues and announced, "No harm done."

But Naomi bounded off the cushions, bunched and wired to the point of quivering both in body and voice. "I'm sorry. I'm sorry. It's late. I've got to go."

A knock at the door interrupted her babbling. Rita's pronouncement of, "That must be Gabriel," did little to calm Naomi's approaching hysteria. She stood, rooted to the spot, painfully aware of her crumpled appearance and rattled manner and of the urgent need to flee that still hammered through her.

Gabriel.

The thought of him caressed along her frayed and frazzled nerves, quieting them in an instant.

"Rita?"

The sound of his voice warmed her senses like a lover's sigh.

"Gabriel, nice to finally meet you. Rae's told me things that had me imagining a cross between a Greek god and a superhero."

"Not too big of a disappointment, I hope."

"Not hardly."

He stepped into the room, still grinning wide when his dark-eyed gaze touched upon Naomi's. The result was immediate combustion. Silence scorched the air, making it a long moment before either dared to breathe.

"Hello again." His greeting rumbled like a low grade earthquake.

He'd been the stuff of dreams the first time they'd met - more ethereal rescuer than flesh and blood man. But here, now, in the suddenly too small hotel room, he was all too real, suddenly too hotly masculine and all too virile to be contained within the chaste embrace of her memories. She took a cautious step back even as her emotions goaded her to lean into the blaze of his sexuality if to do nothing more than be seared by his intense heat. She could feel the power and strength of him emanating in palpable waves. Before, when he'd come to her aid on the street, she'd been comforted, but here in this suffocating room, she felt intimidated. Instead of trust, there was confusion.

He made no advance toward her either in movement or conversation, as if he sensed her panic. Instead, he smiled faintly and turned his attention toward the less agitated Rita.

"I just wanted to see if you'd settled in all right."

"Just fine, thanks to you and the job here. You've been a lifesaver. Rae said that about you, too."

His laugh was warm, managing to thaw some of Naomi's paralysis. "Rae exaggerates."

"She didn't strike me as the type to sing praises without merit. I think I'll give her the benefit of the doubt."

Then his focus returned to Naomi, and her legs got all wobbly to match the consistency of her stomach.

"And how are you? No ill effects from the other night?"

Rita's intuition honed in like a hawk's. "What happened?"

"Someone tried to steal her purse on the street," he mentioned casually, intent upon glossing over his own part in it.

"And Gabriel stopped him."

Naomi's breathy conclusion brought the shivery tension back between them.

Being in the same room with her, so close it would take only a couple of steps to sweep her up in his arms, put an unbelievable pressure on Gabriel's self-control. All he had to do was reach out. He could have her now and for always. She would be his to love and protect as she should have been all those centuries ago. But at what cost? She didn't know him. In fact, he could sense her wariness, even her fear of him, for reasons he didn't understand. To act aggressively now could backfire, escalating those uncertain emotions to place an even greater barrier between them.

No. She would have to be courted slowly, with gentleness and delicacy, just as he'd done with the shy, orphaned girl left in his family's care. It would take time, time that had always been in his favor but now seemed an enemy he couldn't control. If he pushed, she would run and perhaps he would never find her again.

No. Take it slowly. Rae's friend had wasted no time forging a bond with the skittish Naomi. Now, he needed to step back and let things develop at a more cautious pace. Rita would protect her. She had that capable look about her. If Rae trusted her, he would do no less.

The greatest threat to his plan was now his own weakening will. The need to touch her, to inhale her fragrance, to hold her close and cherish her forever…

The strength of his needs must have somehow translated to her, for suddenly she looked wary and alarmed. Her fear was the last thing he wanted, but before he could conceive of how to defuse it, she was in frenetic motion.

"I have to go. I have to go. Thank you for your kindness, Rita. I won't forget. I won't forget." She repeated that almost fiercely as she skirted the both of them to make a dash for the door.

"Naomi."

His voice stopped her in the hall. She turned back toward him, her eyes huge, her slender body trembling like a doe's caught in a hunter's site. Gabriel smiled determinedly, letting her feel the power of his will.

"I will see you again."

She bolted then, racing down the hall and into the elevator standing open at its end. And she was gone.

Gabriel's breath released in an anguished shiver.

He started at the sudden strong clasp of Rita Davies' hand upon his arm.

"You were right to be concerned. Something's going on with her that's not quite right. I'll make sure she's all right and keep you posted. I'll be discreet and learn what I can without alerting her."

"I didn't bring you here to spy on her."

"Just consider that a freebie. Call me naturally curious. And I'll watch over her for you. Don't worry."

Easier said than done.

FIVE

"Miss Bright, where have you been?"

Naomi straightened slowly from putting her purse in her bottom desk drawer. Her employer's icy tone had her trembling. Before she could speak, he continued harshly.

"Not another purse snatching, I trust."

"I'm sorry, Mr. Zanlos. I was ill."

"Too ill to pick up a phone to inform those who were worried about you?"

She blinked. "You were worried?"

"Of course, Miss Bright. Where would I be without you?"

The smoothly rendered praise rinsed away her apprehension. Her tension eased, but regret remained. "I am sorry, Mr. Zanlos. I hope my absence didn't create any problems for you."

"On the contrary. Miss Granger was happy to fill in for you."

Naomi glanced toward the reception area. Vera Granger sat at her desk, her hands hanging loosely at her sides, her impossibly red head listing to the side as blue eyes stared more cluelessly than normal. One of Kaz Zanlos's pretty print scarves was knotted at her throat.

A pang of envy clenched Naomi's middle, compounding the guilt with which she already wrestled. Vera Granger had been there to serve and now would reap the reward of blissful vacancy, while her own thoughts remained agonizingly clear. There would be no numbing escape for her on this night.

"Are you sure you are all right, Miss Bright? You look…distracted."

She smiled at her boss, trying to appear cheerful and unconcerned. "I'm fine now. Perhaps something I ate."

He continued to stare at her, his gaze growing eerie and luminescent. Before his mind could begin to probe hers, she pushed up a wall of quickly erected blankness. His thoughts bumped against it, roaming the outlines but unable to find a way around it, a sly cat trying to find its way into a fishbowl. A sweat broke out upon her brow, but she held firm until he withdrew. Then the barrier collapsed with an imploding relief.

Where had she learned to do such a thing?

With all she owed Kaz Zanlos, had she the right to keep secrets from him?

But what purpose would it serve for him to learn of her confusion? After he'd placed so much trust in her, how disappointed he'd be in the return of her instability. She couldn't let him down. He was her only link to sanity.

"If you're sure you're all right, Miss Bright, you can go downstairs and get a progress report from Marcus. Time is growing short and there's much to do."

Naomi hesitated. There was so much they had to do, so many contracts and clauses to scan, so many decisions to discuss. She hadn't expected to be shooed away.

And then, through the partially opened door to his private office, she saw a whisper of movement. Then she understood. He was already involved in business, and that business didn't include her. It was business she'd prefer to avoid. She averted her gaze from the tantalizing slit of open doorway and the mysterious figure lurking behind it. Just another secret she'd rather not know.

"Certainly, Mr. Zanlos."

She didn't need to trouble herself over what went on behind closed doors. A trip to the casino floor would ease her restlessness and disguise the worries she couldn't hide for a prolonged period. And with activity, there was no time to think. And to try to remember what was no longer there.

***

The Amazon.

She'd watched the lush landscape take shape over the course of the past few months with a nurturer's pride. By the time they were finished, nothing on the Strip would match its ambitious scale.

There were no walls at the Amazon. Rooms seemed carved out of jungle thickets and backed against the cascade of rocky waterfalls. With the banks of slot machines standing silent and the construction crew on their break, only the sounds of the rain forest intruded. Water roared down into gurgling pools and sighed in fine mists resembling frequent showers. Music of the wild pulsed beneath—the chatter of monkeys and birds from the fronds entwined overhead, the rumble of stalking predators within the realistic thickets, frog songs trilling a resonant beat from each stand of water, all playing harmony to the primal instrumental renderings. Even the air thickened with the cool humidity of a South American evening, as artificial atmosphere spun through a shortened cycle of fresh-breaking dawn and steamy midday before slipping into the fragrant and mysterious shadows of night. Closing her eyes, Naomi became a part of that wild and dangerous setting. But only for a moment.

"We're never going to get these damned machines to work right with all this humidity. It's like a frickin' sauna in here. How are we supposed to keep things running smooth in a damned steam bath? Zanlos must be nuts."

Naomi opened her eyes slowly then slit a stare at the grumbling and enthusiastically profane electrician who'd been toiling to bring the animatronic elements of the jungle to life.

"I'd be happy to tell him you said so."

Harry Bishop's expression froze into an almost comical caricature of alarm. To see such fear etched into the face of the brawny professional reinforced the powerful influence Zanlos' name carried from the top of the towers to the sprawl of the game floor. He wasn't the type of man one wanted to anger. "Oh, no, Miss Bright. That won't be necessary."

Her features relaxed at the big man's obvious distress. "I'm sure it won't be. If anyone can work miracles, it's you, Harry. That's why Mr. Zanlos hired you. He said he wanted the very best to bring his vision to life."

"Is that what he said?" Harry's pride nudged his complaints aside. "It's one helluva job, if you don't mind me saying so, Miss Bright."

"But you make it appear so effortless."

"Yeah, well." A flush crept up into the unshaven cheeks as quiet praise reduced him to foot scuffling boy before the dainty administrator and her gentle flattery.

"You'll have everything ready for the opening?"

"If it's a damned miracle Zanlos wants, it's a damned miracle he'll get."

She touched his arm lightly. "We have every confidence in you, Harry."

And her light touch was all it took to defuse the situation.

She left the casino to the sound of Harry barking obscenity-laced orders to his crew. As she moved down the corridor leading to the main show room, a shiver rippled up her arms and spine. The humidity was gone, replaced by a chill that seeped to the bone. But Naomi's response was more instinctive than reflexive. The place gave her the creeps.

Constructed to look like faux stone blocks, the vine-draped walls seemed to narrow uncomfortably. In the flickering of pseudo-torchlight, the greenery crept upon those rocky walls like thousands of squirming snakes. She drew a constricted breath in hopes of flushing the claustrophobia that came with this portion of the hotel.

Kaz Zanlos had asked for an ancient tomb, and his architect had more than delivered.

When the echoing silence of the halls was replaced by the chattering, nervous energy of the showgirls inside the cavernous hall, Naomi's comfort level returned to normal. She paused just inside the door to watch, an almost maternal smile etching her lips. Like a bunch of gangly, gorgeous kids, the young women struggled to work through an elaborate dance number while their choreographer hurled orders and insults.

"'Evening, Miss Bright."

Without a side glance of acknowledgment, she replied, "They're looking much better, don't you think, Marcus?"

A snort. "If you say so. I'm making book on which breaks first, the girls or Miss Gestapo."

Naomi's smile crept out unbidden. "Marcus, Miss Parsons is only doing her job."

"Some job. I'd rather take on dog or monkey training than try to get that lot to stay in line."

"Don't be mean, Marcus."

But in spite of her remark and despite his position as bouncer, she didn't believe Marcus Sinclair had a mean bone in

his body. Most said he hadn't a brain in his head, but Naomi
didn't think that was true, either. He was a huge, industrial-
sized Dumpster of a man with a closely cropped head seeming
to grow right out of bulging shoulders. His black-eyed glare
and the way the light glinted off the sharply hewn mounds of
muscle in his frequently bared and deeply browned arms was
enough to intimate all but the most stalwart…or stupid. Rumored
to be part Samoan, he fit nicely into the exotic stylings of the
hotel, missing only a loincloth and feathered headdress. Instead,
he favored Armani tailored slacks. Hired for his bulk and brawn,
he had no real need to show off his intellect. He was there to
threaten outsiders with mere presence and to dictate order by
virtue of booming voice and bulging biceps. But with Naomi,
he was more gentle and awkward mastiff than snarling pit bull.
As unlikely as it would seem, Marcus Sinclair was one of the
few people with whom she felt completely at ease.

They stood side-by-side in companionable silence at the
back of the empty auditorium. His mammoth size dwarfed her
like a Clydesdale next to a dainty gazelle, but oddly enough,
when Kitty Parsons turned her acerbic tongue to him, it was
Naomi who bristled protectively.

"Marcus, you dumb hulk, how many times do I have to tell
you to keep those photographers out of here?"

"Sorry, Miss Parsons," he rumbled. With an apologetic nod
toward Naomi, he lumbered around the back of the hall to chase
off the bold newsmen who'd managed to sneak in for a peak at
Vegas's most hush hush revue.

The choreographer unwittingly broke the concentration of
her girls by bringing Marcus and Naomi to their attention. Once
the petite assistant manager was spotted, there was no bringing
them back to heel. Like exuberant pups, they bounded off the
stage to swarm around Naomi.

"Miss Bright, what do you think of my new hair color? Is it
too orange? I was trying for copper penny, and I think I ended
up with glazed carrot."

"Naomi, has Mr. Zanlos said anything about getting my
boyfriend a job in the kitchen yet?"

"What did you think of my kick? I've been working on it

all week."

"Naomi, would you say something to Mr. Zanlos about our schedule? How's a girl supposed to have any kind of life with the hours he makes us keep?"

"Could you get Miss Kitty Kat to pull in her claws? We can't learn a routine when she has us all raw and bleeding."

One at a time, Naomi patiently addressed the questions as if she were dealing with a gaggle of girls instead of with women who were mostly the same age.

"It looks vibrant, Molly. Newly minted. Have Jack come in for an interview, Jeannie. We're taking on staff at the end of the week. Grace, you put Jackie Chan to shame. Marty, Mr. Zanlos wants you to get your beauty rest, and about Miss Kitty…"

"She's too old to get declawed."

All the girls snickered at the spiteful comment, and even Naomi had to smile. She felt like a den mother to the young dancers and was amazed that they turned to her for advice so readily when her own experience with life was more limited than the most sheltered of their group. Each and every one of them was dear to her and, sensing her fondness, they responded with unconditional devotion and oftentimes an embarrassing honesty when it came to their own escapades. Naomi listened and empathized and consoled, and that was why they came to her with both problems and accomplishments. Perhaps, Naomi thought with a ruthless honesty of her own, it was because they felt no threat when they were with her. None would worry about competition from Naomi Bright, the quiet, librarianish assistant who was tap water next to their vivacious spray of uncorked champagne.

But Naomi loved them too much to let it matter.

They were her family.

"Miss Bright, if you are quite through interrupting, we have a lot of work to do."

Naomi stepped in front of the suddenly cowering show girls, a mother hen fully ruffled. Though her voice was pitched low and soft, the authority behind her words was unmistakable.

"If you push them too hard, you increase the risk of injury and none of the girls is replaceable this close to our opening.

Mr. Zanlos wouldn't approve of slave driving, Miss Parsons. Besides, I thought they looked marvelous. You've done a wonderful job." That last remark took the sting from what came before it and gave the ruthless choreographer permission to back down.

"All right girls, take a short break. I mean short."

Naomi withstood their squealy hugs then, when the girls had scattered in search of cigarettes or other forbidden pleasures, she was left to face Kitty Parsons. She was a cool ice sculpture with a stare that froze on contact.

"I don't appreciate your undermining influence." It was hardly a purr. "I'll have to speak to Mr. Zanlos about it."

"Perhaps you've forgotten that I speak for Mr. Zanlos. For him and to him about things I don't approve of. And though I admire your skill, I can't say I like your methods. If there's one thing I can't abide, it's a bully." The quiet reproof efficiently put the overbearing woman in her place.

"I get the job done, Miss Bright. That's why I was hired."

"Hired. Fired. Just a simple change of consonants."

And with that, she turned her back on the seething choreographer, pretending not to feel the virtual daggers the woman thrust into her back as she left the room.

***

"She's amazing, isn't she?"

Kaz Zanlos didn't respond to the comment right away. He watched his assistant through the one-way glass from their high up overview of the auditorium. Finally, he had to agree.

"Yes. She is very efficient. And invaluable to me."

A lusty chuckle. "In what ways?"

"In all ways. And it would upset me greatly if that were to change for any reason."

"I will not interfere there. At least, not yet. Not unless she betrays us."

"She won't."

A dark chuckle. "You don't understand the power of fate, my friend."

Zanlos frowned. "He's being watched. If he becomes a threat, I'll deal with him."

Alex Cross turned from the window to regard Zanlos with a thunderclap of displeasure. "Oh no. That I'll not allow. If one hair on his head is disturbed without my direct order, you'll know why the night fears me and those I represent."

Though Zanlos appeared outwardly unmoved by the warning, he took it very seriously. There weren't many who'd ever scared him in the past, and that number pared down to next to none now that he'd assumed this supernatural state. But Cross was one of them. He made Zanlos' hair stand on end, just like the proverbial footsteps passing over his grave. Only he wasn't in the grave, and that's how he preferred for it to remain. Revenge could wait. He'd learned patience, just as he'd learned to deal with those like the casino's mysterious owner—with confidence underlaid with caution.

"What do you suggest we do about him, Alex?"

"I want him closer," his quixotic companion said at last. "Keep your enemies closest, I always say. He makes me nervous out there. I want him in here where it will come as no surprise when he decides to make his move."

"This is about him, then?"

A nod. But Kaz was not convinced. He knew his benefactor had his own agenda, and Kaz had no intention of letting himself or his assistant be crushed when its gears were put in motion. He'd played out that losing hand before. So he pushed for a stronger commitment.

"It's agreed then that both Miss Bright and the policeman are off limits for the time being."

"Agreed."

So why didn't Kaz believe it?

***

The sound of water woke her.

She could hear the waves crashing below, angry and seething, much like the emotions pushing upon her.

Where am I?

The sensations of tearing grief and fright were so familiar they no longer had the power to surprise her. Anguish surged in a violent tide, sucking at her soul with its relentless rip and ebb. Dampness froze against her cheeks as an icy wind burned her.

Defiantly, she turned into that harsh blast of air, letting it chill the hot ache of loss weighting her heart.

How could she go on knowing what lay in store for her? Knowing the misery of the years to come because she had seen them enacted through her mother's tears.

Her mother? She'd never known her mother.

Gathering her courage, she looked below. How far down it was, how bleak and cold and final that solution. But what else was there now that he was gone?

She leaned into the steady thrust of the wind, letting it support her body like the strong line of a lover's form. Her eyes slipped closed as if in bliss. For it would be bliss to escape this awful sorrow.

But the scream that jerked her back to awareness sounded of terror not liberation.

Naomi glanced about in alarm, disorientation glazing her eyes and shortening her breath. It took a panicked moment to realize she stood on the small balcony of her rented house, overlooking the little garden below. Her cotton nightgown clung coldly to her body, plastered by the spray of early morning rain that blew in from the distant mountains. Her pulse pounded in her ears. Her temple throbbed in time. Nausea swelled then slowly receded as she began a fitful trembling.

What did it mean, this recurrent dream with its emotions and sensations so vivid she could scarcely believe they weren't real.

Were they real?

Was it more than a dream but rather a memory?

She took a shaky gasp as understanding struck her. With a wobbly rush, she just made it to the bathroom as sickness tore up through her middle to burn her throat and eyes. As the raw spasms finally abated, she sat back on the tiled floor and slumped upon her forearm where it draped along the edge of her tub.

If it wasn't dream, it was truth.

She'd just relived her attempted suicide.

***

From his vantage point in her spearlike yucca thicket, Gabriel witnessed once again the chilling tableau played out from Naomi's past. He'd tucked himself away from view within her backyard oasis, held there by the fomenting emotions writhing through her dreams. He could feel her panic, could sense her agitation in the soft whimpers and moans she made in her restless tossings. Though he couldn't see into her private hell, couldn't personally experience the dreams that so tormented her, the friction they stirred matched the violent chafe of a lightning storm about to tear loose within her soul. He didn't need to see the images that drove her toward her grim and very final decision. They were etched against the stark white canvas of her face as she tore open the doors leading to her darkened bower. She raced to the balcony rail, not a moonstruck Juliet come to seek her lover but rather a woman pushed to the very brink of self-destruction by the demons that pursued her. His own face was wet from more than the rainfall as he suffered her anguish and her pain-wracked indecision when she paused before taking that fateful leap.

And he watched her wake as he had on countless nights before. He saw the surprise then the horror twist her expression.

His first instinct was to go to her, to wrap her in his embrace and console her with the fact that on this night, he'd been here to catch her. But would she accept that from him at this tenuous point? He didn't think so. His presence would create questions and a demand to know a truth he could not yet reveal. A truth about himself and his reason for watching over her. To rush that telling would bring ruin to all his hopes and careful plans, but seeing her in such pain of confusion was too much to bear.

How could she trust him once she knew the extent to which he'd failed her? He hadn't been there to catch her the first time. He was here standing out in her bushes because he'd failed to keep her safe when a second chance had arisen in Washington. He should have been more aggressive, more swift to act on her behalf instead of allowing his investigation of Zanlos to play out just a little bit farther in hopes of snaring him in a web of his misdeeds. Instead, he'd been the one snared, and Naomi again had suffered for his over-confidence. He'd been so careful in his court of her in her role as Zanlos' secretary, so careful not to let his emotions get in the way of his duties. He'd held back, keeping his distance so as not to give himself away to the clever lawyer and his unknown and much more dangerous partner. There, as here, Zanlos had wreathed himself in secrets and shadows and had hidden himself behind the trusting innocence of the woman who worked for him.

Gabriel had discovered too late that Zanlos and his vicious partner had taken advantage of that cautious distance to make Naomi their thrall, to steal her free will and make her their pawn. But the scheming lawyer had underestimated the strength of Naomi's spirit. He'd been misled by her fragile appearance and gentle manner. He hadn't known a fearless and fiercely protective female resided within that delicate shell. Though Gabriel had managed to wrest her from Zanlos' grip, she'd returned there of her own accord, driven by the noble intention of saving Gabriel and his friends from betrayal at her hands. And Gabriel had lost her. He'd been helpless to prevent a newly-made Zanlos from snatching her away. Gabriel's frantic search, aided by a tip from Rolland, had brought him to Las Vegas, where he discovered to his dismay that Zanlos had snatched away more than Naomi's freedom. He'd also stolen her memory of all that came before. Of him. What had become of the spirit she'd shown in that brave act of sacrifice? Did it still flicker within the frightened and haunted woman on the balcony above? Or had Zanlos managed to steal that as well?

He had no answer as she turned and went back inside. Only the intensity of her sadness remained, lying heavily upon his heart like the repressive blanket of humidity left behind now that the rain had passed by.

If he couldn't comfort her within his arms, he'd do the next best thing. He reached out with his mind, thinking to apply a little vampire magic, just enough to quiet her turmoil and allow her to seek rest. Nothing dramatic. Just a soft layering of calm, emotional sedative. He let his thoughts stretch toward her, opening like arms widening for a hug.

And that's when he smacked up against her defenses.

Mentally, he reeled back, stunned, surprised by the cold shield she'd erected about her own psyche that prevented him from getting close to her. He frowned in the darkness, distressed by her rejection of his comfort. Had Zanlos taught her to protect herself in such a fierce fashion? He reached out again, seeking signs of the other vampire's web of control, but there were none. He could sense Zanlos, but it was a vague residue compared to the impenetrable wall she'd placed about her thoughts.

Lest she be alarmed by his attempted intrusion, Gabriel withdrew his probe. Forced to observe her from the impersonal distance, he brooded in the night. This gift she'd acquired would keep out tampering powers. That was good. If she could shield herself from his mental inquiries, perhaps she could resist Zanlos as well. But however strong her external shell, he knew the inner crumbled with each passing moment. And would continue to disintegrate unless he could find a way to make her whole.

It was his fault.

His pride had pushed her to that pinnacle of self-destruction, but his determination and his love would keep her from going over that edge again.

He'd been given a another chance. He couldn't afford to waste it. Not when more than just her life hung in the balance.

He was bartering for her immortal soul.

SIX

"Hello again."

Naomi looked up in alarm, but her startlement eased when she recognized the woman with the serving tray.

"You look awfully pale. I'm not going to have to escort you to the ladies' room again, am I?"

"No." Naomi managed a wan smile. "I just didn't get much sleep is all."

"Tell me about it. In this noisy place, I don't think I've managed more than forty winks myself since I got here. I've got to get out and start looking for some place quiet. Someplace away from the Strip. Someplace, you know, normal. Do you know of any place like that?"

And it came to Naomi in a flash.

"Yes. Yes, I do."

"Great. I get a break right after the first show. Let's grab some coffee."

"Okay."

And Naomi began to think that maybe it would be okay. That maybe there was some degree of normal to be found in her life if she didn't have to live it with only her tangled thoughts and shadowed memories for company.

Maybe she wouldn't be so afraid if she wasn't so alone.

"You're serious? You wouldn't mind a roommate?"

"Do you snore?"

"Like a sailor." Rita Davies grinned wide and swabbed up another gob of ketchup with her French fry. "These are terrible for you," she pronounced before popping it into her mouth. She chewed with relish. Everything she did, she did with gusto.

Naomi knew she'd made the right choice.

"I'm a hopeless slob, but I'm a great cook. I don't have time to do anything but work, so you don't have to worry about me bringing unwanted guests home. I don't have family, so I won't be running up the phone bill." Rita paused for a moment, looking concerned. "I do have one ongoing relationship that I hope won't be a problem."

Naomi waited. How bad could it be? A boyfriend in prison?

"It's Mel. He's getting on in years and is losing his hair. Sometimes he gets pretty grumpy, but mostly he's a real lover."

"Mel?"

"You know, as in Gibson.

"You have a relationship with Mel Gibson?"

Rita nearly choked on her cherry cola. "Don't I wish. Mel's my cat. I've got him boarded for now, poor baby. He's declawed and has had all his shots. He doesn't go out and kill birds. He prefers to watch them on Animal Planet. You aren't allergic or anything, are you?"

Her look was so genuinely pleading, what could Naomi say?

"I'll be expecting you and Mel tomorrow."

After Rita returned to work and Naomi began the walk to the Amazon, she had time to consider her impulsive choice. A virtual stranger and her cat would soon be invading the privacy of her home. What did she know about Rita Davies other than what she'd seen and liked? And even envied a little bit.

But then what could be worse than spending another night in a cold sweat, waking to her own demons in her own prison of solitude?

Rita would bring life and noise and energy back into her silent, pastel existence. What could be wrong with that? Of all the risks she'd been afraid to take, what could be bad about this one?

Unless she woke her new roommate while screaming like a mad woman.

***

"Come in, Miss Bright."

Naomi entered the office cautiously, wondering why he'd sent for her so early in the evening. Kaz Zanlos was a creature of habit, as easy to read as the face of a clock. With the advent of evening, he'd hold private meetings with his investors and staff. Her presence wasn't required until later in the night, allowing her time to pursue her own compulsion. But on this night, his call came almost immediately upon her arrival, and she had to question the reason for his break in routine.

"Sit down, Miss Bright."

Obediently, she took the chair angled before his big mahogany desk where he sat with the glitter of Las Vegas spread behind him. For an instant, she recalled another office, one with walls of glass, with another city as a backdrop, but the image flickered just out of reach and eluded her. She didn't try to retrieve it. That was another life. What did it matter?

Zanlos stood and came around the massive desk to lean casually upon its edge. He was an elegant man. Naomi had always found him attractive in a sharp, inapproachable way. In his expensive silk suit and Italian leather loafers, he presented a picture of success and power. The darker elements of what he was roiled beneath the surface, always a part of his internal makeup, brought into keener focus by his altered state of being.

He wasn't a good man.

She's sensed that about him from the start, from the beginning of a work relationship that she could no longer remember. He involved himself, and by doing so, involved her, in things that crossed the boundaries of law, both manmade and unnatural. He walked confidently with danger, preferring its company when he could have made himself a fortune along legitimate lines. His associates came in big cars with bulletproof glass, flying in from either coast to check on their investment in the Amazon. He spoke with them behind closed doors, and she preferred not to know the content of their conversations.

But it was Alexander Cross who concerned her the most. Cross, the unseen and unheard owner of the Amazon and holder of the purse strings. The man she'd never seen except in fleeting shadow.

Perhaps so she could never identify him in a police line up.

But even knowing what Zanlos was and what he was probably doing, Naomi's allegiance stood unwavering. Kaz Zanlos had saved her from madness by bringing her here, by giving her a job she loved and a purpose that carried her from day to day. And for that reason, she could never betray him.

"Have I done something wrong, Mr. Zanlos?"

He smiled tolerantly at her uneasiness. "Miss Bright, you

never do anything wrong. That's why I value you so greatly. This is not about business."

"Oh?"

"I realize that your private life is none of my business, but it is still my concern. I am concerned about you, Miss Bright. Something has happened recently that has upset you and that, in turn, upsets me. Is it something I can help you with?"

He'd brought her into his office to discuss her personal dysfunctions, Naomi realized in a surge of sudden panic. How could she answer? By telling him that her dalliances with insanity had returned and threatened to control her life? That she couldn't trust the reality of what she saw from one minute to the next?

"I met a man," she heard herself blurt out in response to his request. It wasn't what she'd planned to say, but it wasn't exactly a lie, either. He would detect a lie from her in an instant. Of all the confessions she could make, this one seemed the safest.

"Oh? And who is this lucky fellow who distracts you from your work?"

A flush of heat stole up into her pale cheeks, doing more to convince him than any words could have. "His name is Gabriel. He is one of the knights in the show at the Excaliber."

"Ah, your knight in shining armor. And is he, Miss Bright?"

"Is he what?"

"Worthy of your affection?"

She stared for a moment, not knowing how to answer. Then she admitted with a hush of embarrassment, "I don't know."

Then the other shoe dropped. Hard.

"But I do. This man, this Gabriel McGraw, he hasn't sought you out for the reason you suspect or perhaps hoped."

The slap of his words took her unaware, stinging her upon impact then reminding her of her naivete with their harsh, lingering burn.

"What do you mean?" And she didn't want to hear his answer, to hear what she already knew…that Gabriel, her guardian angel, wasn't interested in her at all but only in how he could use her to forward his own interests. A cold lump, hard as a fist, settled in her belly as she waited for Zanlos to destroy her illusions.

"This man is no stranger to us, Miss Bright. You don't remember him but it's true."

She believed him. She'd known there was something about Gabriel that went deeper than a chance meeting, something that suggested history and emotions she could no longer recall.

Had they been lovers? Before she could think of how to phrase that delicate question, Zanlos continued his evisceration of her dreams.

"Mr. McGraw is a policeman, Naomi. His only goal is to see me punished for a wrong perpetrated by my former partner. But since she is out of his reach, he's decided I will do. He thinks to use you to get close to me. He means to use you as an instrument to my ruin."

"No."

"I'm sorry, Naomi but it is the truth."

"I meant, no, I would never betray you."

And though there were tears in her heart and glistening in her eyes, she spoke the with a candor he could not doubt.

And he allowed himself a small, satisfied smile.

"I will never see him again."

There. It was over. She'd closed the door on the tantalizing threat of Gabriel McGraw. Part of her was relieved to put the stress and strain of emotions behind. But another whispered that knowing him could have led to wondrous things, things worth the agonies of doubt and indecision. Things she'd envied from afar in the lives of the others but was afraid to seek out for herself. Now, she didn't have to struggle with whether or not to take the risk. The decision was out of her hands. She'd numb her heart and accept it. Just as she numbed her mind to all the rest. But her staunch claim didn't please Zanlos as she'd thought it would.

"No, Miss Bright, you will see him and often. You will let him get close to you and let him believe you'll get him closer to what he most desires."

"And what is that?" Her words rasped from a soul wrung dry.

"Revenge. A petty, self-serving revenge that will only harm

the innocent, you included, Miss Bright. And that, I cannot allow."

No. Don't ask me to do this. Don't ask me to betray this man. Don't ask me to abandon honor and self-respect in order to serve you.

Even as she thought those things, the rebellion inside her was already dying.

But I will serve. I will serve.

Leadenly, she asked, "What do you want me to do?"

***

It took Rita Davies less than a day to make herself completely at home in Naomi's cozy bungalow on the outskirts of the city, and her presence infiltrated every available surface. Her blender and power drink mixes crowded Naomi's colorful woven basket collection back against the ivy designed tiles, where they huddled together as if in alarm and insult. Already dishes filled the sink basin, stacked in a precarious pyramid with half-filled glasses, coffee cups and skillets that smelled of sauteed onion and green peppers. An open package of flour tortillas lay on the counter, drying out like a lizard in the heat of day. Various jackets, shirts and even a stray coral-colored lace bra re-decorated Naomi's couch and chairs, and a row of unmatched footwear marched out from under the coffee table, interwoven with an assortment of socks and knee-highs.

The light was on in the bathroom. As Naomi reached to turn it off, she grimaced at the sight of wet towels mounded on the floor and at the thick residue of herbal-scented bubbles still frothing in the tub. The water was dripping. Naomi tightened the faucet even as her features tightened. She tripped over a lone sandal as she stared in amazement at the assortment of products now commandeering her sink. Every fragrance-free, organically grown, environmentally safe beauty aide she could imagine and then some.

Perhaps she'd acted too impulsively in opening her home to a stranger.

A very messy stranger.

She snapped off the light.

She couldn't hear the music, only the relentless thump of

the bass. Her eardrums winced at the merciless assault even before she tapped on the door to her newly occupied spare room. Occupied like France after the Germans marched through it.

Because of its sunny eastern exposure, Naomi had used the room to showcase her collection of black and white photography. The contrasts came alive in the pure, unforgiving light, and she had spent many a morning unwinding with a cup of tea, admiring the plays of darks and whites. The simplicity relaxed her. But there was nothing relaxing about what Rita had done to her former retreat.

The delicate wrought iron day bed frame was tipped up against the wall and out of the way. The mattress rested on the floor next to the heap of every article of clothing Rita owned…other than those already strewn through other rooms of the house. A massive stereo system was stacked on the other side in the midst of a litter of CD jewel cases. Rita lay in the center of it all, headphones engulfing her reality as she bobbed in time to some aggressively clinical techno beat. She wore a purple sports bra and boy-cut briefs. Her toenails were painted to match.

Spotting her, Rita wrenched off the headset. The harsh searing of a dance mix pounded out.

"Hey, I didn't hear you come in."

"I knocked," Naomi murmured by way of apology.

"I wouldn't have heard a wrecking ball if it was knocking." She switched off the CD player and gazed up at her roommate with a naked honesty. "I can't thank you enough for taking me in like this. You're an amazing woman, Nomi. I've never met anyone as good hearted."

Flushing at the effusive compliment, a part of her whispered cynically, "Or as soft headed."

"I made you a no-yolk omelette and some wheat-free muffins. I thought you might be hungry when you got home."

The thoughtfulness crushed her churlish sentiments of moments before beneath a regretful heel. Emotion at the unexpected gesture thickened in her throat.

"You didn't have to do that, Rita."

"I know, but Mel doesn't really appreciate my mother-henning. I told you I love the kitchen."

The cooking part but obviously not the cleaning part.

"Thanks," she sighed. "I'm too tired to make anything for myself this morning."

Without a trace of self-consciousness, Rita bounded up and into the kitchen in her underwear. Blushing for her, Naomi followed, hoping she wouldn't discover that her shameless guest vacuumed in the nude.

If she vacuumed.

While Rita buzzed about the small galley-type kitchen reheating the healthful offering, Naomi carried two plates to the table only to stop dead at the sight of the most mammoth cat she'd ever seen lying in a butterscotch lump right on the middle of her place mat. The animal regarded her with an indifferent blue-glass gaze before closing its eyes, obviously considering her not worth the worry.

"That's Mel. Just give him a shove. He has no table manners."

As Naomi reached out a tentative hand toward the yellow glob, Mel gave her a low rumble of warning. She jerked her hand back.

"He's all right." She decreed faintly and set the plates on two other place mats.

You're damn right, all right, the cat seemed to say with a twitch of its tail.

"How was your night?" Rita asked with an almost June Cleaverish cheerfulness.

"Long," Naomi admitted. "And over."

"Like a bad date."

And that reminded Naomi of her unpleasant purpose.

"Speaking of dates, have you seen your friend Gabriel again?"

"Not since he helped me move."

Gabriel had been in her house? Alarm and a vicarious sense of excitement skittered through her.

"He has a huge trunk in that old car of his, and I had a ton of junk in storage. I hope you don't mind."

"No," she croaked out, thinking of Gabriel McGraw in her

private spaces "Of course not. We should have him over for dinner to thank him for being so kind to you and for rescuing me from that purse snatcher. Do you now how to get hold of him?"

"Yeah, he gave me his cell number in case I needed anything."

An unworthy pang of jealousy splintered into Naomi's thoughts. With what she planned, she had no business harboring possessive feelings. She shouldn't have any feelings about the matter one way or another. Freezing her emotions until no resonance of regret trembled, she smiled at Rita narrowly.

"Find out when he's free. I have something I want to ask him."

***

He was just using her.

Naomi tossed from one side to the other in her restless search for escape in slumber. It eluded her.

Using her, using her tangle of emotions, her vulnerability, her loneliness.

An awful thought paralyzed her breathing.

What if he'd arranged the purse snatching just so he could play the hero?

There were no heroes. Hadn't she learned that lesson once before? When? When had she learned it?

She'd known him before, before the blackness sucked her memory away.

Flopping onto her back, she stared through the darkness toward the ceiling, as if trying to find some answer there. What had their relationship been? She should have asked Mr. Zanlos, but she'd been afraid, then, to hear the truth. Instinct told her they'd been close. Then why hadn't Gabriel mentioned a shared history when they'd met on the street, and later at Rita's room? Did he know about her collapse? Did he think to trade upon her lapse to rebuild what still simmered between them? She hugged herself, suddenly cold in the climate-controlled room.

Had they slept together?

A shudder rippled to her toes. His hands on her body, his hot breath upon her face. Sensation surged to supply the rest—

not the erotic images she expected but rather panic, desperation, fear.

Her gasp sounded raw and loud against the soothing hum of the air conditioner.

With sleep out of her reach, Naomi rolled from her bed and padded into the bathroom. Under the rosy glow of the night light, she opened the medicine cabinet and was delayed for a moment by the sight of all Rita's vitamins and mineral supplements surrounding her own small bottle of relief.

She shook two of the tablets into her palm and washed them down with a swallow of tasteless tap water. Zanlos wouldn't like her taking them, but she'd been so deprived of rest, she'd sought out help in a suburban clinic. Just to help her relax. Just to ease her way into slumber.

Just to keep the dreams at bay.

And it worked.

Sometimes.

Returning to her room, she started to pull back the covers only to have the action halted half way. A low growl of protest told her the reason. Mel was plopped in the center of her bed and wasn't pleased with the idea of moving.

"Scat," Naomi hissed, but the beast simply reiterated his response.

Out of patience, Naomi tugged on the covers and was rewarded by the seismic thud of the animal hitting the floor. She slid under the sheet as Mel waddled from the room in disgust.

Sighing softly, Naomi closed her eyes, willing sleep to hurry. But even the drug couldn't overcome her anxieties immediately as long minutes ticked past.

Get close to him, Zanlos had told her.

Easy to accomplish, but how difficult to endure?

SEVEN

He'd stood in her little backyard Eden before, but this was the first time as guest rather than unseen observer.

She'd made the small space into a desert oasis complete with palms, richly scented flowering shrubs and lighted koi pond. But what made it true paradise was the sight of her approaching with a frosted glass of ice tea. The lights from her patio doors shone through the gauzy dress she wore, illuminating the sleek line of her body and the graceful mechanics of her walk. He stood, mesmerized, he with the power to enchant, suddenly the helplessly enchanted.

"I hope it's not too sweet."

He took the cold glass. "I'm sure it's fine."

Sweet was this moment so long desired.

When Rita had told him of Naomi's request that they meet, his hopes soared. Time for the courtship to begin. But now that he was here, and with Rita conveniently absent, a strange undercurrent of tension threatened his expectations.

Why had she invited him? He'd wanted the reason to be emotional interest, but Naomi's rigid movements and taut smile telegraphed some other motive. He scented her uneasiness, could hear it in her shallow respirations. At first, he'd thought it was fear but now...

Anger. He sensed anger but couldn't understand its cause. The brief eye contact they made snapped with it. Had he done something? Did she suspect something? He couldn't lay a cause to the fierce set of her soft lips. They hadn't had enough time together, at least in this lifetime, for her to form an opinion of him one way or another.

And that, he meant to change.

He smiled, letting the gesture spread like a sunrise across his face, letting the wattage build until she couldn't help being warmed by it.

She resisted for a moment, clinging to her stony facade, then slowly, with great reluctance, those edges of ice began to melt away. Her gaze dropped, and when it flirted back up to his, he found all the emotion he'd wished for simmering there. Hope, curiosity, desire, need. Yet still, that discoloring trace of wariness. Well, he'd just have to woo that away.

"You haven't tried your tea."

"I've been drinking in a more satisfying sweetness."

As he raised the glass to take a sip, he was rewarded by the flush of pleasure stealing into her cheeks. But she wasn't to be so easily won.

"You speak flattery well."

"Only to you." He caught himself before he'd added, *my lady*. That she'd think those words sounded sincere because of frequent use on others couldn't be farther from the truth. He'd always had his share of fair ladies crowding for his attention, but only with Naomi had he felt comfortable and at ease enough for poetic sentiment. "You inspire me."

"I'm supposed to believe that?"

When had his gentle Naomi become a cynic?

"It's my plan to convince you of it."

The nervousness crept back into her glance. "Of what?"

"Of the rightness of what's between us."

Her head reared back, her stare growing fixed. But he could hear her heartbeat quicken, its tempo becoming fast and frantic. *Not with fear. Please, don't let it be with fear.* "I wasn't aware there was anything between us. I don't even know you."

He forced a confident grin to coax away her alarm. "Ah, and therein lies the convincing."

"Ummm."

Clutching at her glass with both hands, she slipped away from him. Though it was his first instinct to follow close, he held his ground and simply trailed her with his stare. Her tension had returned, lending a stiffness to the fragile slope of her shoulders and a jarring rhythm to the natural glide of her walk as she circled the gurgling little pond.

"I didn't ask you here so you could dazzle me with your pleasant but a bit too polished charm."

He pursed his lips at the tartness in her words but couldn't contain his smile. "Too bad. Then why, may I ask, am I here?" So much for romance.

"I don't know if Rita's told you that I work at the Amazon."

"The new hotel at the end of the Strip. Yes. She said you were the manager's assistant. A very prestigious job."

"A very demanding job," she corrected without a hint of boastfulness. "I make things run smoothly for everyone else."

"And you've hit a snag."

"Yes." Her quick glance conveyed her gratitude at his immediate grasp of the situation.

"And how can I help?"

She ceased her restless travels, coming to a stop on the other side of the pool. The iridescent lights seeped up the cool pastel of her dress to illuminate her fair skin like Carrara marble. Gabriel struggled to breathe.

"I've seen you at the Excaliber. You are very skilled with a sword."

"It's a show."

"No. It's more than pretend with you. I'm sorry I can't explain it better, but there is a oneness with you and your weapons that makes the battle…real."

"I'm well trained to make it appear so."

"You've been in the military."

"Is it that obvious?"

"You have that kind of discipline. Can you train others?"

"Train them to do what, exactly?"

"To move with the same kind of confidence."

"Sure. After about eight months."

"How about three weeks?"

"You're joking, right?"

"I'm very serious. That's when we open at the Amazon."

"And what has one thing to do with the other?"

She looked around then sank down onto one of the pretty little wrought iron benches as if suddenly needing the support. A touch of entreaty stole into her uplifted gaze. "Our Amazon is filled with Amazonian women. The female warriors, you know." He nodded, and she continued. "Only our female warriors are about as aggressive as puppies."

"And they need to be pit bulls."

She smiled. "Exactly."

"You want me to train your show girls to become GI Janes?"

"Could you? I mean, not really, but just teach them the attitude, the toughness, the control, how to swing a sword without cutting off each other's limbs."

"This was your boss's idea?"

Her hopeful gaze flickered downward in evasion. "No, it's mine. Mr. Zanlos doesn't come down onto the floor. He's busy in his office with investor meetings. He leaves the details to me. And it's my job to make those details..."

"Go smoothly. I get the picture."

"Can you help me, I mean, us?"

"And I'd be working closely with you?"

She looked uncomfortable, and that was his answer before she spoke a faint, "Yes."

"But I have a job already."

"We can pay you twice what you're making now."

"You don't know what I'm making."

"Yes, I do." Then she put her hand to her mouth. "Please don't say anything. I wouldn't want to get Rita in trouble."

"Rita found out how much I get paid?"

"I have a feeling Rita is very resourceful."

"Good old Rita."

He was silent, letting the moment build with suspense while inwardly he reined hard on his eagerness. Working closely with Naomi. Close but out of the sight of Kaz Zanlos. This was perfect. Perfect. Finally, he ended her wait.

"Three weeks at twice the pay. How can I refuse?"

Naomi had hoped success would relieve the tightness crushing within her chest, but the pressure squeezed mercilessly. Her heart was beating much too fast. The evening heat went straight to her head, making it swirl while her thoughts spun around like revolving satellites. Faintly, she heard the sound of glass shattering, but she didn't associate the noise with the drink she'd been holding as all her senses seemed to suck down into an endless vacuum.

She said his name, and he was there.

Her field of vision filled with his handsome, angular features. Gabriel McGraw but not...not quite. The tousled mane of blond hair was the same, and the rugged symmetry of his face. And his smile, his smile like the promise of a new day dawning clear and bright and ripe with possibilities. The difference was in his eyes. The gaze that bewitched hers was deep and dark and dreamy, untouched by harshness, by evil. The gaze of an innocent, of a idealist, a romantic as yet untarnished by the ugly truths of life. Shy, hopeful, respectful.

This was the man she'd fallen in love with.

But it wasn't the same man who shared her garden and threatened to break her heart.

Images, sensations, sounds swirled about her with tornadic force. Laughter, a light caress of lips upon her palm, the tickling of lute strings, and quiet words, spoken with fierce intention and intensity.

"I will return for you. You have my pledge, as you have my heart."

She sat up with a gurgling gasp for breath.

"It's all right. You're all right."

The quiet assurance brought her focus back to the small garden, to the delicately scented night and to the man who now held her close.

Her gaze darted about in a panic. All was as it should be, but could she say the same about herself and about Gabriel McGraw?

"What happened?" she asked to give herself time to recover.

"You fainted."

He'd joined her on the wrought iron bench. It's size forced them into intimate proximity. His arms wrapped about her, binding her to his chest in a possessive curl, both comforting and claustrophobic. Too disoriented to struggle, she sagged against him, limp and trembling, until small slivers of awareness began to reassemble. Alarming things like how his silky shirt warmed to the heat of her body, how his scent reminded her of tall grasses and cool meadow breezes. The bend of his arm formed a supportive cradle about the small of her back, and the hollow between his chest and shoulder, a secure nave in which she could hide forever. She closed her eyes, her senses soaking up those oddly familiar details. How could she know the exact way his lean jaw fit against the top of her head? Or recognize the muscular sculpting of his arm as if she'd ridden those impressive highs and lows before and often? Why did the sound of his breathing console with the steady cadence of the tides, so regular, so solid, so eternal?

Her hands were knotted in the loose folds of his shirt, clutching for security against the ebbs and rips of her awakening senses. Slowly, her grasp relaxed and her fingers spread along the taut and hard textured plane of his midsection. His breathing stopped. She felt his fingertips trace the curve of her cheek. When they curled beneath her chin to encourage an upward tilt, she didn't resist.

He was going to kiss her. And she was going to let it happen.

She wanted it to happen. Had wanted it to happen for so very, very long.

Only it didn't.

When it didn't, she opened her eyes. His features swam into focus, so close she could map the laugh lines feathering from the corners of his eyes and notice a tiny scar on the bridge of his nose. His dark stare swallowed her like warm, blanketing evening, engulfing her world with the compelling secrets of its own. This close, his eyelashes seemed impossibly thick and his mouth irresistibly soft. She touched his lips with trembling fingertips, lightly charting their mysterious curves and tempting swells. His gaze brightened, firing with something so beyond simple passion that she was consumed in that complex combustion. His mouth moved gently against the pads of her fingers, moistening them, sucking lightly at them. Intrigued, she flirted with the feelings sparking between them, until the sudden harsh draw of his breath startled her from her musings.

She stumbled away from him, backing off the bench on unsteady legs to protect emotions that were more wobbly still. Her hand went automatically to the sheer scarf knotted at her neck where a hard pulse pounded in denial of what she'd been about to do. Her fingers twisted tight in the loose ends of silk, as if clinging for her very life against the attraction she held for this man.

But it was a lie.

He was there to use her, to abuse her heart, and she'd had quite enough of that.

"I'm sorry to be such a bad hostess, but I really think I should go lie down. There's a bug going around at work, and I think I may have picked up a touch of it."

"You need to take better care of yourself, Naomi."

Whenever he spoke her name, an electric charge prickled along her bare arms, as if she were standing in the path of a fierce storm drawing danger like a lightning rod.

"I will. About that job? Can you be at the hotel tomorrow afternoon?"

"Nothing like short notice."

"As I've said, time is something we don't have." Talking business felt safe, and she gathered courage from the uninvolved nature of it. This was familiar ground. Desire was not.

"It will have to be in the evening. I'm afraid I'm just not a day person."

"That will be fine. I'll arrange things for you. Mr. Zanlos will be so pleased."

"I'm not doing this for him."

Again, she experienced that current of longing, that wish that his words were true.

But they weren't.

"Tomorrow night then, Mr. McGraw."

"Gabriel."

She swallowed and said his name, wishing it didn't sigh from her lips as if a spoken answer to prayer.

***

As he climbed into his big Mercury, he saw the telltale flutter of the curtains in the front of the bungalow. *A bug going around.* That bug was the disease of Zanlos' influence, and the sooner he dealt with Zanlos, the sooner Naomi would be cured of it.

As he sped toward the glow that hung over the city like the aftermath of an atomic detonation, he recalled of the scent of her hair with the wistful inhalation of his breath. The petal soft fragrance of violets drew him across the centuries to her side. And her skin, so smooth and flawless. And much too pale. He frowned. Was she ill? Was Zanlos overeager in his possession of her? His own protective instincts rumbled. To drain her to such a weak state was madness, but perhaps it was necessary to maintain his control. Was she aware of what Zanlos was, of what he did cloud her mind and manipulate her actions? Was she even now a pawn drawing him into some clever trap? It didn't matter. He could take care of himself. It was Naomi's survival that concerned him. No, consumed him.

Whether Naomi wished to act upon it or not, her subconscious was reacting to the past they'd shared. That was all the encouragement he had, and truly, all he needed.

Tomorrow night, he'd be close to both his love and his enemy. And it would be his impossibly difficult job to keep the two separated in both heart and mind while he saved the one and destroyed the other.

EIGHT

"You're going to go in there right under his nose?"

Gabriel paused in the brisk stuffing of his gym bag and tried to soothe his friend's worry with a confident smile. "He takes no interest in the running of the casino, only in the business matters above. He won't even know I'm there."

Rolland snorted his disbelief. Gabriel felt compelled to calm his doubts.

"I'll use a mild mask so I won't be recognized by anyone beyond the room. If my old friend should happen to glance my way, he'll see a stranger."

"And you have the power to maintain such a disguise?"

Reluctantly, Gabriel admitted, "Yes, I do."

"So you'll mask your identity and cloak your presence from our kind and be on guard every second against danger?"

"It's what I do, Rollie. It's what I've done for centuries."

"I could help."

"Stick with your studies, my friend. This is my battle. I can't do what I must do from the outside."

"My studies, as you call them, are not without their own risks," he said. His tone prickled in his own defense.

Gabriel pressed his shoulder. "I'm not making light of how you've chosen to lead your life. Our paths have gone in different directions, but I'm glad they've crossed once again. I have missed you, Rolland. So many times I could have used your sage counsel to keep me from rushing into trouble. You've always been the tug of restraint to my own impulsiveness."

"Yet you won't listen to me now any more than you would then."

Gabriel shrugged. He glanced about the locker room, feeling a strange sadness at walking away from the familiar, away from his companion of another era, another lifetime. He was always walking away. It was the pattern he'd made for himself to better accept what he was. No ties, no involvements. He couldn't afford to linger with humans in a world that didn't have a place for one such as himself. If he stayed on the outside, constantly moving, he had no time to miss what had escaped him.

Until now. Until Rolland and the excitement of this place fired his spirit with memories of a past he could no longer claim.

Until Naomi.

Now that he'd found her, he'd have to adjust his preternatural world to include her. He'd worry about how exactly to accomplish that once he'd freed her from Zanlos. He wouldn't consider the possibility that their worlds would never mesh in harmony. It could be done. He'd seen it happen with his human partner, Rae Borden, and her new husband, newly made vampire Nick Flynn. He and Naomi would have the life they had been denied. He hadn't conquered time to let it slip away from him now.

"So, you go there for him or for her?"

"For both," he admitted quietly. He closed the bag with a loud rasp of the zipper. "I think I have everything."

"Everything except your reason. Gabriel, no good can come of this."

Gabriel forced a smile of patience. Rollie - always the cautious one. But he owed his friend the courtesy of his attention. That, and so much more. More that they had never spoke of. "Why do you say that?"

"As a student of history, I listen to what history tells me. You should do the same."

"I'm listening."

Rolland scowled at his friend's obvious indulgence. "No you're not. You never listen, Gabe. You just rush in. Think first, Gabriel. Remember the past."

Yanking the bag straps up over his shoulder, Gabriel gave the morose prophet an impatient look. "Remember what?"

"What happened the last time duty and love collided. Your pride destroyed her, Gabe. Would you do that again?"

Wincing as if from the unexpected thrust of a sword, Gabriel turned away from both his companion's sincerity and the truth he spoke. But Rolland wasn't ready to let him go.

"Gabriel, she belongs to him. How can you think to bring him down without her suffering as well?"

"I won't let that happen."

"How can you prevent it any more now than you did then? You can't fight what was not fated to be."

Gabriel confronted him with a fierce expression. "What was fated was a future Naomi and I shared together. I will have that future, Rollie. I will."

"At whatever the cost?"

"What else could I gave that I have not already surrendered?" He concealed the pain in his eyes behind a pair of dark glasses. "Thank you for all you've done, Rollie."

Seeing their parting was imminent, Rolland sighed. "You'll return for a rematch, won't you? Our fans demand it."

"Anything for the crowd."

Rolland's voice deepened in anguish. "Don't do this, Gabe, not alone."

"I'm not alone." He slapped his hand down upon Rolland's shoulder, offering no further explanation. "You worry too much."

"And you not at all."

"You see, people don't change with the passing of time. Only the scenery does."

"You'll call if you need me."

"You are a good friend, Rolland."

"That's not a answer, Gabe."

"I'll call."

But as Rolland watched him leave the locker room area, he shook his head. "No you won't," he said to himself. "Not until it's too late."

***

"Come on, Grace. My grandmother can kick higher than that. Grace...who gave you that unfitting name?"

"I'm trying, Miss Parsons. I had it yesterday."

"And lost it today. Concentrate. Again."

As the girls started the routine over, Naomi bit back her opinion of how Kitty Parsons handled her charges. Bullying and insults to gain cooperation sat poorly with Naomi, but the choreographer was a professional, well-known for her flashy show numbers. Who was Naomi to question the methods if the results earned rave reviews?

But she didn't have to like it. And she certainly didn't like Kitty Parsons, but the woman had put together a dynamite dance routine…until Grace turned a beat too late and collided with Marty, bringing the rehearsal to an awkward halt.

"Grace, you move like a breeding cow. If you can't get this down, you can get out."

As the other girls shuffled in embarrassed empathy, Grace stood alone, all teary humiliation. "I'm trying, Miss Parsons."

"Trying doesn't cut it here. This is not your first grade dance recital, though even those children could do better in your place."

Enough.

"I don't think a first grader could fill out the costume as well as Gracie does, Miss Parsons."

Grace looked toward Naomi as she approached the stage area, her mascara beginning to run as she wiped at her eyes and gave a grateful smile. Kitty Parsons' expression was much less welcoming.

"Miss Bright, to what do we owe *this* interruption?"

"There's going to be a little change in plans this evening, something new I think the girls will enjoy."

Parsons narrowed her eyes, obviously doubting that she would. "No one told me about any change in schedule."

"I'm telling you now, Miss Parsons."

"And I'm telling you we are too far behind already to indulge in any foolishness you've come up with."

"I'll be sure to tell Mr. Zanlos that you considered his idea foolish without even hearing what it was."

Kitty took a deep, irritation-cleansing breath. "Let's hear it."

The girls had gathered into a tight group to silently cheer Naomi's confrontation with their nemesis, but one by one, their attention was drawn away from the tense discussion as they noticed a shadowed figure coming down the center aisle. The closer he came, the more riveted their focus, until the two verbal combatants were distracted into following their rapt gazes.

Naomi's system jolted as if hit with a charge from jumper cables as she watched Gabriel McGraw's mesmerizing approach. She could understand the dancers' uncharacteristic

gawking. Her own tongue would have lolled out as her jaw
hung unhinged if she hadn't found the presence of mind to snap
it shut.

There was something about Gabriel McGraw…something
more. More than just good looking, with his rumpled blond
hair and brooding poet's expression. More than just great pecs
poured into the sculpturing hug of a black tank top under the
loose flow of a gaudy, comic book character shirt. More than
just powerful in the way he moved with such leashed control.
Las Vegas was full of handsome, buff and beefy men. But none
of them had seen anything like Gabriel. He was man to the max.
And then there was still that 'more' that made it impossible to
look away.

And he was a liar and a schemer, too. Naomi couldn't afford
to forget that.

"Ladies, Mr. Gabriel McGraw. Mr. McGraw is going to
teach you to add a little something extra to your routine.
Something that will mesmerize the audience and keep them
coming back for more."

No one seemed to notice that she sounded a bit like a carney
shill with that pitch. They were too busy goggling over Gabriel
as he set down the bag he was carrying and stripped out of his
shirt. There in the shadows, etched into sharp relief by the glare
of the stage lighting, his arms and shoulders looked positively
lethal. A collective sigh whispered from the group on stage.

"We don't have time for this," Kitty Parsons hissed at this
renewed affront to her power. "I'm going to go up and talk to
Mr. Zanlos myself."

"Don't let the screen door smack you on your way out,"
came a naughty murmur from one of the girls. Kitty glared but,
unable to discern which one had mocked her so openly, she
stormed away intent upon putting a stop to Miss Goody Goody
Bright's interference.

None of the dancers even noticed she was gone.

"So, Mr. McGraw," cooed the carrot-topped Molly, "what
are you going to teach us?"

"That the best defense is a good offense."

While the girls puzzled over that, he unzipped his bag and

drew out a short staff of wood. He twirled it with increasing speed from one hand to the other until the air whistled and hummed while he talked.

"Any of you do any boxing, karate or self-defense?" He met with blank stares. "How about Tae Bo?" Hands came up. "All right. That's a start. It's balance, control and timing more than strength. Naomi—Miss Bright—asked me to pack some punch into your number, so we're going to learn to punch."

"You mean like Bruce Lee shit?" Candice, the chronic grumbler, interjected.

"No, more like Xena Warrior Princess shit," he corrected with a grin that melted them down like the froth on a steamy cappuccino. "Who wants to be a Xena?"

"She's bad," Candice conceded, and the others nodded. "But we're lovers not fighters."

"Be both. Strong is sexy. My job shouldn't be too hard since you're all in good shape." He allowed a charming leer that had the girls giggling in their skin tight spandex, and Naomi shrinking silently within her boxy K Mart Jacklyn Smith skirt and jacket special, feeling neither strong nor particularly sexy. "But you don't have to be an Amazon female to learn self-discipline and power. Anyone can."

"How about Miss Bright?" Jeannie suggested, drawing unwelcomed attention to the bookish assistant.

"Even Miss Bright," Gabriel insisted. His gaze locked on Namoi's, warming, compelling, challenging. "If she wants to."

Naomi started to shake her head.

"Come on, Miss Bright," Grace coaxed, and the others took up her plea until they were all clamoring for Naomi's participation. Alarmed yet secretly intrigued by the idea, Naomi held up her hands.

"I'm not dressed for it, ladies.

"Next time, come prepared," Gabriel suggested with a wink. *Next time.*

The thought of being in close proximity to him each night stirred a rash of apprehension and its less welcome kin, anticipation. But she'd get over it. She wasn't here to flirt. She wasn't here to learn to fight. She was here to set a trap. And

Gabriel was the big rat she planned to catch when it snapped. Resolve firmed her stance and her expression.

"So…Mr. McGraw, are you going to handle us all by yourself?" Marty's question was a purr of innuendo.

"As intriguing an idea as that might be, I've asked a friend to help me out.'

Who, me? Naomi was about to shake her head again when Gabriel turned, not to her, but toward the back of the auditorium, to where another Xena-ish woman entered.

Naomi's jaw dropped a second time. "Rita?"

"Ladies, this is Rita Davies. She has an intimate relationship with self-defense, and she'll help you look like lean, mean, fighting machines."

"Don't forget the sexy," Molly added.

Gabriel laughed. "Trust me. Nobody's going to forget the sexy. Now watch the way Rita moves while we go round."

Flashing a grin to Naomi, Rita slipped out of her oversized shirt. She wore a citrus green unitard beneath it. She and Gabriel hopped up onto the stage area, and the girls fanned out to observe and to shamelessly eye the gorgeous Gabriel. Naomi stayed in the shadows, also considering the sparring pair with new awareness.

When had he asked Rita to join him? Why hadn't her roommate mentioned it?

Was there more to their supposed friendship then either had bothered to bring to her attention? An unsettling jealousy rumbled through her as she admitted that they did look good together, both fit and confident and aggressive in their movements. A couple. Perhaps. Drawing the flaps of her beige jacket together over her less than spectacular bosom, she faded back further in the auditorium to take a seat at one of the tables on the fourth riser. From that elevation she had a clear view, and she wasn't sure she liked what she saw. Gabriel McGraw controlling her girls. Rita Davies, her friend, partnered with Gabriel.

Soon they wouldn't need her at all.

Rubbing at the tension pounding through her temples, she paused in sudden surprise.

It was gone.

She'd been so busy and preoccupied that she hadn't noticed until now.

The hour was early evening, a time when her unexplained restlessness typically came calling. Calling until she couldn't ignore the summons. But the compelling urge hadn't come, nor had the chills of desperate yearning and knotting anxiety that wouldn't ease until she was caught up in the pageantry at the Excaliber. She'd associated the compulsion with the place, but maybe she'd been wrong.

She stared down at the two faux combatants and explored the sense of calm so foreign in conjunction with the setting sun. A disquieting notion rose like the pale moon beyond the jarring city lights.

Maybe it was the man who drew her.

***

Kitty Parsons stopped at the private elevators, reaching out to stab at the button just as the doors opened. She stumbled back to avoid being knocked over by the exiting bulk of Marcus Sinclair. He caught her by the forearms in an instinctive move to protect her from a fall. Instead of displaying gratitude, she slapped at his big hands until he released her.

"Get out of my way, you moron."

As she shoved by him, which was rather like pushing at a granite wall, to enter the elevator, Marcus threw up his forearm to block the closing of the door.

"Mr. Zanlos is in a meeting. He won't like being interrupted."

"I don't care what Mr. Zanlos does or doesn't like. And it's none of your business, anyway." The smack of her hand upon his arm was only slightly harsher than the snap of her tone. Shrugging, Marcus stepped back so the door could soundlessly close.

"Idiot," she muttered to herself. "I don't need this crap."

Kitty smoothed down her sleeves just as she smoothed her ruffled ego. She'd left a prosperous gig at the Mirage to pull this show together. Her resume boasted of successes everywhere from Caesar's Palace to the MGM. She worked with the greats, and she'd made greats. No way some little accountant was going to throw her scrawny weight between her and another hit show. And she was going to let Zanlos know it.

Squaring her shoulders and drawing up to her regal model-perfect 5'11" height, Kitty marched from the elevator and across the marble floors of the office suite as if sweeping down the fashion show runways of her youth. She was well aware of the impression she made and expected the nitwit girl at the reception desk to be flustered by her approach. As well she was.

"Miss Parsons, you don't have an appointment."

"I don't need one, twit."

And she breezed on by, never pausing to knock at the restricted barrier of closed doors. She barged in with an imperious disdain for those rules. Rules Kaz Zanlos was not pleased to have broken.

"Miss Parsons, weren't you told I was in a meeting?"

"This can't wait. There's a problem with the show, and I need it taken care of right now before your meddling assistant ruins everything."

"Oh? And just what has Miss Bright jeopardized?"

"The autonomy of my authority."

She glanced from Zanlos' rigid expression past the easeled rendering of the creepy tomb that would eventually take center focus for the production number to the second man in the room. She didn't know him, but she wouldn't forget his face. She never forgot a face, just in case it was necessary for her to court investment clout at another hotel if this meeting went south. He didn't look like the typical money man. There was something about his eyes…something both intense and at the same time wonderfully dreamy. She couldn't seem to look away.

Vaguely, she was aware of Zanlos' response.

"Miss Parsons, you seem to have overlooked two very important facts. One, Miss Bright is an extension of my authority, which I assure you far outranks your own. She does nothing without my knowledge and consent. Mr. McGraw's arrival shouldn't have concerned you. He is no threat to your control. He's only here in his thin disguise which, though very good, fooled no one, to serve our purposes. You should have minded your own business and stuck to doing your job instead of thinking to meddle in mine. Two, 'no interruptions' means no interruptions. Pity a clever girl like yourself couldn't grasp those simple dictates. Too bad for you and irritating for me. Now I'll have to find someone to replace you."

He was going to fire her? She knew she had only moments to argue her case, to sell herself as irreplaceable and beg forgiveness for her obvious gaff, but the words wouldn't translate from frantic thought to basic speech. A cold sweat of effort broke upon her brow as she sank deeper and deeper into the dangerous enchantment of the stranger's stare. She couldn't move.

"This is going to be a major inconvenience," Zanlos was saying with only mild annoyance. "But I suppose it can't be helped."

"I can't be recognized. Not yet."

And the silky voice, like the cold velvet gaze, pulled her down, down into a sleep from which there was no awaking.

She never felt the sharp teeth tear into her.

NINE

An hour passed, then two.

Sipping at the diet soda Marcus brought her, Naomi glanced nervously from stage to rear entrance waiting for Kitty to return either with her shield or on it. But she didn't return, and instead of feeling relieved, Naomi worried.

Worry over what havoc Kitty Parsons might be wreaking was safer than worrying over the turmoil Gabriel McGraw churned up inside her.

He was great with the girls, and they adored him. Kitty's sharp tongue never encouraged half the sweat and effort that one of Gabriel's sly smiles elicited. They couldn't do enough to please him. Not that she could blame them.

Rita quickly won a spot of respect and camaraderie as well. She was amazing. For all her ample size, she possessed swift and fluid reflexes and a balanced stance built for boxing if not for dance. Capable, cool and agile, she embodied the Amazonian spirit of conquest and self-control. And on her, muscles were sexy. Gabriel seemed to think so as he teased and taunted her and the others good-naturedly through a series of martial arts routines. He spent a particular amount of time with the high-kick-impaired Grace, coaxing, cajoling and building the esteem of the target of Kitty's frequent rants. And even though unusually weak in her routine, by the time they put the power into the program, she was keeping up with the others.

And Naomi had to admit that by the time they'd finished and were toweling off the moisture of accomplishment, she could see the difference blossoming already. Gone were the giddy and prissy movements of a flock of prima donna showgirls. They exuded a new sense of unity and composed confidence. And she could envision what her boss had in mind when he suggested Gabriel McGraw. A finely tuned team of women in control of themselves and similarly the situation. The Amazon was going to have a huge hit on its hands. What audience could resist such lethal power and feminine beauty all rolled into one?

Oddly, Marcus seemed to be able to. Usually, he doted on the girls and was slavishly attentive. But tonight, he watched with a curious intensity, half frowning and uncommunicative. Perhaps it was concern over the problems Kitty Parsons could cause, but Naomi sensed it was something more serious. She didn't ask, and he didn't offer.

When the girls trotted by on their way to the showers, Marcus leapt up to catch Grace as she went suddenly boneless. As her head lolled back, Naomi saw, as did her beefy companion, a set of odd marks upon her throat. As Marcus bent to get a closer look, Naomi tugged up the towel that lay draped about her shoulders to conceal the ragged punctures.

"Poor dear," she murmured. "Probably on another one of her silly diets and living on nothing but kale and cucumbers."

"'m all right," Grace muttered groggily as she stirred and finally was able to get her long legs untangled to support her. "Just got a little woozy there for a minute."

"Have you had a decent meal today?" Naomi scolded.

"Yes, Mother, and I'm on my way out for a stack of burgers that would embarrass Marcus." She smiled faintly as the big man helped her to her feet. But Marcus wasn't easily distracted from what he'd seen.

"What's that on your neck?"

Her hand went up to the raw looking marks. "Some sort of bug bite, I guess. My new boyfriend and I were getting back to nature the other night, and something must have nailed me."

"Other than the new boyfriend," Marcus muttered, and Grace squealed in objection.

"Marcus, you're terrible. And for your information, he's a gentleman and smart, too."

"And the two of you were discussing Plato under the stars."

"Who?"

"Never mind."

Naomi cut in. "You'd better put something on that bite before it gets infected. If it's not any better by tomorrow, maybe you should go to the clinic."

"Geez, it's a mosquito, not airborne syphilis. Get a life, you two." And with a touch of uncharacteristic irritation, she pulled away from them and their concern to join the others on their way to the dressing room.

Naomi glanced up at Marcus. Though his features were a familiar blank, she could see a flurry of activity going on behind his dark stare.

Plato, indeed.

"Hey," Rita called out as she bounded up the aisle. "Can I catch a ride home with you?"

Naomi's reply was cool. "I'm leaving in an hour."

"Great. I'll be ready."

After she'd hurried by, Marcus gave her a long, assessing look.

"You know her?"

"My roommate, Rita Davies. Just moved here from Detroit."

"Mmm. And our action hero over there?"

Naomi risked a glance at Gabriel, who was tugging on his shirt. He caught her gaze, and she quickly averted it. "Friend of a friend."

"Nice to have friends."

She regarded him curiously. "Jealous?"

He made a disparaging noise then faded back as Gabriel approached. But he didn't go too far.

"Well," Gabriel prompted. "What do you think?"

Honesty overcame her other prejudices. "Great. They look great. The critics are going to eat them up."

"How about you?"

"Excuse me?"

"Would you like to go out for something to eat?"

He had slipped in the request so smoothly, she almost didn't catch herself in time. A date? He was asking her out?

Just for a meal, nothing sinister, nothing dangerous. And just what Zanlos had ordered.

But when she met his stare, all sorts of dangers simmered there.

"I can't. I'm giving Rita a ride home."

"She can come along."

"No, I mean, not tonight. Thanks." And she scrambled up and away from the table, leaving Marcus to smirk in the face of

Gabriel's defeat.

"She's not your type, slick."

Gabriel lifted a doubting brow. "Why would you say that?

"Because if you bother her, the only type you'll be interested in is the type they replace at the hospital when I get through with you."

Gabriel didn't look impressed. "Very subtle."

"I prefer to lay things right out in the open. You mess with any of these ladies, and I mess with you. Get it?"

"Consider it gotten."

"Good."

***

"Why are you so angry?"

Naomi slid a fast glance at her passenger as she angled her little Neon into traffic. "What?"

"Why are you so mad at me?"

"I'm not mad."

"Yeah, right. You hold onto that steering wheel any tighter, and you're going to bend it."

Naomi consciously relaxed her hands, but the tension remained through her shoulders and jaw.

"Is this about Gabriel?"

"Why would it be about him?"

"Because usually when a sane woman does a Jekyll and Hyde there's a man involved."

"Are you involved with him?"

Silence greeted that blunt request.

Blushing fiercely, Naomi stammered, "I mean, are you and he…"

"I know what you mean. And no. Why would you think so?"

Feeling foolish now that her petty envy was out in the open, Naomi blundered ahead. "The way you showed up tonight. A rather sudden change of jobs."

"Some guy at the Excaliber was getting too pushy, and it was either push back or push on. Gabriel found out I had a background in self-defense training, and he asked if I'd be interested in helping him out. He was doing me the favor, bless him. But if you'd rather I look for work someplace else…"

"No. No, that's fine. It'll be fun."

"You're sure?"

Naomi displayed a genuine smile. "I'm sure. And I'm sorry."

"Girl, you've got to see that that boy only has eyes for you."

Instead of being reassured, Naomi's heart leapt with alarm. And her grip on the wheel tightened.

"I mean, you might have to worry if I were into looking for a man at the moment. But the opposite sex is off my list. Permanently." Rita paused, then laughed at Naomi's wide-eyed stare. "Nomi, you need to get out more. Life holds way too many surprises for you. Start by taking Gabe up on his next offer. He's a good guy. You might surprise yourself and have fun."

"I don't date."

"Why the hell not? You running from some secret marriage or something?"

"I don't know."

"What do you mean, you don't know?" Rita turned halfway in her seat to give Naomi her full attention. "That's an awfully strange thing to say."

"I'm an awfully strange girl." She took a chance and blurted out her carefully held secret to her only friend. "I don't remember anything of my life before coming here."

After a long, shocked moment, Rita asked, "Car accident or something?"

"I don't think so. Just no memories. My boss, Mr. Zanlos, brought me with him from out East. He said I'd had some kind of breakdown."

"Pardon me, but you don't seem the type to suddenly go crackers."

Naomi smiled wanly and shrugged. "So now you know why I don't want to get to know some man. I don't even know myself." She glanced at her passenger. "Maybe now you'd like to think about finding someplace else to live."

"Naw. I like strange. And besides, Mel likes your backyard. He thinks it's better than watching Animal Planet."

Feeling ridiculously grateful, Naomi kept her focus on the

road. Marcus was right. It was nice to have friends.

But she hadn't been totally honest with Rita, and she wasn't being totally honest with herself. She did have one memory, if not stored in her mind, then imprinted upon her emotions. Her heart remembered Gabriel McGraw.

And if she remembered him, then why wasn't he admitting to a relationship?

She would never know unless she did Zanlos' bidding and let the undercover policeman get close to her. Close enough to share secrets and tell tales.

***

"He's up to something; I just don't know what yet."

Marchand LaValois paced his Virginia warehouse office as he processed this scant information given by his best operative. "How can you stay close to him? He knows you."

"I've been careful to keep my face hidden. And besides, I have someone else in place."

"Someone you can trust?"

"Yes."

"This man is dangerous. I needn't tell you that."

"I know well what he is."

"And the woman, she's there?"

"Yes. She's his assistant. She got me a job at the hotel. So far, I've been undetected."

"We must know what he's doing. If it's something as ordinary as criminal activity, we don't care. If it's something unnatural as well as illegal, then we must step in and step hard. He escaped us once. He will not be so lucky again. If Zanlos can't be brought to heel, he must be ground under it."

"I understand."

"And Gabriel, you understand that if the woman if a part of it, she must be dealt with, too."

"I'll see to her."

"Gabriel." The warning was no more than the soft speaking of his name.

"I will do what needs to be done to protect what we are."

And Gabriel opened his eyes, severing the contact before

his mentor could delve any farther into the complexities of that vow. In an instant, he went from chill coastal air to the dry scorch of Nevada, from who he was to what he must do. Bring down Zanlos and protect Naomi.

But if he had to pick one...

Dawn was near. He could smell it on the horizon where it climbed the mountains that ringed the desert playground. Time to seek his shelter and leave the turmoiled thoughts for another night.

Hide in plain sight. That lesson had been learned during centuries of warfare. The obvious was always the least suspected. When he'd come to Las Vegas, Rolland offered to see him safely housed, but Gabriel preferred to arrange his own accommodations. Not that he didn't trust Rolland, or at least the Rolland he remembered, but a secret couldn't be betrayed if no one knew it.

He glanced into the night, where a beam of light from the dark pyramid shot into the heavens. He didn't remember the pyramids. He wasn't that old, not as old as she who made him, but he always took comfort among things of ages past. He was one of those antiquities, born of another time, destined to search the years, the decades, the centuries.

But now that that search was over, time was no longer his friend.

Moving with the flow of late night revelers returning to their hotel, he entered the regal Luxor, but unlike those who walked beside him, never really recognizing his presence, his objective wasn't a nice, air conditioned room beneath the slanted glass walls. It was a slab of marble in the entry hall.

The walls of the Pharaoh's tomb were painted to resemble a world that pre-dated his own. Beneath those murals were stone boxes guarded by statues of majestic lions and mythical beasts meant to hold the sarcophagi of kings. What one would hold until the next sunset was no king, but rather a vampire.

He waited until the dribbling flow of tourists dwindled. One moment, he stood outside the marble encasement and the next, he thinned to become a vapor that could seep beneath its rim into the protective darkness within. There, he closed his eyes, shutting out the questions and the conflicts of what he must do. And summoning the features he'd held to his heart while kings rose and fell, he let go of his consciousness to remember a dream.

A dream of fated romance.

TEN

"What's that all about?"

Gabriel followed Rita's nod toward the back of the auditorium to where Marcus was in brisk conversation with a rather pale woman with startling red hair and too much makeup. Fearing the discussion might have something to do with Naomi's absence, Gabriel tuned his preternatural hearing in to catch the last of the words. Relief made him careless.

"It would seem our choreographer decided to quit without notice." He noted Rita's surprise and added, "Lip reader."

She quirked a brow at his explanation but didn't question it. "Well, no great loss there. The woman was a witch with a capital B."

"But where's that going to leave the show without anyone at the helm?" But he was thinking about Naomi, wondering if this new crisis had taken her away temporarily or, perhaps, permanently. "I need a way to get upstairs to find out what's going on."

"An extra pair of eyes, you mean." Rita toweled off her forehead and neck with her sweatshirt, then knotted it loosely about the waist of her lipstick-red leotard. "You're just lucky I have other pairs that are distracting, McGraw. It's time for me to do a little reconnaissance." With that, she hopped off the stage and swaggered up to the manmade mountain by the exit door.

"Hi, Marcus, is it?"

He regarded her unblinkingly. With a sigh, she forged ahead.

"I'm trying to find Naomi Bright. She's my roommate, you know, and I need to talk to her about Mel's plans for the evening. Do you know where I can find her?"

At first, she thought she might as well be talking to one of the support pillars, then his dark eyes narrowed slightly to assess her. "She's probably upstairs with Mr. Zanlos."

"Oh, then I probably can't talk to her. It was really urgent. Could you take a message to her?"

Marcus glanced from his leggy charges to the beseeching

gaze of the woman in front of him. He'd noticed her before. She had the nicest shoulder development he'd ever seen this side of Madonna.

"I can't leave."

"Oh." Her expression fell.

"But I guess there's no reason you can't go up as long as you don't get in anyone's way and come right back down. Vera, the redhead I was just talking to, is the receptionist for the offices. She can help you find her."

It was Vera for the receptionist and Miss Bright for Naomi. Interesting.

Rita squeezed his forearm. She had a good grip. "Thanks."

He glanced at her hand then grunted a response. With a wink at Gabriel, Rita followed him to the private elevator and watched as he turned his key in the panel. The door sighed open.

"Now don't go poking around where you don't belong. You're my responsibility while you're up there."

She saluted in response to that dire warning. "Yes, sir." And the door slid shut. Then opened moments later upon chaos.

The seams of the reception area bulged with desperate humanity. Workmen with rolled plans. Electricians with belts weighted down by the tools of the trade. A chef trying to make himself understood through dramatic gestures and broken English to a frazzled and incomprehensive secretary. A pair of suits with sleek briefcases impatiently regarding their Rolexes. No one noticed her standing on the fringe of the harried crowd, but everyone turned immediately to the tiny woman in the ill-fitting suit who slipped in quietly, then with her first soft syllables, took control of the room.

"Thank you for your patience everyone. We've had a bit of a crisis to contend with, but Mr. Zanlos is anxious to meet each and every one of you as quickly as possible." She turned to the head electrician with a calming smile. "Harry, I've put the inspection off another two days. I'm sure that will give you the time you need a take care of the problem. I can't tell you how much we appreciate your crew's willingness to put in the overtime on this." Then to the architects. "We'll have those revisions down to you on the floor within the hour. Nothing drastic, and I think you'll approve of the changes." While the appeased workmen headed to the elevator, she addressed the chef in flawless French, soothing his histrionics while the bubble-headed secretary gaped in mid-gum snap. Then she spoke to the businessmen, this time in Italian, gesturing that they follow her. She paused when she noticed Rita and put up her index finger as she shepherded the gentlemen into the inner office. Rita exchanged a look with the wilting secretary.

"She's good."

The brightly dyed head nodded. "Everyone here thinks she walks on water."

"You, too?"

"I think she could if she wanted to."

Naomi returned, still as crisply efficient as the knife-edged pleats in her skirt. "Sorry to keep you waiting, Rita. It's been crazy up here. We open in less than two weeks, and everyone has last minute jitters."

"You seem to be just what the doctor ordered."

Naomi allowed a self-effacing smile. "I'm great at handling every crisis except my own." Then she took a breath, and her shoulders slumped. Suddenly she appeared frail and weary. "Thank goodness we've managed all of them except one for the night."

"Kitty Parsons?"

Naomi sighed. "Can you believe that woman? Just up and walked out when we've got so much to do to get the show ready. I don't know where we're going to come up with a choreographer on such short notice who can just step in and carry on. I'm fresh out of miracles on that one."

"You look like you're all out of everything." And it was the truth. The willowy girl was swaying like a reed in a harsh breeze. "Call it a night and trust a miracle to happen in your absence."

Naomi placed a pale, slender hand on her forearm for a squeeze. "I can't abandon ship, Rita. Someone has to—"

"What? Go down with it? Why does it have to be you?"

"That's my job."

And she turned expectantly as one of the huge office doors opened.

"Miss Bright, I don't wish to be disturbed." Shrewd obsidian eyes fixed upon Rita and held. "Oh, forgive me. I did not realize you had a guest."

Before Naomi could stammer an excuse, Rita thrust her hand out. "Not a guest, her roommate. Rita Davies. I'm working with the show downstairs."

"I'm surprised we haven't met before. Not much escapes me, especially not someone so noteworthy."

His fingertips were cool and smooth as he lightly curled hers into his palm. His accent, soft and sensually seasoned with the warmth of South Africa, compelled attention just as his direct gaze mesmerized. Hawkishly handsome and slick as sin. Rita distrusted him on sight.

"Since you're going to be in a meeting, do you mind if I steal Naomi away for a while?"

"As long as you return her. Miss Bright is my most valuable asset."

"But I still haven't taken care of the Parsons matter."

Kaz Zanlos brushed away her protest with a flick of his hand. His nails were square cut and as white is if they'd been polished. "There's nothing more you can do tonight. I'm sure you have other business to attend. Or should I say pleasure."

His stare captured Naomi's for a long moment, until she gave a faint nod. Watching, Rita got the uncomfortable feeling that with that silent exchange came an incredible amount of exerted pressure. She'd seen that kind of control leveled in abuse situations. Seeing Naomi's meek acquiescence, she wondered about the relationship between employer and employee. And she didn't like the way his intimidation caved in the confident woman Naomi had been only moments before. That animation drained away until not a trickle of independent will remained. Whatever he was forcing upon her, Naomi accepted his dominance with enough uneasiness to make Rita despise him for his silky bullying.

"Very good, Miss Bright," he pronounced once he was sure she would follow his unspoken edicts. Then he smiled at Rita, all liquid charm. "It was a distinct pleasure meeting you, Ms. Davies. Remember your promise to return her."

Was there a slight implied warning there?

After he disappeared to resume his meeting, Rita shook her head. "Whatever he's paying you, it's not enough."

"Mr. Zanlos has been very good to me." The tight, almost defensive tone made Rita blink in surprise. Then the tension eased to genuine gratitude. "After all he's done, I could never take advantage of his kindness."

"People can only take advantage if you allow them to," Rita observed as they walked toward the elevator. Naomi gave a cursory wave to the fast fading secretary then looked up at her roommate with a sudden shrewd understanding.

"And that's what I do. I let them."

"I didn't say it was a bad thing."

"No, not like world hunger or venereal disease."

Rita laughed at Naomi's tang of sarcasm as they stepped into the elevator. After glancing about, Rita remarked, "Strange. Most elevators have a least one mirrored wall. You'd think with all the vanity running rampant in Las Vegas that they'd be everywhere."

Naomi wasn't thinking about mirrors. She was thinking about what Rita had said. Was everyone taking advantage of her? Did she foster that needy behavior by enabling their dependence? She thought of herself as efficient and capable. Was she instead a willing doormat? Or a passively aggressive control freak?

Like Rita said, she had to get out more.

And she had to start tonight. Kaz Zanlos' subtle prompt wasn't to be ignored. Tonight with Gabriel McGraw.

When she saw him on the stage leading the dancers through a complicated set of fighting techniques, the swell of sensations came close to drowning her. Need, longing, hurt, distrust. So many things for a man and a relationship she couldn't remember.

From a safe distance—if any distance from which she could observe him could be considered safe—she enjoyed watching him. Strength, power, and lethal beauty—things he exuded, things he was passing on to the women he taught so that when they moved together it was graceful, controlled poetry. Though he seemed relaxed and focusing on the movements, she knew he was instantly aware of her, just as she'd been able to feel his presence on the streets. It had been him. She knew that now. But why? Why was he following her? Why were they so attuned to one another? What had they been to one another for the connection to remain so strong? She had to know. Gabriel was one of the pieces to her past. If she could find where he fit in, perhaps other sections would begin to fall into place.

"They look great, don't they?"

"You've done a remarkable job," Naomi admitted. "Now if we just had someone capable of putting it all together."

The girls saw her then, and the number came to an uncoordinated end as one by one they rushed to the edge of the stage to all talk at once.

"Did you hear about Miss Parsons?"

"What's going to happen to the show?"

"Are we going to be able to open on time?"

"That bitch. Wouldn't you know she'd pull something like this at the last minute."

Naomi held up her hands to halt the verbal barrage. "Ladies, we're working on it. You just keep working on what you have to do."

"Miss Bright, I finally got that kick."

She smiled at Grace with the pride of a parent. "I knew you could do it. How are you feeling? Did you get that bite taken care of?"

The girl looked confused, then put her hand to her neck where only the faintest of marks still showed. "I forgot all about it. I feel fine. I went through a sack of burgers and about twelve hour's sack time."

"Alone?" Molly chided.

"Yes, alone."

Naomi did a quick head count and frowned when the numbers didn't add up. "Where's Jeannie?"

"She called in sick. The flu or something. We've been working around her."

"I hope it's nothing serious." That's all she needed. Another problem to solve.

"Her boyfriend got that job in the kitchen. They were

probably out celebrating a little too enthusiastically." Molly demonstrated with a graphic triple pelvic thrust.

Molly's conclusion seemed logical. Naomi only hoped it was something that simple. She could use simple about now.

Rita climbed up onto the stage and did some limbering stretches. "Come on, ladies. Time's a wasting. Gabe, Nomi needs some R and R. Why don't you take her out for a walk, and I'll put these gals through their paces."

Just like that, all Naomi's anxious worries about how to approach the subject of being alone with Gabriel were gone. And he didn't seem to mind the matchmaking one bit. He snapped up his colorful shirt and waved to the dancers.

"Work hard, ladies. Don't try to think about me out there having fun while you're in here straining your little buns off."

Several rude comments made him grin, not at all as shocked as Naomi was by the blatant and colorful vulgarity.

"Sticks and stones, ladies."

"If we had them, we'd throw them," Marty replied with cheerful malice.

When Gabriel hopped down off the stage, the reality of spending time with him hit Naomi like the push of desert air upon leaving the climate controlled hotel. It took her breath and left her gasping. But she didn't resist when his fingertips lightly capped her elbow. She waited for the usual rebellion to a man's touch to rear its objecting head, but no protest came. Her defenses lay strangely silent.

"Shall we?"

She preceded him up the aisle, aware of the girls' speculative and envious gazes. Aware as well of Marcus's hulking presence in the shadows and of the feel of his disapproval. Was he aware of who Gabriel really was? Of what their employer had asked her to do? How could she ever feel comfortable with Marcus again if he did?

As they walked through the cavernous lobby, she fielded the questions and comments from more than a dozen workmen before they finally escaped. Out in the sapping heat of the night, she expelled a grateful breath.

"Out of the pressure cooker and into the fire?"

"That obvious?"

"Where would you like to go? I'm at your disposal."

Oh, if only that were true.

"Someplace to unwind. Someplace I've never been before…which should be easy since I've never been anywhere."

He whistled down a cab and whisked her inside, not speaking after he directed the driver to the end of the strip. She sat stiffly beside him, studying her side of the street with a fierce intensity. What was she going to say to him? Did Zanlos expect her to seduce him? To pump him for information? She had no idea how to go about either thing. With men, when she wasn't issuing orders as their superior, she was completely at a loss. And Gabriel McGraw didn't look like the type to take orders.

How did I get myself into this?

Up ahead, she could see the orb of the Stratosphere soaring above the strip atop its impossibly high tower. Was that where they were going? A trickle of alarm shivered through her belly as they grew too close to see the top of the 1,149-foot tower. Gabriel paid for the cab and handed her out.

"Are we going up for a drink?" Apprehension tightened her voice. Because she didn't want to admit to a crushing fear of heights, she could have told him she didn't drink. But he smiled at her, and the power of speech suddenly left her.

"No questions."

While she waited by the elevator, he stood at one of the ticket windows. If he thought she was going to be catapulted into space on the Big Shot…

"Ready?"

"As I'll ever be," was her cautious reply.

In a matter of seconds, the express elevator had them at the top.

And Naomi saw what he had in mind.

The High Roller. The roller coaster that looped around the pod of the Stratosphere.

"You did say something you'd never done before."

"I didn't mean dying."

"Trust me."

And he put out his hand to her in a gesture that suddenly

meant more than a few loop-de-loops one hundred stories up. And he smiled again as her palm slid over his.

Strapped into the car, perhaps the very worst moments came with inching ahead as the rest of the seats were filled with the daring and gravity defiant. With her pulse hammering in her ears, each hard thrust shooting adrenalin through her the way they'd soon be hurtling through the night, she gripped the safety bar until it grew slippery. Then Gabriel's hand slipped over the top of one of hers. The cool comfort of his light squeeze gave her a final instant of calm before the cars rocketed forward toward outer space. Of course, at the last second, they whipped into a tight curve so only her liver went sailing into the blurring heavens.

Wind stung her face, forcing tears from the corners of her eyes. She could hear the screams of those around her but didn't think her voice added to theirs. She was too busy trying to remember to breathe through clenched teeth as momentum flattened her against Gabriel's side. She heard his words shouted into her hair.

"Open you eyes and fly."

For a moment, all she could see was a smear of colors upon a dark pallet. Then the distinct pattern of constellations appeared. She was flying, her spirit riding currents of air with a freedom unlike any other.

How wonderful. How delightful.

Then all too soon, they were slowing, surrendering back to the pull of reality.

She turned to Gabriel. His hair spun wildly about his head as if a mixer had been applied, and his eyes glittered with exhilaration. That gaze quieted and deepened as it fixed upon her own. Their stares mated in a strangely communicative silence.

Did you enjoy it?
You know I did.
There's more to come.
I'm afraid.
Don't be.

"Why are you here?" she demanded suddenly, never

expecting an answer and especially not the one that stole her senses all over again.

"I came for you."

ELEVEN

I came for you.

Before she could process his answer through the sensory overload stirred by the ride, their car was stopped so they could exit on shaky legs. While part of her was afraid to pursue what his comment quickened within her, another had to know what was behind it. What was this past they shared? She wasn't thinking about Kaz Zanlos and his covert orders. She was focused upon the emotions left quaking by Gabriel's simple response. Raw feeling was the only force strong enough to subdue the power of Zanlos' commands.

For you.

She couldn't let it alone. She had to know.

"I think I need a drink."

When they were seated in the elegant revolving restaurant with its 360-degree panorama of the jewel box city below, Naomi's agitation returned. Self-consciously smoothing through the tangle of her hair, she ordered a white wine and leveled an unswerving stare upon her companion.

"Who are you?"

"Gabriel McGraw. I'm a former cop from D.C."

If he'd said anything else, the evening would have been over, and she would have known him to be the liar Zanlos claimed him to be. But this first truth left her hopeful that more would follow.

"Former?"

"A slight conflict of interest between my job and my conscience. I took a leave of absence to take care of some unfinished business."

"And that business would be?"

She clutched her wine glass in both hands. One of his layered over them. His touch was cool yet sparked fires of yearning from a source she didn't recognize. A self-preserving panic cried out for her to pull away, but his touch soothed more than it upset, just as his reply did.

"You and me, Naomi. I couldn't let so much go unresolved.

I had to follow."

"But I don't know you." Anguish tore through that claim. His answer only deepened the riddle.

"Don't you? Don't you feel the bond between us? The pull you can't resist? Naomi, you are my soul mate, and even if you can't recall the circumstances surely you remember the feelings. I know you do." More of a plea than a prompt, he spoke with a passion as unsettlingly direct as his dark stare.

"I remember the feelings but not the facts." With that admission, she drew her hands away and gulped the wine. But there was nothing as potent as the urgency of his gaze. He waited, wanting more, more than she could give him. "What were we to each other? Lovers?" She blushed as she asked it, but she needed to hear his reply.

"Regrettably, no."

Disappointment speared her heart. She hadn't realized until this moment how much she'd wanted there to be some healthy, normal link between her and this enigmatic man. But nothing in her life was normal.

"Why not?"

He smiled faintly at her demand. "Not for lack of interest, that's for sure. Call it bad timing." And he chuckled as if that was some great sad joke. "You might say we were courting."

Courting. How quaint. How sweetly satisfying.

"You trusted me, Naomi."

Her neck prickled warily. "And was that a mistake?"

"Perhaps. But only because I wasn't completely honest with you."

"And you'll be completely honest now?"

His smile took a skewed bend. "No."

"I see."

"I can't be. Not yet. But you can trust me, Naomi. Trust in what you feel."

"I feel confused and afraid and uncertain."

"And love?"

"I don't know."

That wasn't what he'd wanted to hear but he recovered well. "I'm patient."

Why did that claim frighten her so? Had she expected him to give up and go away? Was that what she wanted, or did she secretly thrill to the thought of his pursuit?

"Why don't I remember?" Frustration tore through her voice.

"What has Zanlos told you?"

Her gaze lowered to the empty glass she rolled between her palms. "He said I had a nervous breakdown. He brought me out here with him and helped me get better."

"And did he?"

"Yes." Defensively stated, but in the back of her mind, she wondered. Was she better? Was knowing nothing better than finding the strength to accept the truth, no matter how ugly that truth might be? "I was suicidal."

"That's what he told you." It wasn't a question.

Challenged by his tone, she said, "It's the truth. I don't know where I'd be without him. Probably in some state institution somewhere. He saved my life, Gabriel." She met his stare fiercely. "I won't let you harm him."

He was silent for a moment, thinking of how to continue. He approached the subject cautiously. "He's not one of the good guys, Naomi."

She'd always known that, so there was no surprise in her response, just the same dogged insistence and loyalty. "I don't care. He's made me feel safe."

"Safe? He's made you a prisoner to his plans. Who is he working with, Naomi? Who's partnered in this plan of his?"

"I don't know."

"Don't know or won't say? Or can't say?"

That last provoking question bothered her because of what it implied. "I'm not afraid of Mr. Zanlos. I've never seen him do anything wrong, so don't expect me to help you with your harassment." She began to push away from the table, so he leaned forward, hoping his earnest look would slow her.

"Naomi, he's behind what's wrong with you."

She stared at him, aghast then angry. "He's helped me."

Gabriel rose up at the same time she did. His stare burned into hers. "He's made you his slave."

Her head jerked from side to side. "No."

Her head began to pound—hammer on anvil behind her eyes. She reached into her bulky purse for the pills she wasn't supposed to take. But they helped, the way a little more truth and a lot less stress would help. She swallowed two down with the last of her water. One stuck half way, forcing her to cough and gratefully accept his untouched glass of Chardonnay. She gulped it down until her windpipe opened, allowing her hoarse objection.

"You don't know what you're talking about."

But she heard Rita's prophetic claim. *They can't take advantage unless you allow it.* Angrily, she emptied the contents of the glass. The thudding between her ears became an annoying buzz, like whispers behind turned heads and shielding hands. The buzz of gossip, the pitying glances. She tried to deny them with a shake of her head. The pain was almost unbearable.

"You know I'm right, Naomi. You just can't admit it to yourself. He's used you. He's lied to you."

"No." Strength gave way to a deeper confusion as she tried to reject the destruction of her orderly world. She couldn't let him chip away at the cornerstones to her sanity.

He was the liar.

She couldn't breathe. She had to get away. While he was left to pull bills from his wallet to satisfy the check, she rushed from the restaurant. Stumbling blindly, she sought a saving calm to the turmoil in her head. Panic beat against her temples. Sound roared within her ears. Not even when she staggered out into the chill wind on the open air observation deck, did the fever cool within her brain. Escape. She had to escape the jarring noise and sudden blur of visions streaking across her view like scenes playing out in fast forward. For an instant, she saw Kaz Zanlos, but before she could focus upon his image, it bled to become another—a monster of blazing red eyes and feral teeth. She gasped, trying to draw air into the constriction of her chest. It wasn't the truth she saw. It was the nightmare that pursued her. The madness returned by Gabriel's relentless words.

She bumped into the first restraining rail and clutched it with quaking hands. Beyond was another fence then darkness, cool darkness broken by the tiny glowing dots of suburbia as she faced the mountains instead of the city. She saw only freedom from the crushing pressure of sound and sight, the blissful freedom she'd experienced on the ride only minutes ago. She strained for a taste of that sweet release, leaning, lifting her face toward the beckoning heavens.

A hand touched her elbow, a voice called her name. She began to turn toward the dizzying smear of visuals, seeking a focal point upon which to cling. But the features that crystalized out of the mist of memories and dreams didn't offer salvation.

They promised hell.

Her nightmare had found her.

Shrieking, she lunged backwards. Momentum sent her tumbling over the rail to fall between the two barriers.

"Naomi! Don't be afraid. I won't hurt you."

Naomi! Fear me not. I mean you no harm.

Choking on the bitter bile surging up to burn her throat and nose, she scrambled to her feet, thinking only to evade the hands reaching for her.

Hurtful, pawing hands.

She whirled and flung herself over the next rail.

And was free.

Darkness and an oblivion that was her friend. She spread her arms wide to embrace it, to give herself to that cold, final peace.

Until a sudden remembrance shocked through her heart and mind.

Gabriel, my love!

Before she had a chance to scream out in objecting terror, he was there, strong arms encircling her, cinching her up tight to his solid form. There to save her.

This time.

The burn of the wind rushing by her face eased to a gentle caress. Time slowed to the pace of shared heartbeats, hers rapid with amazement and fright, his anything but steady as they spiraled down with the graceful loops of blossoms entwined upon a light evening breeze.

And while he held her and listened to the raw pulls of her

breathing saw across the edges of his heart, he could see again and again in damning slow motion the flutter of her skirt and the disappearance of her slender ankles and sensibly clad feet as she went over the edge.

Again.

Because of him.

"I'm sorry. I'm sorry," he repeated in a broken litany that could never assuage the horror of that instant when he witnessed the event that had previously writhed only in his imagination.

How fragile her psyche. How damaged the spirit that had evolved through centuries without redemption. And the blame was his just as the responsibility was his. His task was to bring her peace. He'd thought it could be done through a mending of their torn destinies, that reuniting their lives as one would make her whole and him forgiven.

But he'd been wrong. So wrong he'd been shocked almost into inaction when she flung herself over the rail to face death rather than the truth he represented.

Her faith in him hadn't been enough to sustain her. Had Rolland been right? Had he always expected more than she could give? Had his wish that she match him in strength of head and heart been beyond that of which she was capable? Had the pressure of his wants driven her to such a drastic end?

Not again. Never again, he swore on her soul because his was already forfeit.

Perhaps the kindest thing he could do was to remove the turmoil he caused from her troubled life.

Right after he freed her from Zanlos.

Then, if fate had decided he was not to bring her happiness and her the answer to all his prayers and dreams, she could find those things with another.

His search for fulfillment of a centuries' old promise was gone. All that remained was for her to find peace.

And as Gabriel saw her to a cab and instructed the vehicle to see her safely home, a figure far enough away so as not to be detected smiled with self-satisfied pleasure. Things couldn't be going better on the course of well-suited revenge.

***

"What the hell happened to you?"

The sound of the cab had woken Rita from her light sleep. Oddly, she'd been keeping a half ear open for the sound of Naomi's return. Just to make sure she got home safe. The maternal instincts amused her. And perhaps were unnecessary. Somehow she didn't think her little roommate was as fragile as she looked. She'd sensed steel there, no less honed for protection than the sword Gabriel had wielded at the Excaliber. Strength wasn't Naomi's problem. She had backbone to spare. It was the streak of vulnerability that had Rita concerned. Hawks were drawn to a wounded bird. It was nature at its most elemental. And Rita meant to protect Naomi from predators, not just because of her promise to Gabriel and her debt to Rae. She genuinely enjoyed the other woman's company.

And if Naomi brought company home with her, Rita meant to discreetly withdraw.

But Naomi came in alone. And it was obvious from one look at the trembling, shattered creature slumped against the door jamb like a refugee of a natural disaster that things hadn't gone well.

Rita received no response to her first demand and only a vague reaction to her second alarmed entreaty. Dazed eyes remained fixed and vacant for a long moment, then Naomi's gaze lifted. Rita gave a soft cry. Never had she seen such pain and anguish in another's face.

"Nomi, what happened? Are you all right?"

Seismic tremors began in her slender shoulders, jerking through them before shuddering down her spine. Her teeth chattered. Recognizing the ravages of shock, Rita enveloped her in a supportive embrace, the only thing that held her together as her knees gave way. Rita half dragged her to the sofa and eased her down upon it after a sweep of her forearm sent a contentedly dozing Mel lumbering under the table, where he glowered in displeasure. Rita gathered a comforter up about the spasming shoulders and began to chafe the limply hanging arms. Then Rita took quick inventory. Despite the disheveled hair and zombie-like expression, Naomi looked as impeccable as always. The seams of her skirt and her pantyhose were smooth and hopefully undisturbed. But Rita had to make sure.

"Sweetie, talk to me. Where's Gabriel? Did you get separated? Why didn't he bring you home?"

"He—he tried to h-hurt me. I said no, but he wouldn't stop and he was too strong." The horrible words hiccuped from her, telling a story that had Rita's jaw clenching. Naomi continued to stare off into space, the shadows swirling in her eyes as the moment played back within her head. "I was such a fool. He'd always been so n-nice to me."

"That son-of-a-bitch." Growling that epithet, Rita hugged her quivering roommate close and vowed, "No one will hurt you again. Not ever, if I have anything to say about it."

But Naomi didn't respond. She continued to stare with that wounded intensity off into the horror of her memories.

TWELVE

Where's Gabriel?"

Marcus looked up in surprise as Rita flung her bag down upon the stage. She was sleek as a seal in her black unitard, but her manner befit a more dangerous animal.

"Haven't seen him yet. The girls are all waiting. All but Jeannie. She didn't show up. And Gracie's dragging again."

Rita nodded absently at the news because at that moment she caught sight of Gabriel McGraw striding down the center aisle. An almost feral snarl from her startled the big bodyguard. Something was up. And he hit it with his first question.

"Where's Naomi tonight? She usually checks in before she goes upstairs."

"She's staying home. A migraine."

That was said with all the force of a chipper shredder as she pulled on her fingerless gloves and pounded knuckles to palm.

"You look ready to take on the world tonight," Gabriel remarked as he slid out of his loose shirt.

"Maybe some of its less savory elements."

The snap of her tone had him raising a brow in question, but Rita whirled away and challenged, "Go a few rounds with me to loosen up."

Alerted by her sudden tense aggression, he hedged. "I'm already pretty loose."

"Yeah, but I'm wound tight enough to break or break something. Come on, tough guy. Not afraid of the weaker sex, are you? I thought guys like you liked to show women who's boss. Come on and show me." And she spun back, tossing him a staff. He caught it deftly and climbed cautiously up onto the stage as Rita addressed the curious showgirls. "Ladies, tonight Mr. McGraw and I are going to demonstrate how the weak sex can fight back and fight to win. Surprise is our first and best weapon."

And she struck. The staff cracked against the side of Gabriel's head, sending him stumbling to one side. He righted himself and took a defensive position.

"See," she explained fiercely. "Even the biggest bully will think twice before attacking a capable opponent. So don't let him get his bearings. No fear. No mercy." And she jabbed the end of the staff into Gabriel's sternum, then into his gut. Another man would have been on his back, gasping and throwing up his dinner, but Gabriel only shuffled back a few steps and regarded her with a perplexed furrowing of his brows.

"What's going on, Rita?" he asked in a low aside.

"Like you don't know, you bastard."

Pushed by emotion, she attacked rashly, and Gabriel was ready for her. He feinted to one side then used his staff to sweep her feet out from under her. Before she could scramble up, he placed the heel of his staff at her throat. She lay still, glaring up at him.

"Combat is an emotionless endeavor," he told the dancers without looking away from Rita's livid expression. "Anger, fear, revenge, jealousy—those things cloud the mind's clarity. Don't put yourself at a disadvantage. Cool and in control wins every time." He moved the pinning stick and put down his hand to his fallen opponent. Rita ignored it, rolling to one side and onto her feet.

Restless in her anger and unresolved retribution, Rita snatched up her towel. "Run through the hand to hand routine. No sloppy movements. Mentally tough, ladies."

As the women paired off to spar, Rita finally confronted a confused Gabriel.

"You shit. She trusted you."

"Who?" Then the weight of consequence took hold, and his features turned to granite. "Is she all right?"

"How do you think she is after what you put her through?" Rita leaned closed to hiss. "You stay away from her."

"I plan to. She doesn't need to worry that I'll bring her any more pain." Though his words were low and ripped through with his own inner agony, they had no effect on the stoic Rita. He sighed heavily and petitioned, "Just watch out for her, Rita. Will you do that for me?"

"Not for you, but because she's my friend."

Before they could continue their conversation, Jeannie's boyfriend Jack, still dressed in his kitchen whites, approached in a frenzy. "Have you seen Jeannie?"

Grateful to turn to something less volatile, Gabriel told him, "She hasn't been to practice for the past two nights."

"She hasn't been home either. I was hoping…I thought maybe you'd know where she was."

"Me?" Gabriel looked perplexed.

"She said she was getting some extra help on the routine, the same kind of help Grace got. What kind of private lessons did you give my girl, McGraw?"

"I haven't seen her since she left with the others two nights ago."

The distraught man gripped Gabriel's upper arms. "If she's with you, for God's sake have the decency to just tell me. I've been going out of my mind with worry, what with her coming home and acting all strange like I wasn't even there, talking about finding some new kind of heaven. What have you done to her?"

"Nothing." Gabriel shrugged out of the man's grasp then pressed his shoulders in earnest. He stared straight into Jack's frantic gaze until slowly the anger and panic came under his control. Only then did he continue, his tone as compelling as that dark, mesmerizing stare. "I haven't seen her. I have no relationship with her other than what's gone on right here. We're worried about her, too."

That broke the young cook's control. He seemed to crumple, fighting back the sobs.

"Have you filed a missing persons report?" Rita injected gently, but she was watching Gabriel, her attention speculative and keen.

Jack shook his head. "Not yet."

"Then that should be your next step. Do that now, and we'll let you know if any of us hears from her. Okay?"

He nodded and after mumbling a frazzled apology to Gabriel, wandered rather aimlessly out of the theatre.

Rita turned to the girls. "If any of you hears from her, I want to know about it, okay?" Then she looked to Marcus who'd been standing off to the side not interfering. "And what's with you? Weren't you supposed to do something? The man was almost homicidal."

"I'll do something," Marcus promised quietly, but Rita whirled away, dismissing his vow as inconsequential.

And as the rehearsal started back up, Marcus watched Gabriel McGraw, planning exactly what he would do.

***

"Look at them. Lovely, aren't they?"

The two men stood at the two way glass looking down upon the energetic run through on the stage below while Kaz Zanlos hung back with the investor's three bodyguards. Zanlos preferred to stay out of the way when his partner was pitching a deal as he was tonight. They'd been feeling Mob muscle since taking on the Amazon project, and now they were carving out a niche for themselves so they'd be left alone. A rather specialized niche if he did say so himself.

"Yes, they are, but Vegas if full of lovely ladies. What's your point?"

Alex smiled at the mobster's gruff dismissal. "Oh, but they're not just lovely. They're lethal, too."

Tony Gianbano smirked at that. "Those little cream puffs? Get odda here."

"You would, perhaps, like a demonstration?"

Gianbano shrugged. "It's your dime."

A whisper of movement was all the warning they had. A shriek from one of his bodyguards brought Gianbano around in alarm but it was horror that froze him to the spot. A woman, one of the tall, leggy dancers had his best shooter by the head. Only the man wasn't facing forward any more. She'd twisted his head a clean, quick 180, then dropped him to the floor.

By then, the other two came out of their shocked immobility. One even managed to get off a couple of shots in the soundproof room. The creature—she no longer looked like a woman, let alone human—took the slugs in the chest, but they had as much effect as a pea shooter. The gun was torn from him, hand and all, and cast across the room. Then she ripped the scream from his throat with the slash of razor-sharp teeth. Gianbano stumbled back as blood geysered up, splattering the glass and his three thousand dollar suit. The other guard grabbed the demon from behind, initiating a choke hold. But suddenly he wasn't standing behind her any more. They were face to face. Her crimson-smeared mouth opened wide to swallow up his cry of terror and just as quickly his life. When he was nothing more than a shell, she let him fall and whirled toward Gianbano. A damp stain spread across the front of his pleated trousers.

Cross held up a hand. "That will be all, Jeannie."

And the ghoul transformed before their eyes into a beautiful showgirl who just happened to be showered in gore. She took the handkerchief Zanlos offered and delicately wiped her lips and chin. As she turned away, a glimmer of red glinted in her eyes, just enough to convince the quivering Gianbano that he hadn't imagined the whole thing.

"Forgive the rather graphic demonstration, but I wanted to make sure you got the full picture," the elegant hotel owner continued. "We'll take care of the clean-up and your suit, of course."

Gianbano slid to the floor, whimpering like a baby.

"Now, to business. We offer a unique service—you might say the disposal of your problems. You send that problem to us, to see the show, that problem is gone without a trace. As you've seen, my girls can overcome any opposition. And who'd suspect any threat from…a cream puff?" He paused, but Gianbano was still in a gelatinous state of shock. "My associate has taken the liberty of preparing some contracts granting us exclusive disposal rights, if you will. I think you'll find us reasonable. Since I'm sure you've seen enough proof of our capabilities, shall we just get down to the signing?"

Gianbano reached up shaking hands for the pen and paper. The two men standing over him exchanged thin-lipped smiles, and when they looked down at him, their eyes glowed blood red.

"What are you people?" the mobster cried.

Zanlos chuckled. "We're entrepreneurs."

The rehearsal went as well as could be expected with Rita

on the warpath, Jeannie missing and Grace stepping on everyone's feet including her own. Finally, Gabriel had her sit it out, dismissing her complaints of light-headedness and chills with a sympathetic tolerance.

The marks were back on her throat, raw and fresh.

Perhaps if he could spend some time alone with her away from the noise and distraction, he could learn something of who had initiated her and why. But before they were finished for the night, she disappeared, stating she was sick to her stomach. Just as well. He was too on edge to conduct a subtle probe of her subconscious. His concentration waned beneath his concern for Naomi.

Rita would take care of her, freeing him for his pursuit of Zanlos. Unfortunately, he was almost out of a reason to remain in the hotel. The girls had picked up the martial arts moves with an amazing ease. Already trained in grace, timing and balance, teaching them how to channel control into personal power wasn't like learning a new language but rather how to understand a specific dialect within something they already spoke.

He'd taught them everything he could without going into a more serious competition mode. They walked through the drills with concise moves and an alluring rhythm. Now they just needed someone to convert that force into dance.

Without Naomi at the helm, he wondered if it would ever happen.

Where was she? He wanted to ask Rita, but her cutting glances said she'd just as soon take off his head as answer his questions. Maybe it was better this way, for the break to be quick and clean. And permanent.

As long as she was safe.

"That's a wrap, ladies," Rita called after they completed the workout.

"When are we going to get costumes?" Molly wanted to know.

"When do we try it to music?" Candice echoed.

Rita held up her hands. "You're asking the wrong person. I'll check with Naomi and let you know."

"Tell her we hope she's better soon," Marty said for all of

them. "There sure is a lot of funky stuff going around." All the girls nodded, their expressions somber and more than a little anxious.

Funky stuff, indeed.

Gabriel packed up his bags and headed for the door. He'd never felt quite so isolated before as the women flocked together on their way to the dressing room. He'd made them into a group independent of him. That had been his job and it was over. Now his real job took precedence. He hadn't been approached by Zanlos since his arrival at the hotel. He'd felt no vibrations, no mental sniffings about, so apparently his cover was intact.

Or maybe Naomi had already told Zanlos everything.

Perhaps that was best. All the cards out in the open. Gabriel never shied from a fight. But tonight he was weary in both body and mind. The image of those slender ankles disappearing over the rail wouldn't give him any respite. Maybe he'd stop in to see Rollie and let his friend coax him from his morose mood. He'd been avoiding his friend and felt bad about it. Rolland, the poet, always had some soul-stirring remedy for what they now called the blues.

He was about to enter the spacious casino when something hard jabbed against his spine. He stopped, not as much alarmed as puzzled.

"Head for the parking garage, slick. We've got some things to discuss."

Marcus?

Curious as to what the big bouncer might want, Gabriel played along. He stepped out into the steamy parking structure. In a few weeks' time it would be overflowing, but tonight there were just a few workmen's trucks and a line of dumpsters.

"What's this all about, Marcus? I step on somebody's toes?"

"Not just toes, pal, my whole foot, and I'm going to plant it hard."

"On whose orders?" Had Zanlos ordered him destroyed? Did that mean Marcus knew who…or rather what he was? If he did, would he think he could hold him captive with a .38 handgun? No, this wasn't about Zanlos. Zanlos wouldn't have sent one of his own in so unprepared. Marcus was going rogue.

But why?

Before he could ask, Marcus looped one of the fancy neck chains he always wore about Gabriel's neck and pulled tight. It wasn't the fierce twist of the heavy links that cost him his breath, it was the chain itself.

Silver.

The links were silver.

The metal bit into his skin like acid, the allergen it contained closing off his windpipe as effectively as a garrote about the neck of a human. As he gasped and tried ineffectively to struggle, Marcus maneuvered him easily into the trunk of his Bonneville.

Once the deck lid was closed and the big car on the move, still there was no relief. The contaminant spread through his system like poison, crippling his body and blurring his mind. Ravaging chills enveloped him. He tried to loosen the chain, but it seared his fingers. And after a few minutes passed, he no longer had the strength to struggle. By the time Marcus dragged him out and let him drop face first into the sand within the glare of the headlights, fever consumed him. Hauling himself up to hands and knees, he surveyed his surroundings. Desert. Miles and forever of it in every direction. And worse, the eastern horizon showed the pinks of approaching dawn.

Whether it was his plan or not, Marcus Sinclair was going to kill him.

"All right, McGraw, now that there's no distraction, let's you and me talk."

Gabriel groaned mightily as Sinclair's expensively shod foot caught him in the ribs. He collapsed full length on the hard packed ground. What seemed like an eternity later, he found the strength to get to his knees, where he wavered and blinked groggily up at his attacker.

"What do you want, Sinclair? What is it you think I've done?"

"I told you not to harm them. I warned you, but you didn't listen."

"Who?"

"The girls. You just couldn't leave them alone. What is it, drugs, sex, both?"

"I don't—"

Sinclair kicked him over onto his side. "You don't need to feed me a line of bull. You show up, and things start happening. Parsons resigns, or did you arrange that so you could bring your Amazonian friend on board? Then the girls start acting strange and disappearing. And now Naomi. That was the last straw, pal. She so above you, so above the both of us, she's on another planet. You understand?"

"I would never hurt Naomi or any of the others."

"That's right. Because you won't get the chance. Did you think this was going to be a warning? Think again. You were warned. This is the end of the road for you." And to prove his point, Sinclair drew his pistol.

Gabriel dove into him. It wasn't a forceful attack, but it was effective enough to topple the vengeful bodyguard. The gun discharged, sending a streak of fire along Gabriel's ribs. Then he was scrambling, burrowing into the low, prickly scrub brush, using the night to his advantage.

"Where do you think you're going to go?" Sinclair taunted after him. "We're in the middle of the fricking desert." He bent to touch his fingertips to the thick dampness dotting the sand. "You won't get far, my friend. There are worse things out here than me, and I hope you run into every one of them."

Pocketing his revolver, he got into his big car and headed back toward the lights of Las Vegas, leaving the rest of his work to the less kinder elements.

Gabriel waited until the sound faded, until those of the night resumed their natural cadences. He tried to stand and found he could not. Fire and ice chased through his system, weakening him with disorienting pain. To a lesser degree, his side burned. Both things would heal with time, but time was not his friend. Not with the way the palette of pastels seeped over the distant mountains. If the sun found him upon the desert floor, it would consume him like dry tinder.

He tried to shape shift into something light and fast that could escape the approaching day, but pain and confusion kept him from holding the image for long enough to transform. He had one more option, but did enough strength remain to send a summons?

Agonizing minutes ticked by. He began to burrow into the softer surface sand but quickly reached the rock-like dirt that refused to absorb moisture just as they refused to absorb him. His insides cramped and quivered. His exposed skin began to prickle, dry and crack. To distract himself from the pain and pending fiery destruction, he summoned the calming image of Naomi Beorththilde seated at his family's table as he told them of his plan to wed her upon his return. She's looked up through eyes great and round with surprise and shy delight. And hope. There'd been such hope in her trusting gaze.

What hope would Naomi Bright have if he died here in the desert without ever giving her the chance to truly live again?

And then he heard it, the deep, full-bodied rumble of a big block V8.

By the time they reached him, he was curled into a tight protective ball to reduce his vulnerability to the first few pools of dawn spreading along the desert floor.

"Help me with him. Quickly, girls."

And then the heavy trunk lid closed, and blissful darkness took him in its embrace.

THIRTEEN

She heard the sounds the minute she opened the front door. Soft, snuffling sounds of distress.

Instinctively, her hand dove for her handbag, but there was nothing in it except house keys, Tums and sunglasses. No .38 Special to back her play.

Rita advanced quickly through the living room, doing a visual check of the perimeter as she moved. The noises originated from Naomi's bedroom. Was she alone, or was there an attacker?

A quick pass through the kitchen and she wielded a knife serious enough to make sushi out of anyone threatening her home. And she thought of the neat little bungalow with its tasteful beige accessories as home for the moment, as much of a home as she'd had in a long time. And she'd be damned if anyone was going to come party crashing.

Even if it was the charming and no-longer-to-be-trusted Gabriel McGraw.

Naomi's room was dark. The only movement was beneath the antique satin and lace coverlet, the restless movements of someone caught in the throes of a nightmare.

With a sigh of relief, Rita lowered the knife. There were no bad guys to slay here.

Or were there?

"Please. You mustn't. I cannot. Please stop."

The words moaned from the woman thrashing through the tangle of her dream. The idea of withdrawing silently was abandoned. Rita sat on the edge of the mattress and placed a hand on one slender shoulder. Naomi cringed beneath that touch as if it had become a part of her frantic ramblings.

"Sweetie, you're having a bad dream. Wake up."

"My lord, you mustn't. Let me grieve. I have yet to grieve."

Frowning slightly, Rita gave her a shake. "Nomi, wake up."

Instead, the fearful cadence grew stronger, more forceful. "Nay, I say nay. I must mourn my love. There will ne'er be another for me save Gabriel. No other can assume his place, not in my heart nor in my bed. Honor my wishes if in truth you honor me."

The strange dialect, the anguished words so ripe with regret and sorrow. *Gabriel?* She spoke as if they were lovers and he was dead. Naomi's dreams were certainly more colorful and creative than her own. Hers were of slow-motion chases and forgotten locker combinations.

"If I cannot be lady of this manor, I will give myself to God." And she lunged forward, coming off the bed to sit for one long minute, eyes open and unseeing. Her body strung tight, her breath caught. Then the tension dissolved into a jerky trembling, and her breath released on a sob.

Rita gathered the wailing figure into a comforting embrace, rocking her slowly as her mind raced along a scary path she'd once traveled alone.

Now she knew what demon plagued Naomi Bright.

***

"Naomi, when did it happen?"

Naomi frowned at her roommate and took another sip of the rich black coffee, hoping it would clear away the fog from her brain. Even a shower hadn't helped. She felt like the tissue coaster beneath a cocktail glass, all limp and worn thin. The last thing she could remember clearly was sipping wine with Gabriel McGraw. Then, if Rita was correct, she'd lost a day and a night to some kind of hysteria. *Madness.* Her sense of self was slipping away again. Rita sat in the opposite chair, watching her as if expecting her to snap at any second.

Perhaps she wasn't too far off the mark.

"When did what happen?" She was cautious now. Dates and time were her secret enemy, an enemy hidden from her by her own blank memories.

"When were you raped?"

That was the last thing she expected to be asked, and she stared at Rita, her expression mirroring her utter disbelief. "What? I don't know what you're talking about. Why would you think such a thing?"

"You were out with Gabriel the other night," Rita continued carefully. "When you came home, you were acting strangely...as if something bad had happened. Did he...Nomi, did Gabriel hurt you?"

Startled by the idea, she blinked as if slapped. "Gabriel? Gabriel would never hurt me."

"How can you be so sure? You hardly know him."

That wasn't true. She'd known him...forever? But then again, what did she really know?

She tried to remember. The restaurant. The wine. The pills she never should have combined with alcohol. Gabriel asking questions that disturbed her, forcing her to think back to a past she couldn't access. She'd tried to deny what he was saying...what had he been saying?...denying first in words, then by running away, by escaping. Her head pounded. Nausea curdled in her stomach.

"I wasn't well. Gabriel sent me home in a cab."

"He never touched you?"

The feel of Gabriel's arms around her. The scent of his clean shirt and cool skin. The sense of safety.

"No."

"Oh, shit."

Naomi regarded her more closely, alarm sharpening her concentration. "Why? Did something happen with Gabriel?"

"Now I'm not so sure. Maybe just me making conclusions in giant leaps and bounds. Nothing that can't be fixed with a good apology. I hope."

Naomi rested her forehead in the well of her palms. Her headache roared. "Why all these questions about Gabriel?"

"I thought—I assumed when you came home all disoriented that he'd—that he'd done something he shouldn't have. It wasn't like I couldn't recognize the signs."

"Signs of what?" She peered at a curiously subdued Rita through the spread of her fingers.

"Physical assault. Honey, if Gabriel didn't harm you, someone must have. I'm not off base here. I've been there, Nomi. You don't have to be ashamed. It's not your fault."

Confusion swirled through the agony in her temples. "But I've never been attacked."

"Nomi, I've lived with it, too. I've watched you shy away

from contact with men. You make yourself unattractive so they won't notice you. You live for your job. You have no life. You're hiding from the pain. You're blaming yourself. Nomi, it's okay. Those are normal reactions to a terrible crime. But you have to control it. You can't let it control you."

After Naomi continued to stare with a frightening vacancy, Rita probed deeper.

"You don't remember, do you? Sweetie, it's eating you alive. I know. I tried for the longest time to hide what had happened from those who cared about me, even from myself. I tried to pretend it never happened, that it didn't matter, and, God help me, that it was somehow my fault, that I'd asked for it. Nomi, no one asks to be raped.

"He was my supervisor. I thought he was going to go over some test scores. He wanted to start with a drink, then when he suggested we go to his apartment, I said no. He said he'd take me home. He didn't. When he finally dropped me off hours later and in shock, he told me if I said anything, he'd tell my superiors that I'd used sex to try to bribe him for a promotion and that when he'd said no, I threatened to cry rape. And I knew everyone would believe him. Everyone except Rae Borden. She knew something was wrong. She got me to take her self-defense class, and eventually the truth came spilling out. She made sure they listened to me. The bastard was fired. And I stopped being afraid of who I was."

"But you're still afraid to let a man get close to you," Naomi surmised with a surprising empathy.

"Well, I'm working through that. But for now, I'm concentrating on me, on finding my strength, my center. And that's what you have to do, too."

Naomi was silent, taking in all Rita said. Could it be true? Could a savage assault have stolen away her memories? A lot of the pieces fit, especially the physical evidence she'd so determinedly ignored.

"What am I going to do, Rita? How do I know if what happened to you happened to me?"

"You need to talk to someone. A professional."

Her defenses shot up, surrounding her behind a wall of

suspicion and fear. "You mean a shrink?" Someone who would pry into her private agonies, push into her life, prod for reasons, real or imagined, behind her pain. Someone who would strip her emotionally naked and leave her vulnerable to a truth she might not be strong enough to hear.

There were things she mustn't tell, things no one could know.

"A shrink, a priest, Oprah. It doesn't matter. Talk to Mel. Talk to me."

"And if I don't have anything to say?"

"There's hypnosis to reach repressed memories. Just don't think you can do it alone, okay? Turn to someone you can trust."

"And who's that?"

"Me, for starters."

Naomi nodded. She could trust Rita. And Kaz Zanlos. But Gabriel? Why did she automatically pause when she considered trust and her handsome knight in the same equation? Had he done something to make her doubt his sincerity? Had he done something to betray her belief in him? How was she to know when she couldn't remember the last two days let alone twenty-seven years?

"There's more, Rita. It's more than just the not remembering. It's the dreams, too."

"What dreams?"

"Dreams of the past. Not my past but one from centuries ago. So real. I feel all the emotions, all the fears. Like I'm living them myself. Not just when I'm sleeping, Rita. I see things and hear them when I'm awake, too."

Rita frowned slightly, saying nothing. So Naomi hurried on, letting it spill just as her friend recommended.

"It has something to do with the Excaliber and Gabriel. Something pulls me toward them that I don't understand. But not Gabriel as he is now. Gabriel, the knight he played in the arena." She blushed. "I told you I was strange."

"Honey, I've seen strange. This isn't strange. Odd maybe in a twisted, Freudian sense."

"Feeling more comfortable in a world that existed centuries ago is only a little odd?"

Rita shrugged. "I'm no psychiatrist, but my guess would be that to deal with the trauma, you've created a safe, sanitized world to live in. One with unrequited romance that's no danger to you."

"But I'm afraid, Rita. I'm afraid I'll forget which is real and which is pretend. I don't understand why this is happening to me."

"There are answers out there, Nomi. You have to have faith."

"And what if I don't like what those answers tell me?"

Rita sat silent. She had no pat response.

And that left Naomi all alone. Unless her boss or Gabriel McGraw could be convinced to reveal all.

***

Only Gabriel wasn't at the Amazon that evening. None of the girls had seen him. No one had heard from him. And only Marcus didn't look surprised. He explained the reason for his unconcerned attitude when Zanlos called him to his office. Naomi sat off to the side, anxious and pale, so much a fixture at Zanlos' side that she wasn't even noticed.

"What do you know about Mr. McGraw's disappearance?"

"I know he won't be coming back any time soon."

Sinclair's smug certainty quickened a shiver of panic around Naomi's heart.

"And why is that, Mr. Sinclair? What have you done?" Zanlos' tone was still civil, but Naomi wasn't fooled by it. Fury vibrated beneath the surface. Sinclair was in mortal danger without realizing it.

"I took initiative, Mr. Zanlos, like you're always encouraging. McGraw was trouble. When he showed up, strange things started happening with the girls. I don't know if he was feeding them drugs or what it was. Grace is a basket case and Jeannie disappeared. He was the last one to be with either of them. We don't know anything about him. He just shows up out of the blue with that pretty-boy smile and everything goes to hell. Ask Naomi…Miss Bright."

Naomi froze when her boss's black stare leveled upon her.

"Miss Bright? What do you know of this?"

"I—nothing. Mr. McGraw was very good at his job. That's

all I know about him."

"But he upset you," Marcus interrupted. "You went out with him, and when you didn't come in and your roommate got in his face, I just assumed—" He broke off, finding no support in Naomi's blank features.

"You assumed?" Zanlos purred. "Do you know the meaning of assume, Mr. Sinclair? You make an ass out of you and me. That's what assume means. And what did this brilliant assumption of yours lead you to do?"

Marcus glanced nervously at Naomi then back to the chill-eyed Zanlos. "I took him for a ride."

"A ride? And the destination?"

"The desert."

"Am I to *assume* that Mr. McGraw did not return from this ride with you?"

"He slipped me in the dark. I don't know where he is. He might be...dead. He took a round when we struggled."

There was a soft thump. Both men looked toward the gentle sound to see Naomi Bright in a heap on the floor. Marcus, for all his bulk, reached her first, lifting her limp form up and steadying it in the chair. He patted her hands and, more awkwardly, her chalk-white cheeks. Slowly, she blinked and gazed at him with a horror that pierced his soul.

"I don't know that he's dead, Miss Bright," he assured her in a rush. "All I know is that I hit him. He'll turn up. I'm sure of it."

"He'd better, Mr. Sinclair." That ultimatum from Zanlos needed no chaser to go down with a harsh burn all the way to the pit of Sinclair's belly. "You'd better pray he does. And from now on, don't take the initiative unless you check with me first. Is that understood? Or do I have to draw you a picture?"

"I understand, Mr. Zanlos," Marcus mumbled, straightening to his formidable height that somehow seemed dwarfed when compared to the magnitude of Zanlos' cool anger. "I just thought—"

"I don't pay you to think, Mr. Sinclair. Thinking is not what you do best, so leave it to others to do for you."

After Marcus had withdrawn, Zanlos turned his attention

to his assistant. His manner gentled.

"Do not worry, Miss Bright. I'm sure no harm has come to Mr. McGraw. It would take more than Sinclair's bumbling best intentions to remove him. Considerably more. When he does arrive, I think it's time he and I had a discussion. Would you arrange that for me, my dear?"

Naomi nodded.

"Very good. It's time Mr. McGraw knew exactly what was at stake."

Naomi didn't puzzle over what that statement might mean. Her entire being ached with the thought that Gabriel might be lost to her. Anguish dammed up in her throat, but while her emotions ran wild with grief, her thoughts remained oddly calm.

She would know if anything had happened to him.

How wasn't important.

Gabriel McGraw was very much alive. And she would see him again soon.

**

While Zanlos and Naomi were busy interrogating Marcus Sinclair, Rita took advantage of the distraction to do some exploring on her own. She couldn't believe she'd mucked it up so badly. Gabriel McGraw had called her in for help, one professional to another, and instead of help, she'd betrayed him unfairly to the woman he loved beyond reason. Perhaps that was it, the reason for her flagging judgement. No man would ever look at her that way, with the kind of devotion that provoked sonnets and sacrifice. Gabriel had it bad for a woman who was too obsessed with the past to see the future he offered along with his heart. Poor Naomi. There had to be some way to get them together. And if she could find some information that would aid in Gabriel's case against Zanlos, he would have more time to court his lady love.

She could smell dirty doings all over Zanlos' operation. Investment money to the tune it would take to build a jungle palace like the Amazon didn't come without strings attached. So who was pulling those strings? The mob? Drug lords? Did Naomi know? She wanted to avoid bringing Naomi into the picture, at least until she discussed things with Gabriel. Naomi needed some serious mental help. Rita was a pragmatist. She understood a soul tortured by scars of the past. What kind of scars had so warped Naomi's psyche that she would seek to hide from a life that had so much to offer? Zanlos had some kind of hold over her. Something nasty and unnatural, she'd bet her shield. Naomi would have to be freed from that situation before she could recover. And that meant bringing down Zanlos. Quickly.

Rehearsals were over. The stage sat dark and quiet. The huge ancient tomb that would be the focal point of the show was almost completed, but it already gave her the shivers. The cold stones—and they were real stones, possibly the real deal—and pagan carvings smacked of another time, another existence, where superstition ruled with a violent hand. She couldn't help wondering about the finishing touches. They'd yet to do a costumed run through, but the tone of the dance, of the whole show, was growing increasingly fierce. Women warriors. A sacrificial temple. How Spielburgian.

Because the storage rooms behind the stage were strictly off-limits and usually guarded by the hulking Marcus Sinclair, that was the first place she'd decided to nose around. She was a sucker for locked doors. The forbidden fruit or something of that nature now that Naomi's problems had her thinking with a psychological bent.

The lock was a good one. It took her a while to pick it. Someone wanted something hidden. Her pulse began to rev like a finely tuned engine on the starting line. The room was big, dark and absolutely silent.

When she was sure it was unoccupied, Rita risked flicking on the slender mag light she carried. It's powerful beam cut through the blackness to reveal boxes and crates, obviously from some source outside the country if the extensive customs stamps were any indication. These were the completing touches for the temple. An archeologist's wet dream, perhaps, but nothing of interest to her. She'd have preferred some nice, juicy incriminating evidence that smacked of smuggling illegal weapons or nose candy. Then she studied the bounty lifted from several opened containers. What she was looking at? Were these priceless antiquities, slipped into the country and now available for a ransom of wealth to some closet collector? She stepped in closer to examine the large pieces so she could describe them later to someone who would know their worth. Old, definitely, but valuable, she had no idea.

One item drew her attention. It was a sarcophagus of stone, ornately etched and set with jewels that looked like they might be worth an old king's ransom. And holding its secrets in was a heavy chain and serious padlock that now lay curled upon the lid like some snoozing deadly snake. Now that looked ripe for housing naughty business. What might it contain that required such hefty security measures? She weighed the sophisticated lock that could have only been breached with a jackhammer. Or a key. If she opened the lid, she'd be contaminating the evidence. But it might be worth it to see what was inside. She could ask Gabriel about a warrant. But that would take time. What if whatever was inside was no longer there when she returned? Just a little peek…Her fingertips caressed along the edge of the cold stone. It looked heavy, but she could probably lift it without too much trouble.

Then an annoying voice of reason intruded upon her treasure hunting fervor.

By the book. Stick to the rules and do your job.

She patted the lid and sighed. Whatever it was, it could wait until she did things right.

Flicking off her light, she started to turn toward the door. From out of the blackness, a crushing force caught her by the throat. She tried to cry out, but the superhuman grip effectively stifled any sound of alarm. As she was lifted up off her feet, she tried to kick at her assailant, but with the breath stolen from her lungs, her strength drained too quickly away. She hung in the powerful grasp, limp and gasping.

As the world swirled in a pattern of bright-colored pindots, she could see two spots of red that remained constant.

And over the frantic heartbeats pounding in her ears, she heard a low hypnotic voice.

"It's not time for you to see into that Pandora's Box. Soon. Have patience. But in the meantime, you know what they say about curiosity, my little tiger cat."

A swift, stinging pain, then Rita Davies' world went black.
Then red.

FOURTEEN

Her head throbbed, and Rita was nowhere in sight.

Naomi waited near the entrance to the parking garage. The hour was early, nearly morning. Paperwork had kept her occupied, that and worry, for most of the night, and now she just wanted to go home to mentally and emotionally crash.

She stepped back inside the huge empty hotel where the climate control brought an immediate parade of gooseflesh to her arms. No one. Obviously Rita had found another way home. She rubbed at her aching temple, wishing her roommate had found the courtesy to let her know. But that wasn't fair of her. They'd made no prior arrangements. She was just tired and feeling bitchy and a bit jealous that Rita wouldn't be sitting in front of the television with her cat for company. She had a life, even if that life didn't yet include dating. Naomi wondered what it would be like to be included in a group of friends, like the gregarious dancers, just going out and having fun with no set agenda or schedule to keep. Exhausting, she decided. Fishing her car keys from her new handbag, she said good-bye to her work world in favor of what she prayed would be a long, untroubled sleep.

The garage was almost empty, a few utility vans near the doors then nothing but oil puddles on pavement beneath the pale yellow glow of suspended lighting beyond. Her footsteps echoed, sounding as slow and dragging as her thought processes. What did she have in the refrigerator at home? Her brow furrowed. When was the last time she'd gone to get groceries? Such a simple thing, such a normal, everyday task, and the answer eluded her. She wasn't hungry anyway. A shower and a good eight hours of sleep. That's all she required for the moment. Maybe she'd shop in the afternoon. Maybe Rita would like to go with her to add to her supply of healthy additives and odd, non-food group items. Like bean curd. Who could actually think of that as sustenance?

Her car was parked halfway down the center aisle, the little white Neon waiting forlorn and abandoned. A statement on her life, as well.

She never actually heard anything. It was more a feeling, a sensation of movement coming up behind her like the chill of an air conditioner suddenly turned on full blast. She looked over her shoulder, and her blood went as cold as the frost on those cooling coils.

"Jeannie? Is that you?"

She stood in the shadows of one of the squat support pillars. The arrogant body language was pure Jeannie, but something was wrong. Naomi's nape prickled. Instead of rushing to the other woman with questions and concern, she stayed where she was, spooked into immobility.

"Hello, Miss Bright. Out kind of late, aren't you?"

It was Jeannie's voice but then again…The soft syllables hissed slightly, as if the young woman had a mouthful of new orthodontia.

"Jeannie, we've all been so worried. Where have you been?"

"Here and there."

"Jack's practically frantic."

"Oh, I've seen Jack. He's not worried anymore."

"Why haven't you come to rehearsal?"

Jeannie swayed away from the post, her body undulating with the forward movement like a model…or a stripper on a catwalk. She'd always had the grace of a dancer, but her motions now were fluid and oozing with sensuality, a seductive Salome wearing a secretive and cunning smile. "I've got other interests now."

"But this show could have been your big break." Naomi began backing up, her hand with the car keys behind her, searching for the door to her compact.

"Oh, Miss Bright, there are things in this world and beyond that you can't imagine. I could show you. Let me show you." That purred invitation stirred quivers of warning up and down Naomi's spine.

"Not tonight, Jeannie. I'm very tired."

Jeannie drew closer. Her fever-hot stare bored into Naomi's, and it was impossible to look away. Sparks of light and magic glittered in that gaze, as mesmerizing as a kaleidoscope. Naomi bumped into the door panel. The key scraped along paint surface, desperate to find the lock.

"And I'm hungry." That was almost a growl that grew petulant. "It's your job to look after us, Miss Bright, to see to our needs. Give me what I need."

The key slid into the lock and turned with an audible click. The sound brought an immediate sharpening to Jeannie's features, features that hardened into harsh, unnatural angles as she suddenly rushed forward without seeming to actually move.

Naomi jerked open the door. The chrome bit into the calf of her leg, slicing through her stockings and skin. She hobbled in a tight circle, trying to get inside before the hyper-enraged Jeannie was upon her. Too late. With the thrust of one palm, Jeannie slammed the door shut, cutting off her exit.

"Not trying to run out on me, are you, Miss Bright?"

So close, Naomi could see the strange pallor of Jeannie's skin where it stretched taut over jutting cheekbones and razor-sharp jawline. The complexion the girl was so proud of for its creamy smoothness appeared almost transparent beneath the unflattering light. Tiny veins spidered beneath the shallow surface, pulsing angrily. This wasn't Jeannie. It couldn't be!

Suddenly, the unfamiliar creature was snatched back away from her and spun out into the middle of the parking aisle. She crouched there, hissing like something venomous as Gabriel yanked opened the car door.

"Get in."

Trembling wildly, Naomi obeyed, scrambling across to the passenger side after fitting the key in the ignition. She couldn't see Gabriel facing the furious woman with a feral show of teeth. He jumped behind the wheel and slammed the door, punching the universal lock. Jeannie flattened against the window, her fingers clawing at the edges, nails scraping the glass with a nerve-shredding screech. Gabriel started the car and gunned it forward, squealing the tires as he spun around the nearest pillar.

"Look out!"

Even as Naomi screamed the warning, she knew it was too late for Gabriel to react. Jeannie was just there, right in front of the vehicle. The bumper and grill struck her in the abdomen. Her features crumpled with surprise before she went down and out of sight.

Hands clapped over her mouth to hold back her hysteria, Naomi twisted in the seat to see a form sprawled on the pavement. Then, incredibly, as they sped away, she saw the supposedly broken figure gather up and stand.

The car shot out of the garage and onto the side street to a cacophony of horns and curses. Gabriel battled the wheel, bringing the vehicle under control and into line with the steadily moving traffic. Only then did Naomi sag back in the seat, shocked beyond measure by what she'd seen. Or had she imagined it?

"Are you all right?" Gabriel asked without looking for himself. "She didn't hurt you, did she?"

"No and no." Instinctively, she wrapped her seat belt around her, fearing she might dissolve right to the floorboards in a quaking, gelatinous glob. Her mind started to function, spinning madly to explain what she'd witnessed. "Was it drugs, do you think?" She'd heard that PCP lent its users abnormal strength and the ability to ignore pain. But that didn't explain away everything as neatly as she wanted. "What would make her act...and look that way?"

"I'll take you home."

For the next few blocks, as horror rattled through her, she didn't realize he never offered an answer. Then another revelation hit.

Gabriel!

Her gaze flew over him to assure herself that he was indeed real and unharmed. Real, yes, but her stare snagged upon a dark blackish stain beneath his arm where a jagged hole had ripped through the front and back of his loose-fitting shirt. Marcus Sinclair hadn't missed.

"You've been shot!"

"What?" He glanced at her as if startled by the idea. Following her wide stare to the gore mingling with the bright pattern of material, he understood and shrugged. "It's nothing."

"Nothing?" So much blood! "Gabriel, you should be in a hospital."

"I've already been treated for it. I'm fine. Really. It's you

I'm worried about."

"Me?" He was referring to their last meeting where she'd...what? Lost her mind for a minute? "Nothing's changed with me," she claimed with an ironic bite of truth.

"You got home safely? I wanted to take you myself, but I didn't think it would be...wise."

And she could sense him drawing back to become as neutral as those blandly spoken words. But uninvolvement wasn't what she wanted. Not now. Not after so many things had happened. Perhaps the strain of having Jeannie scare her nearly witless kept her usually protective shell from forming up around her. But the last thing she wanted was to be isolated with all her fears and doubts as he turned her car into the driveway.

She didn't give him a chance to say anything.

"Come in. And I don't care if you think that's wise or not."

He shut off the engine without protest and came around to her side to open the door. She got out on absurdly weak legs, feeling as if she'd been on a wild roller coaster ride all over again. Gabriel slipped his palm beneath her elbow for support. Just that, but it was enough to fill her with encouragement.

Gabriel...

And suddenly Kaz Zanlos was there in her mind, manipulating her thoughts, her questions becoming his questions. *How badly is he injured? Why has he come for you? Does he suspect something? What does he know? I need these answers, Miss Bright. You will get them for me.*

As she unlocked the front door to the darkened bungalow, she struggled consciously to shut off Kaz Zanlos' dictates. Tonight wasn't about him. It was for her. For her answers. For her benefit. Tonight she would focus on what was between her and Gabriel. Finally, the voice in her head was silent with just a residual ache to remind her of her duty.

Rita wasn't home. As she switched on the light to the kitchen/dining area, there was a disgruntled hiss as Mel leapt off the table, sending the vinyl place mat soaring like a Frisbee. The huge creature bounded under the coffee table and glared up unhappily, growls rumbling from its massive form.

Seeing Gabriel's hesitation, she said, "Don't mind Mel. He

and I don't get along." She glanced up at him, noting how pale and weary he looked under the interior lights. "Can I get you an ice tea…or something stronger?" She had some wine in the back of the cupboard somewhere. Zanlos had sent it to her for Christmas and, since she didn't drink, it simply aged gracefully back behind her discount store glassware.

"I'm fine. Don't worry about me."

"But I do." She spoke the truth boldly, facing him in her front hall with all the anxieties that had knotted up inside her for the past twenty-four hours. "Marcus told me what happened."

"Did he." Such a cautious statement.

"He said he drove you out into the desert because he thought you were somehow involved in the problems the girls were having. Of course, he was wrong about that." And she waited, gazing up at him expectantly.

"He was wrong."

Her gust of relief was audible. "Marcus gets so overprotective sometimes."

"There's no harm in that when it's you he's keeping from harm."

She fixed him with another unblinking stare. "And would you harm me, Gabriel?"

His answer came with heart-rending certainty. "Never. Nor would I allow any harm to come to you. Which is why it's not a good idea for me to be here."

"I disagree."

And before he could think to react or she could question her actions, Naomi stepped forward so that they were toe to toe. She caught his face between her palms, noting on a periphery how cold his cheeks were. She pulled him down to her. Even as his eyes widened, hers were slipping blissfully closed.

His mouth was a taste of heaven.

His surprise only lasted the instant it took for the reality of their kiss to sink in. Need roared through his body, tightening every muscle, alerting every fiber so it cried out for the feel of her. It was hell to hold himself back from what he wanted, had dreamed of for an eternity. But he remained in fierce control of those desires, with the luxury of her shy overtures as his reward. That she had little experience kissing both delighted and humbled him. Her soft lips trembled as she pressed them to his. The fit was perfect, yielding yet tentatively seeking. He let her search out his response, waiting for her to satisfy her curiosity. His restraint buckled as she initiated a hesitant sliding and sampling. He brought his hands up slowly, touching first the gentle slope of her shoulders. They quivered beneath that light contact. Then he sketched the fragile line of her jaw with his fingertips and her sigh shivered with anxiousness and anticipation.

Gradually, so as not to frighten or upset her, he parted his lips so they could exchange breaths and the first inquiring trace of his tongue. She moaned, not a wanton sound of need but a tender expression of awe that seized his heart like a fist to squeeze unrelentingly. He had never wanted anything so much in his entire life as the sweetness of her awakening passions. To be the one to first stir them within her. The honor overwhelmed him.

He followed that initial foray with increasingly invasive sweeps, to taste, to explore, to lathe along the luscious offering of her mouth, of her trust, of her innocence. A heady bouquet that made his senses buzz and his reason blur. Their only junction was lips and fingertips, but he was aware of her so keenly she could have been poured down his body like hot wax. The centuries' old ache to know her, to claim her as his own, tensed along his forearms and through his thighs, twisting in his belly and flaming in his groin. If their touch grew more intimate, he feared he would explode from all the turmoil massing inside.

Heightened emotions quickened a sharpening to all his other faculties. Above and around the chaste kiss, his desires seethed, the passions of the man warring with the hunger of the beast also residing within. He could scent her mortality, the fragrant tease of it on the tip of his tongue and up his nose, where it provoked a dangerous havoc. Over her soft, hurried breaths, he could hear the enticing beat of her heart beckoning him to follow along that hearty, rich trail pumping through her, to partake of her soul as well as her body, to enjoy both to the limits of ecstacy where they would share what had long been denied them. She would let him. She would enjoy the new experiences he'd bring her. But she wouldn't understand what drove him to cross boundaries he'd placed between love and lust and longing to keep her safe. For him and from him.

Her tongue slipped over and around his. Her palms adored the lean angles of his face. He sampled the delicious prospect of her surrender, sucking and nibbling on her lower lip until she whispered his name with the reverence of a prayer.

And her fingertips traced down the strong line of his throat, over the high neck of the knit pullover he wore. Grazing the gauze protecting the raw burns cut into his flesh. She hesitated, and before her questions could form, he jerked back with a shock of pain and self-preservation.

She gasped at his abrupt withdrawal, staring up at him through eyes limpid with complex demands and uncertain emotions. Her moist lips begged the return of his.

His mind swirled, his mouth wetting for the taste of her acceptance. Of her...blood.

She'd cut herself.

Suddenly, the hot sensations grabbed control of him, bringing an angry ache to his gums and a seething urgency to burn along his starving system to burst within his brain. His nostrils flared to inhale the intoxicating warmth of promise.

He could dazzle her with vampiric magic. She would never know what he'd taken from her along with her trust.

But Zanlos would know. And how much greater danger would that place her in?

The wounds at his throat pulsed and flamed. The effects of the silver still poisoned him, sapping his strength. She could provide what he needed to return to his full potency. Her love. Her trust. Her blood.

His to take. Hers to give without...choice.

He took a hasty step back. In the living room, Mel yowled and skittered for the bedroom. The animal recognized him for what he was.

Breathing hard, aware that his hunger raged in his stare, Gabriel averted his eyes from the tender expectancy offered in her upturned face. Instead, he lowered his gaze to the gash in her calf, to the thin line of crimson staining her torn nylons.

"You've cut you leg."

Naomi blinked to scatter the fog of desire. His words reminded her of the pain when the car door struck her. She felt, for the first time, the sting of the cut and the throb of the bruise rising around it.

"You need to clean that and bandage it tight so nothing will get to it," he told her in a strangely thick voice. Where had the spicy, expectant mood of moments ago gone? Gabriel had pulled back into himself, to the aloof observer, who said little and displayed less of what was going on behind his steady, dark stare.

She wanted him to stay. She wanted him to indulge her with more of what fired her emotions to such an unexpected frenzy.

But he was backing away, evasive, nervous, eager to be gone.

"My ride's here."

His statement startled her. She hadn't heard a car pull up.

But when he opened the front door, she could see his big boat of a car at her curb. And she could just make out beneath the cool gleam of the street light, the figure of a woman behind the wheel.

Hurt and jealousy speared through her. Was this woman the reason for his abrupt change of passions?

Had she been wrong to think he wanted her as badly as she did him at that moment?

He had someone else waiting.

"Good night, Naomi. Lock this door behind me."

She watched him hurry down the front walk. When he opened the passenger door, the driver's face was briefly illuminated. She was beautiful, with creamed-coffee colored skin and striking bone structure.

What was this woman to Gabriel McGraw?

The car sped away, cloaking Naomi's question in a cloud of exhaust and mystery.

Leaving her at the threshold of desire and doubt.

FIFTEEN

Rita never came back to the apartment. The woman who snapped orders at the girls that night was a stranger.

Or at least that was how it felt to Naomi as she watched from Marcus's side as a tough-talking and rough-acting Rita pushed the dancers to their limit. Time was running out. The next night they'd use the full set for rehearsal. Workmen assembled it in the background, causing a constant distraction and hazard to the performers as they worked through their extremely physical routine. Rita yelled and cursed and corrected until each move was sharp and fierce and ultimately warrior-like. And exciting. Naomi's adrenalin raced as she followed the movements. If she knew how to exact such control and confidence, she could have handled the situation with Jeannie the night before. She never seemed to have control. Others always stepped in to rescue her. Gabriel, Rita, Zanlos and even Marcus. Being a victim in their eyes suddenly presented an ugly picture. One she could close her own eyes to no longer.

She watched the violent poetry of self-defense play out before her and compared it to her own placidity. Zanlos had saved her career, Rita her mind, Gabriel her emotions. What had she managed to accomplish on her own? She was a shadow who existed during the evening hours at this hotel. She followed Kaz Zanlos' edicts without question, even though she suspected they were illegal. She'd left her sanity in Rita's hands, too afraid to search out a name for her malady on her own. Gabriel...he created a confusion in her boring routine of service to others because he made her want something for herself. And she was afraid to take it. On the fence. Middle of the road. Afraid of her shadow. How could she expect the respect of others if she had none for herself?

The only thing she had was her work, and Zanlos had ordered her to reel Gabriel into a trap. What was wrong with her that she couldn't recognize right from wrong? Zanlos was in the wrong, yet she couldn't make herself act against him or his commands. Gabriel was a cop, one of the good guys, yet she considered betraying him.

Her hand was at her throat, gently rubbing the faded marks below her ear. They seemed to throb angrily with objection every time her thoughts gave way to turmoil, until it hurt her physically to contemplate her options. Follow Zanlos' orders. That was the path of least resistence, the road that caused no pain of body or conscience. Even if it was wrong.

That's what a weakling would do. A doormat without a mind or opinion of her own.

"I've got to get some air."

Marcus reacted to her curt announcement with alarm. "If you'll wait until they're finished, I'll go with you."

"I don't need a babysitter, Marcus." His wounded frown prompted her to place a hand on his bulging forearm. "But thank you for the offer. I'll only be gone a minute."

He nodded toward the stage. "Is it just me, or do we have a little more estrogen than usual pumping up there?"

"Rita's working them hard because the opening is so close, and we still don't have the number right."

"Right. Must be it. To the casual male observer, it looks like she's out to bash anything with testosterone."

Naomi grinned. "A big boy like you threatened by a girl with attitude?"

"Make that grrrrl. And I'm not the least bit intimidated."

"Yeah, right."

They shared a chuckle over it, but Naomi's brow pleated in concern as she walked through the nearly-ready-for-company casino. Marcus was right. Something was different about Rita. That he'd noticed it, too, made her all the more worried. And another worry wasn't something she needed at the moment.

The night was thick with heat and activity. As she stood on the front walk, she was constantly jostled by tourists rushing to this or that show. Subconsciously, she tightened her grip on her purse. Many stopped to read the "Opening Soon" marquee, and the buzz she overheard was heartening. They were going to make a fortune.

But who, exactly, were they?

The man in the shadows, the one Gabriel had asked her to

name?

An ache started to beat at the back of her neck, beginning its slow spreading toward her temples. She massaged the offending knot of tension, thinking to stem the inevitable headache. She closed her eyes briefly, but against that curtain of black, she saw the blur of black and silver. The rattle of metal and thunder of horse's hooves matched the pulsing rumble in her head.

"Naomi, are you all right?"

At first she thought the voice was part of the hallucination. However, when she opened her eyes, he was there before her, not in knightly armor but in a varsity jacket snapped up beneath his chin. Her initial thought was to wonder why he wasn't sweating in the oppressive desert heat.

"Gabriel, are you coming to work?" Did she sound pathetically hopeful? "Marcus is eager to apologize to you for the misunderstanding."

"Misunderstanding? Is that what he calls attempted murder?"

"He thought he was protecting the girls. And me."

"Did Zanlos send him after me? Or did you?"

Her surprise was too quick and complete not to be genuine. "Me? What reason would I have to want you harmed?"

He avoided the question. "Zanlos then. I'm sure he has reasons aplenty."

Then she heard herself saying before she could hold the words back, "Not really. In fact, he'd like to meet with you to discuss your…differences."

"Differences. An interesting understatement. I think I'll pass. Your boss and I know exactly where each other stands."

"Gabriel, he is a powerful…and dangerous man. Please don't—"

"Don't what? Do my job?"

"Please don't endanger yourself over something that doesn't involve you?" She paused, feeling an odd shiver of déjà vu. When had she said these words to him before? How did she know he'd ignored them then just as he would now?

"It does involve me if he's breaking the law. Is he, Naomi?

You would know that better than anyone. Who's financing this little gig? Where's the money coming from? The Mob?"

"No. There's only one big investor, and there's nothing illegal involved. Can't you believe that and let it go?"

"I can't because you don't. You know as well as I do that something's not right about this whole setup. What is it, Naomi? I'm going to find out with or without your help. If you help me, I can protect you."

"Why does everyone think I need protecting? I'm not a child!"

His gaze warmed suddenly to throw her off her rant. That heated look reminded her of the taste of his kiss. "No, you're no child. But you could find yourself in the middle of something you can't get out of. If you do, call me. Promise you'll call me."

"And how do I reach you should I find myself falling off my fence?"

"Rita knows."

"Rita's not exactly a reliable source these days."

Gabriel's focus sharpened. "What do you mean? What's happened?"

"I don't know. She's just acting odd, angry at the world and happy about it. She hasn't been home. She won't talk to me."

He digested this with more seriousness than she'd thought he would. His advice was strange and alarming. "Be careful around her."

"But Rita's my friend." Her only friend.

"Perhaps, perhaps not. I'm only saying you need to be careful what you say and do around her. She might not keep your confidences."

"What aren't you telling me, Gabriel?"

"That's all I can say."

"Secrets. Everyone is up to their eyebrows in them, and no one can see the truth." She pushed away from him and walked to the curb and back, arms wrapped tight about her bosom. She could feel her heart racing.

"Do you know the truth, Naomi?"

She answered sadly. "If I did, I'd know who to trust."

"Trust me."

"Says you."

"Says your heart. Listen to it."

She saw movement out of the corner of her eye. His big car pulled up to the curb. The lovely woman with the café au lait skin was behind the wheel. Trust her heart. She could feel it breaking.

"I have to go back inside. I'll think about what you said."

"Naomi."

She looked up into his intense dark eyes. She could see more he wanted to say steeping there in those endless depths, but he never spoke any of it. With a wry smile, she turned away and reentered the hotel. Through the smoky glass, she saw him get into the car.

He'd said he would never hurt her.

Liar.

***

"What's wrong?"

Gabriel glanced at the woman behind the wheel. "What makes you think something's wrong?"

Charmaine shot him a chiding look and repeated, "What's wrong?"

"The woman I put in place to protect her has been compromised. Something's going to happen soon, and I'm no closer to finding out what it is than I was when I started. I no longer have anyone I can trust on the inside."

"You could have."

The bland remark captured his full attention. He looked at Charmaine closely, seeing her for the lovely, talented and loyal woman she was. The potential was there. She would never refuse him. She couldn't if she wanted to. But for all the centuries he'd been existing in this world of gray between life and death, he had never manipulated the will of one in his control to knowingly place them in danger. Never. And he wouldn't start now, even when the stakes were so unbearably high. His answer was gruff and final. "I would never ask that of you."

"You don't have to ask, honey."

"You have your daughters to think of."

Charmaine actually laughed. "My daughters? If it hadn't been for you, my daughters would be picking through garbage cans or selling themselves on the street to survive because I'd probably be dead. Sugar, there's nothing I wouldn't do for my girls, and because of what you've done for them, there's nothing I wouldn't do for you."

"You don't understand the danger."

"Danger? Doll, I grew up in the inner city. What does a white bread boy like you know about danger?"

He couldn't contain his grin. Then he was serious once more. "Charmaine, these are not nice people. These aren't even bad people. They are unnatural creatures, like me. They have no mercy. They have no souls."

"And they have your girlfriend."

He looked straight ahead, the agony of that truth tightening every muscle in his face.

"Answer me just one thing."

Hearing the somber quality of the question, Gabriel twisted in the seat to listen. "What?"

"If something was to happen to me, would you see my girls are looked after?"

"Yes."

"Then that's a better deal than anyone else has ever given me, unnatural or not. Have you got a plan?"

"Do you know how to dance?"

"Like Ginger-damn-Rogers with a tan."

"Then I have a plan."

SIXTEEN

"Miss Bright?"

Naomi turned in answer to be confronted by the woman who'd driven Gabriel McGraw's big car. She was even more flawlessly lovely up close. Immediately, Naomi wanted to hate her but found she could not. Because beneath the perfect makeup and stylish clothes was the embodiment of the school of hard knocks. It was evident in the defensive posture, in the nervous glances toward the door that said she didn't belong, in the shadowing of fatigue and caution smudged beneath the straight to the point stare. A kindred spirit in the world of woe and worry.

"My name is Charmaine Johnson. A mutual friend sent me to help you out of a jam."

"And what jam is that, Ms. Johnson?"

"I'm a dancer."

"We already cast the show, Ms. Johnson. I'm afraid there are no more openings." Jeannie's spot was technically open, but Naomi was chafing from the arrogance of Gabriel trying to push another of his lady friends upon her.

Charmaine chuckled, a sound as warm and rich as honey-laced bourbon. "I'm not applying for a job. I'm here to help you do yours."

"Excuse me?"

"Let me put it better. I am a dancer and a damn fine singer, too. But what I have and what this show needs most is soul."

Naomi stared at her blankly, and Charmaine laughed out loud. "See, you don't understand it when I spell it out to you. But you'll see what I mean. What you got now is a bunch of pretty little Denise Austins up there bouncing around trying to look bad. What do those preppy chicks know about survival, about the jungle?"

"You've been to the jungle, Ms. Johnson?" She arched a delicate brow.

"The concrete kind, and it don't get much meaner than that. What you got is a whole lot of attitude without an ounce of soul. Not Soul Train, soul," she amended before Naomi could comment. She tapped her chest with a closed fist. "Soul from in here. Deep down and dirty, hunt for your supper, protect your family instincts. And none of these girls, not even you, Miss Bright, has a clue as to what that looks like."

"Show me."

"Play back that last number."

The moody percussion beat filled the empty auditorium. Tossing off her fitted jacket so she was clad in only a snug white tank top and jeans, Charmaine rolled up onto the stage and to her feet in a fluid tumble. In the center of the other dancers, she picked up their basic movements then made them growl to life with primitive passion. An extra snap of the hips, an exaggerated roll of the shoulders and constant eye contact, bright, wild and burning. Powerful gestures clad in animalistic sleekness, like glossy fur over dangerous sinew. Supple, smooth and even sexier than hell. Something the upper class, classically trained Kitty Parsons couldn't have conceived of in a million years even for a million dollar paycheck.

Jungle soul. Hot. Fiercely rhythmic. Primal strength and sexuality with a little bump and grind thrown in to raise the body temperature.

Perfect.

"Yes. Yes!" Naomi rushed to the edge of the stage. "More like that. Just like that."

Like Jeannie in the parking garage. Predators on the prowl.

And from the corner of her eye, Naomi saw Rita snatching up her bulky pullover, wriggling into it as she marched up the aisle and out of the auditorium.

***

"Who is that woman?"

Rita and her dark lover stood at the one-way glass looking down upon the stage. It took him a moment to focus as he lapped up the rich life's blood from the wounds on her throat. The euphoria of feeding left him dazed and drowsy.

"Who is she?" Rita repeated. The sharpness of her tone finally cut through his lethargy.

"I do not know, my dear. She is very…athletic."

"She just walked in out of nowhere, and Naomi gave her

the job."

"Jealous, love? Of what? Because like all the others, they don't appreciate what you've done, what you offer? Because they exclude you and push you away, even your supposed little friend down there? I know it hurts, my love. I, too, know the sting of their rejection. Good enough to use for their purpose but not good enough to be one of them. You've got a much greater purpose now. You will be my eyes and ears against those who thought to use you against me. Don't you love the irony of it?"

"So I have to stay with that crazy little twit." Her tone was a bit forced, as if she was trying to convince both him and herself with her display of disgust.

His features hardened dangerously. "You will stay where I tell you to stay."

She immediately oozed apology and petition. "But I want to stay with you, to serve you."

"As delightful as that may be, you serve me better where you are. I want to know everything, my dear. You must tell me all. Don't think of it as a betrayal of trust. Does she trust you? Do any of them trust you? She's thrown you aside for him. There is no loyalty there, no trust, no love. Not like I've given you. Rita, she is not your friend."

"She's got some knight in shining armor fetish." Rita spoke that confidence to soothe the bitterness burning about her heart. He was right and it hurt. She had no friends.

"Really?"

"As if there are any real heroes out there who'll come to rescue her. Little fool. The closest she's ever going to get is the make believe at the Excaliber where she dreams and drools over thoughts of chivalry. She has nightmares about it, too, mixing up her pretend heroes with the villain that attacked her. She even speaks lines out of Camelot in her sleep." Her laugh was cruel. "Pathetic."

"I don't know what kind of a policewoman you were, but you have an affinity for evil that quite impresses me."

"You can't work with it all day without some of it rubbing off, you know. I've seen evil. It's no stranger to me." Her talk was tough to harden her heart against those she thought had cared about her. But they'd only been using her, mocking her need for their inclusion. They'd kept secrets, and now she would tell theirs.

"Tell me about this villain. What does she know about him?"

"Nothing. She's blocked the whole ordeal out of her mind and refuses to deal with it. The weakling."

"She's not strong like you."

"No."

"Do not offer solutions to the poor confused girl. Push her, Rita. I need to know what she remembers. I want her frightened and helpless. Feed her panic and pain so that he's busy playing rescuer. That will keep him distracted from what I am doing until the last piece is in place."

She leaned into him, offering the ragged side of her neck for his nuzzling. Finally, he pushed her away.

"You are as greedy as I am."

She laughed. "I like to be appreciated."

"Oh, and your talents are many, my love. You've done an excellent job with the girls. They will be as vicious as they are lovely when they join their friend Jeannie in my little cadre of killers."

"And me? Will I join them, too?"

"Patience. I have not yet decided. Your will is strong. Perhaps too strong for me to control if I gift you with the power of eternity. For now, you please me as you are."

"Frightening a silly girl and placating a vain man's ego."

"Do not underestimate our Mr. McGraw. He may look the love besotted swain but he, unlike myself, is a man of principle and honor. I'm not ready to provoke him to make a choice between head and heart. Not yet. Soon. When all the gold has been moved from Peru into my accounts here, then I will need none of them. She won't scorn my love again. She'll learn, like those before her. And the show will open as a perfect revenge. My revenge."

And Alex Cross glared down at Naomi Bright through eyes red and swirling with madness and obsession.

"Soon."

***

Kaz Zanlos felt a faint tingling of awareness an instant before he glanced up from his paperwork. He didn't express his surprise.

"Ah, Mr. McGraw. I've been expecting you for some time."

"Sorry to keep you waiting."

The detective stood just inside his door. That he had gotten so close without tripping any of Zanlos' safeguards was as alarming as it was impressive. Zanlos smiled blandly. "To what do I owe the honor?"

"I believe you sent for me. If at first you don't succeed, ask for a meeting."

"Oh, you must be referring to that nasty business with Mr. Sinclair. Please be assured that that was none of my doing. Though I can't fault a man for taking his job seriously, Mr. Sinclair went beyond the requirements of his."

"So you want me to believe that it isn't in your best interest for me to be killed?"

"Oh, dear boy, why would I want such a thing? If something happened to you, swarms of your over-zealous brethren would descend upon me like locusts. That's trouble I don't need. I prefer the enemy I recognize."

"Well, you've got trouble whether you like it or not."

"You don't have a very forgiving nature, do you, Mr. McGraw? Can't you leave that unfortunate business in Washington behind us as a mistake on my part? I was unaware of what my associate was planning. Obviously, I didn't plan to become what you see before you now. If nothing else, that should convince you of my former partner's treachery."

"And you were just a Boy Scout in that whole affair?"

"Oh, no. I was a naughty boy. A failing of mine. I see a fortune to be made, and I can't help grabbing for it. My haste and greed lead to some rather unpleasant bedfellows."

"Like now? Who are you in bed with, Zanlos?"

"How indiscreet of you to expect me to kiss and tell. Suffice it to say, I've built this endeavor legitimately. All the I's are dotted and T's are crossed. Remember, in my human life I was a lawyer. Would you begrudge a man an honest living? After all, what did I ever do to you and your people?"

"You stole Naomi Bright."

"Ahhh. Yes. Well you gave me little choice there, did you, detective? As I recall, you and your friends were about to turn me into dust before I had an opportunity to appreciate my new situation."

Gabriel scowled, remembering. He and his friends closing in on the centuries-old Bianca du Maurier who was about to use her vampiric power to enslave a government. Kaz Zanlos, her human partner, was no innocent except when it came to the true nature of the woman's treachery and viciousness. She'd turned on him at the last moment, changing him into one of their kind, leaving him to cover her short-lived escape. And Zanlos, always the clever survivor, had taken Naomi hostage to make good his own exit.

"So you hide behind a woman who trusted you."

"Yes. Blame me for being unchivalrous if you like, but Miss Bright has come to no harm in my care. Good assistants are too hard to find. And so is good insurance."

Gabriel took a threatening step forward. "Let her go, Zanlos."

"She isn't a prisoner here. She's an employee. She comes and goes as she likes."

"She is your prisoner and you know it."

Zanlos shrugged. "A prisoner who has a healthy paycheck, good benefits and an employer who values her work. Not a bad captivity. Truth be told, she would not go with you. Our Miss Bright prefers the safe and familiar to the threat of the unknown. She is a fragile creature, and I see that she is well protected. You see, some arrogant fool in her past did not place her worth above his pride, and she suffered for it grievously." He smiled thinly as that blade of truth stabbed home. "I will not make that same mistake."

"She isn't safe with you, Zanlos. It's all an illusion to abuse her trust."

"You are a fine one to speak of trust. Have you told her what you are and how you've been using her to get to me? Who between us is the honorable man, Mr. McGraw? Which one of us has Miss Bright's interests at heart? If you persist in trying to tear down what I have built here, she will fall with me. There is no way you can avoid that. Is your conscience strong enough to withstand that cost? I think not." He spoke that with a cool cruelty having weighed, measured and determined the type of man he faced. "Honorable men are predictably single-sighted. Though they might protest that they act for the good of all, that innocent 'all' is usually who was caught in the crossfire. You are a warrior, are you not? You understand the terms of war. If you declare it against me and the empire I've created, it's the innocent who will pay the price."

"Not if I take you out."

McGraw took another aggressive step, but Zanlos only chuckled.

"Cut off the head and the beast will die, is that it? It might surprise you to learn that I am not the head. Take me down and you will still be devoured, you and those you care about. You can't win here, Detective. The best you can do is strike a bargain that insures the safety of Miss Bright. If you care for her, as you claim, that should not be too difficult a deal to make. Don't force me to sacrifice her because you are too stubborn to see there is nothing but your pride at stake. I will allow no harm to come to her. She's the only one who knows how to sort my mail properly."

McGraw hesitated and Zanlos continued, confident in his assessment.

"See. Honorable men are no mystery. Do the smart thing. If you care for Miss Bright, leave her in my protection. Return to your righteous tribunal and tell them there is nothing going on here that need concern them. I perhaps have erred as a human being, but I have behaved myself since becoming one of your kind. Isn't that your main concern, that mankind is not endangered by our existence? I have nothing against mankind. In fact, I serve them and their greed most enthusiastically. You have no job to do here, Detective." He held out his smooth palms. "My hands are clean."

He let the young policeman consider that for a long minute,

then he added the *coup de grace.*

"She will be safe and content with me, Mr. McGraw. Can you say the same? Can you guarantee that you will bring her no harm, either mentally or physically, should she go with you? I think not. And I think you know it, too, and perhaps that is why you despise me so. Despise me then. You won't hurt my feelings. Only don't attack me for the wrong reasons. That would not be honorable of you."

"This is not over," McGraw vowed at last, his tone soft with promise.

"I had not assumed it would be. Do not interfere where you do not belong. You have no cause. Your rules, not mine, but I'm not above insisting that you follow them. Good evening, Mr. McGraw. I trust you know the way out."

The way out. An irony, he thought as, unseen in the shadows, he watched the rehearsal wrap up. The sight of Naomi absorbed his senses. Her features were relaxed, her eyes aglow with pleasure as she spoke to each of the girls in her brood. Her attitude toward Charmaine remained a bit stiff, but that was because of him and her curiosity over how he and Charmaine fit together. But it wasn't in Naomi's nature to remain aloof for long, and soon she was chatting easily with the new choreographer.

He could see her as she had been, his lovely, innocent and newly orphaned neighbor who'd come to his family for aid. She'd asked for his help and had claimed his heart. He remembered the details so clearly, right down to the soft dove color of her gown and the scent of violets that sweetened the air about her. He, the bold warrior, was reduced to awkward boy as she gazed up expectantly, waiting to hear what he would say. Her eyes had widened, her lips parted, her breathing trembled as she heard him pledge his devotion and his sword. And he remembered her words now, though he hadn't heard them clearly enough then.

`Tis not your sword I desire, sir knight. The protection I seek comes from the heart, not the hand.

There was a noisy scuffle from the doors of the auditorium as Charmaine's boisterous younger daughters raced down the aisle. The older girl followed at a more sedate and grown up pace. Gabriel watched with heart turning over as Naomi was introduced to the girls. She knelt down so she was eye level with the younger daughters and addressed them warmly, then shook the elder girl's hand with adult propriety. The kids took to her immediately. She was a natural with children. He'd at one time dreamed of their children playing about their feet, had envisioned her tender scolding and comforting embraces, had yearned for the respectful regard of his own son's uplifted gaze as he gave instruction or advice. Had anticipated his prideful and protective emotions as he watched a daughter evolve from shy butterfly to courted beauty.

But that would never happen.

There would be no family for him. He'd settled that when he became what he was, a creature caught between existence and death. No new life could spring from that void, from that suspension of time and reality.

He observed Naomi with the girls, the way she listened with grave attention as they chattered, the way she touched their hair with the fondness of a woman who deserved motherhood. She deserved a man who could gift her with the opportunity to share her love and nurturing with young ones of her own.

He was not that man. Not any more. Not for centuries.

Odd. In his single-minded focus to find her, to claim her, he'd never once thought of whether or not he had anything to offer her once they were together again. All his imaginings were of how things would have been had he returned in time to prevent her from leaping to her death. They would have wed and been blessed by God. They would have lived and loved in his family home, raising children, caring for his estates and his people. An idyllic dream he indulged in every dawn as daylight forced him into his protective slumber. He and Naomi, laughing, loving, growing old beside each other.

It would never happen. Never, no matter how he dreamed, how he schemed and tried to manipulate time and fate to bring them back together.

Naomi Bright was not the woman he'd loved.

And he was not the man to bring her happiness.

Seventeen

It was bad news. Terrible news. The horror of it, the magnitude of it wailed through the castle like a harsh wind on the cries of women and men alike.

What could be so awful? What could creep in and smother the life of an entire community with the spirit-crushing silence of a plague?

When would they come to tell her?

How could she stand to know?

She recognized the footsteps when they finally sounded. She knew the heavy reluctance that issued with it the last information anyone ever wanted to hear.

It was death approaching her door with those slow, steady footfalls.

She'd heard the approach before, carrying life-altering changes and grief and confusion. And pain. Horrible pain.

How much loss could her heart be expected to bear?

She stood illuminated by candlelight, pale and as wavering as those uneven flames. Her heart beat fast, racing as if by its reckless speed alone it could escape the inevitable breaking. But there was no means to flee fate as it neared her door.

Sadness and denial twined about her thoughts, tightening, choking like unwanted vines whose tendrils eventually blocked the nourishing sun. Beneath those tangled doubts she slowly strangled.

The steps continued, growing closer with their disastrous tidings. Along with the echo of boot soles, she also heard another somehow more sinister sound. It was the clank of a scabbard against each stair. Hollow, desolate and dire reverberations clattering to her soul.

And upon the wings of sorrow rose another sensation, the only one strong enough to distract from the agony of loss.

Fear.

Steady. Increasing. Unstoppable.

The price to pay for abandonment.

The wages of being a woman alone.

And a victim of circumstance.

***

"No!"

Naomi sat up, covers clutched to her laboring breast. Fever flamed in her cheeks, yet her body was drenched in icy sweat and trembling with cold.

A dream. Just a dream.

She was awake now, and dreams couldn't harm her. If she lay back down and closed her eyes, a natural slumber would eventually find her.

Just a bad dream.

And then she heard the music. Lute and lyre. Not exactly the type of music Rita had pumping through her speakers. But exactly the kind of spritely tune that provided the soundtrack for her nightmares.

"Rita!"

After a long pause, a light came on in the hallway, and her disheveled roommate stuck her head around the door.

"Is something wrong, Nomi? You could wake the dead."

"What's that music? Where's it coming from?"

"Music? It's four o'clock in the morning," Rita grumbled. "The only sounds I've heard is Mel snoring and me giggling as Tom Cruise sucks on my toes in the dream you just pulled me out of."

Naomi cocked her head, listening. No. It was music. Clear as the organ in church on revival Sunday.

"You can't hear it?"

"Maybe the neighbors," Rita offered doubtfully. Her patronizing expression said what words would not. *Crazy. Loony. Hearing the sounds of a past you don't remember. A past you couldn't have possibly lived.*

"No, the neighbors go to bed at ten. He works at the dam, and she opens a library at seven. They're not the type to spin *Camelot* show tunes and play fair lady and naughty squire."

Rita pursed her lips. "Too bad." Then her mood grew more somber, even cautious. "Do you still hear it? The music?"

Naomi smiled thinly. "No," she lied. "It must have been something from my dreams that was just running through my head when I woke up. I'm sorry I bothered you."

"No bother." Then again, the edge of worry. "Are you sure nothing's wrong?"

"What could be wrong? We open in less than a week, and the show's coming together. What could be better?"

"Thanks to our pinch hit choreographer. Where did she come from, by the way?"

Naomi wasn't sure why she didn't tell the truth, but the lie came quickly and easily. "I'd put the word out to a couple of industry people I know, and one of them came through with a miracle."

"Hallelujah, sister."

Feeling ashamed for misleading her friend, Naomi's instincts still wouldn't allow her to come out from behind the lie. Gabriel's warning was planted firmly. *Don't trust her.* "Scratch a back here, scratch a back there. That's what it's all about."

"So I hear. If you're okay, I'm going to see if I can get back to that dream and Tom."

"Sure. Go ahead. Good night, Rita. And thanks."

Naomi settled back under her covers, but she was wide awake, afraid to close her eyes while the viol was merrily playing.

Rita returned to her room where the stereo light glowed an ominous green. Mel, who had crept in and up on top of her bed, hissed and expanded like a blow fish.

"I don't need your opinion," Rita hissed back.

The cat shot off the mattress and disappeared with a flattening squeeze under the dresser she'd just bought for herself. The dresser and some very high quality sun-blocking blinds.

He hadn't been away that long, but the damp chill of the Potomac seeped into his bones like death. Strange how quickly he'd acclimated to the dry desert clime. If only emotions were as easy to adjust to as atmosphere.

"So you've found no trace of anything illegal going on?" Marchand LaValois made that summation after carefully listening to his report.

"Oh, I'm sure there's something. All the funds are through one unknown investor."

"Whom you haven't been able to trace."

"Not yet. I don't think it's Mob related but I know there's a connection in other, perhaps smaller ways."

"But, as Zanlos said, nothing that justifies our involvement. We aren't the police, after all. Crime isn't our primary focus."

Nick Flynn, Rae's husband, sat on the office sofa, ever the professional in his designer suit and imported shoes. "What about Naomi? Has she been able to tell you anything?" He leaned forward, tented fingers beneath his chin as he considered what he'd learned. Rae's husband, the lawyer and new vampire. "She was very helpful when I was trying to get the inside story on Zanlos' operation in D.C."

Gabriel couldn't stop the protectiveness from creeping into his tone. "If she knows anything, Zanlos' control over her is too strong for her to reveal it to me or to the officer Rae sent out to shadow her."

"I've gone over all the contractual papers regarding the hotel and casino. He's done all the paperwork, gotten all the proper permits. Kaz is nobody's fool when it comes to a paper trail. He taught me a thing or two when I worked for his firm. He knows how to cover his ass. Everything seems legit." Nick chewed on that for a moment, conflict over his former loyalty and betrayal at the hands of Zanlos still a sore spot. He shook it off and went on to another tangent. "Rae wanted me to ask how Rita was working out. She regrets she's unable to be here to see you, but she's kind of under the weather."

"No problem with the baby, is there?"

"Just a bug. She didn't want to take any chances. She sends her love, by the way."

Gabriel smiled. There was just enough annoyance in the way Flynn said that to warm Gabriel's heart. The lawyer apparently still thought his wife's former partner held the hint of a romantic threat. Which of course was nonsense. What he and Rae shared went beyond fragile intimacies. They had a connection of trust and friendship that perhaps the wary attorney couldn't grasp, never having worked the streets with his life in someone else's hands.

"Tell Sugar Rae I'm thinking of her. But don't tell her I'm afraid her friend Rita's been compromised."

"By Zanlos?" LaValois asked.

"I don't know. Who else could it be? I haven't sensed anyone else of our kind close to him, except one of the dancers he foolishly converted."

"That in itself is reason for further scrutiny, but unfortunately we don't have the luxury of time or the personnel to squander on an individual basis."

Squander. Gabriel didn't like the sound of that. It smacked of case closed, time to move on. And he wasn't ready to walk away. Not from Zanlos.

Not from Naomi.

But then Marchand was giving the order he didn't want to hear.

"I think we know enough to back off Zanlos. The crimes he's committed were done as a human, and from what you tell me, he's done nothing to jeopardize our kind with this new endeavor. I need you in Santa Monica, Gabriel. There's a situation there that requires your talents. You can get the details from Nicole tomorrow night. We'll put you up at the house, of course."

That was it. His business in Las Vegas was concluded. Marchand was calling him off a cold scent. He balked at the idea of not going back, of not tying up the loose ends of his past life.

"I'm not finished, Marchand."

"Oh? What's left to do?"

"There's the matter of Naomi Bright," Nick reminded. His own fondness for the administrative assistant helped him recognize the source of Gabriel's distress.

"Is she our concern?"

Gabriel tensed at Marchand's offhanded comment. Sometimes the former patriot and revolutionary was callous in his commands. He and Gabriel were both soldiers. Gabriel respected his instincts and his cause. Finding his elite group which dispensed justice within their own clan of the preternatural, Gabriel had immediately found himself a home, a place of purpose to belong. To atone for the single-minded focus of his youth and the mistakes he'd made that caused those he loved so much pain.

But with all that was at stake in running his organization, the Frenchman had learned long ago not to let the needs of the one distract from the benefit to all. He had to be immune to peripheral matters, or he couldn't contend with the scope of his duties. He left the emotional entanglements to his wife, Nicole, who still was in touch with her vulnerable human half.

"She's my concern," Gabriel clarified.

"Business or personal?"

"Personal."

"I want you back in a week, Gabriel. This other matter can't wait beyond that. Does that give you enough time to resolve your issues with this woman?"

Could he wrap up the obsession of centuries within seven days?

"Yes."

After Gabriel had gone, hurrying to beat the rising sun, Nick Flynn regarded his employer with a justified aggravation.

"He's in love with her, you know."

"She's human. And she's a thrall to Zanlos. What possible good could come of the situation? Unless that connection is broken, she'll never be free to return his affection, and he could never trust her. It's better he end it quickly and move on."

"Better for whom?"

"Oh, for us, definitely. And probably for the woman. For him, there is no way to win."

"What a cynic you've become, March. Don't you believe true love can conquer all?"

"I can't afford to."

"And with a human wife with a child on the way, I can't afford not to."

***

"What do I do? What do you think I should do?"

Gabriel had beaten the dawn back to Las Vegas but was too restless to seek slumber. Instead, he sought out his one-time confidant and purged his tale of woe.

"You're asking me?" Rollie chuckled. "I'm a scholar. I have no knowledge of affairs of the heart."

"How can I let her go?"

"Is it the loss you fear or the lack of a quest to follow?"

"What do you mean?" They were alone in the arena, walking the narrow aisle between the dinner seats and the partitioning wall above the hard-packed combat floor. The lights were off, the huge room in darkness, but they had no trouble finding their way.

"You're an adventurer, Gabriel. You seek out the danger and excitement I read about in books. It's the crusade, not the cause you champion."

"Am I that shallow?"

"No, of course not. But you are one who cannot thrive in inactivity. Decade after decade, you've searched out a war to fight in, a flag to follow. You're a warrior. A hunter. Once a hunter snares its prey, it quickly tires of the conquest."

"Are you saying that now that I've found Naomi, I no longer want her? You're wrong, Rollie. I would spend an eternity in pursuit of her."

"You don't have to. She's here."

Gabriel stared at him, not understanding, and afraid he understood all too clearly. "But I love her."

"Do you? Or are you in love with the ideal of love pumped into your heart and brain as a boy. Courtly love was never meant to be attained, only desired. It was a dream, an unobtainable goal to be coveted from afar. You say you were fated to be with her. It's not fate, Gabriel. It's not love. It's your Holy Land. Your grail. It's the last crusade, and you've no idea what to do once it is over. You can't accept a happily-ever-after ending. You never will."

"You're wrong."

"Am I? Gabe, I know you." Rolland stopped, leaning his elbows back on the top of one of the trestle tables as he observed his friend. Seeing through him so easily even while Gabriel floundered in internal darkness. "I know you better than you know yourself. You and Naomi were never right for each other.

You wanted different things. You wanted windmills to tilt at, and she wanted the security of a home. You wanted battle; she needed comfort. If you had understood her, you never would have left her alone."

Because he couldn't meet his companion's knowing gaze, he stared out into the arena, seeing there all the challenges he'd delighted in as a youth. Now silent, empty. "Don't you think I realize that now?" he asked through gritted teeth.

"No, I don't. Because there are things about her that she never told you, things you don't know to this day. You never had time to listen."

"But you did. She told these things to you." He glanced about, seeing Rollie in a different light – as a steady beacon, a welcoming port. Things that would draw Naomi near.

"I was her confidant, Gabe, while you were her ideal. We shared the same interests in knowledge and books. We'd sit in the gardens discussing philosophy while you were at the lists preparing to destroy the civilizations we admired."

"You were in love with her." He sounded amazed. Rollie shrugged.

"How could I not be? She was all that was gentle wisdom and, for that day, shrewd intellect. But those weren't virtues you would have noticed. Just as she never noticed me when you were there to dazzle her."

"I didn't know."

"Would it have mattered? You were an unstoppable force, Gabe. Everyone naturally followed where you led. I would have preferred to stay behind and court the lovely Lady Naomi and let you fools go off to war against her relatives. But what would my family have said? I had your example to live up to."

"Why have I never heard this before?"

"You would have thought me weak and cowardly back then. Perhaps you still do now. You let nothing sway you from the path of duty and honor, and you would have had no tolerance for excuses."

"What a vain and self-centered creature you must have thought me to be." He said that softly, his tone heavy with regret and apology. "How could you have been such a good friend to me when I was so oblivious to your pain?"

"Gabriel, you were like the sun. When you shone, all else was in shadow. Everyone was drawn to your light, Naomi and myself included. It wasn't your fault, so how could I blame you?"

Yet he had. And still did. Gabriel saw that accusation flicker behind the complaisant expression of the man he thought he knew.

"Go, Gabriel. Now before you hurt her," Rolland continued. "Go before you draw her into your battle and see her destroyed as you did once before. Give her a chance to live."

"Here, with Zanlos?" His tone sharpened with objection and concern.

"Has he harmed her? Is she in any danger except that which you make for her? All you can bring her is chaos and heartbreak. Give her peace in this life, Gabriel, the way you could not in her old one."

Peace. That's what he claimed to want for her, yet he continually distressed and dismayed her with remnants of a past she couldn't recall. He'd thrown her life into confusion by insisting she be who she no longer was - the ghost from a world he remembered, the debt his soul had yet to pay.

He truly didn't believe Zanlos would harm her unless threatened or backed to the wall. And that's what he was doing. His presence put her in peril. What excuse did he have to remain?

Seeing the conflict upon his friend's face, Rollie placed a hand on one slumped shoulder. "I'll watch out for her, Gabriel. I'll see that she's safe. I can make myself a part of her life and act as her friend and confidante as I did once before. Or if you prefer, I can safeguard her from afar without her ever knowing it. I leave that up to you."

With that, all his objections were brushed away. He had no reason to stay. His purpose pulled him in another direction, and his long ago pledge to his lady love would be met by this man he'd trusted with his life. And what had he done but repay him by taking that life and making it into an obscenity? He'd destroyed Rollie's future because of his single-sighted pride and would do the same to Naomi if he didn't walk away. Rollie loved her. He would see her protected and cared for. And didn't he owe his friend, his neighbor, his comrade in arms the chance to realize the happiness now out of his own reach?

With logic as his sword, he lined up the protests created by emotion and knocked them down one by one like opponents on the field until none remained standing. None except the gaping emptiness where his heart should be when he thought of an eternity without her.

"I can't, Rollie. Not yet."

And because his back was turned while he gazed in the direction where the sun would rise, displaying the pinks of a dawn he would never share with the woman he loved, he missed the workings in Rolland's expression. And so was unaware of a plan he might have derailed had his answer been different.

"So be it," came Rollie's heavy summation.

And the plan was set.

Eighteen

The temple was finished.

A chill of uneasiness nibbled at Naomi as she took it in for the first time. Magnificent. Awesome. Frightening. The stuff of pagan legend. And the crowds were going to eat it up.

The lighting crew experimented with atmosphere, creating strobes to effect a jungle storm. A sudden unexpected gust of wind stole Naomi's breath and had her shivering in earnest as the interior of the temple began to subtly glow and pulse with an eerie energy. The music beat like a sacrificial heart in tandem with that cold, phosphorescent gleam.

"Creepy, isn't it?"

After recovering from the cardiac arrest his sudden statement caused her, Naomi glanced up at Marcus and nodded.

"*Twilight Zone* creepy," she agreed.

"They plan to toss virgins down the throat of that thing?"

"I wouldn't want to be a virgin if they do." Then she blushed, realizing what she'd revealed. Usually, her lips were as tightly sealed as Zanlos' vault when it came to anything of a personal matter.

Sensing her awkwardness, Marcus directed his attention away from her burning cheeks and toward the now smoke-wreathed stage. "Is that going to be safe for the girls? With those steep sides and all this smoggy stuff, it looks like an accident waiting to happen."

"We'll make sure it doesn't. The girls' safety is our main concern. I won't have them risking a broken ankle for the sake of special effects."

The quiet authority in her tone must have answered Marcus's worries, for the behemoth relaxed beside her. "Any words from Jeannie?"

Naomi stiffened, recalling the woman's crazed behavior. "I think she's moved on."

"Her boyfriend, too. He just stopped coming in, no word or anything. You'd think good jobs fell from the heavens. And after all the trouble you went through to get him that position."

"I just hope they're all right, wherever they are."

"What do you think of Charmaine?"

His slightly gruff tone alerted Naomi's curiosity. She grinned. "Why, Marcus, are you blushing?"

He tried to glower but ended up grinning, too. "She's a mighty fine looking lady. Refined and kind of tigerish at the same time."

Naomi's brows soared. Tigerish?

"A man likes a woman who's not afraid to be a woman. No offense to your friend Rita, but a man feels like he has to wear a cup around her for his own self-defense. There's not a soft angle on her."

Naomi wanted to come to Rita's rescue, but the memory of her pushing the dancers through their routine with an angry fierceness reminiscent of warriors past got in the way. Instead, she stated, "Rita's just focused. She's been very kind to me."

"That's not hard," Marcus mumbled. "You bring out the best in folks, Miss Bright. Just a natural gift, like the way everyone trusts you right off the bat, knowing that you'll take care of them. You'll make a great mother some day."

Naomi's gaze darted away, and her throat jerked in a convulsive swallow. "I have plenty to do mothering this bunch," she muttered.

"So what's her story?"

"Whose?"

"Charmaine."

"I don't really know anything about her except her timing couldn't be better."

"She's got some sweet kids, smart and not too sassy."

Naomi's smile grew wistful. "She's lucky there."

"Think she'd go out with a hulk like me?"

Naomi quickly controlled her surprise and gave the bodyguard an accessing look. "Well, she could certainly do worse." Gentle, loyal, honest, caring. Yes, a woman could do worse. "You won't know unless you ask."

She was looking about the big empty auditorium and finally had to admit to herself that she was looking for Gabriel. She'd seen little of him since he'd saved her from the encounter with

Jeannie. And they'd shared a kiss. Memory of that exchange warmed through her only to be followed by the coldly vacant reality that he'd made no attempt to contact her since then. Made no attempt to explore the sparks their flint on steel had made with that first enjoyable union. She could blame Marcus for his overzealousness in protecting her, but Gabriel McGraw didn't seem the type to be scared away from something he wanted.

But something had spooked him, when their kiss should have progressed on to more pleasurable pursuits. She wanted to know what it was. Was it Charmaine? Was it her? Did the idea of starting something personal with a woman slightly skewed off her mental center scare him the way a bruiser with a gun couldn't? For the answer she could wait until he contacted her again. Or she could find him and ask him herself.

She could if she had the slightest idea how to get hold of him.

Would Charmaine know? She'd known to pick him up outside her house. She'd come to get a job with his blessing. Tamping down the quick blaze of jealousy with its wont to catch like a wildfire and race out of control, Naomi decided action rather than reaction was required.

"Get the girls started on dress rehearsal, Marcus. I've got a couple of things to follow up on."

"You got it, Miss Bright."

"It's Naomi. You can call me Naomi."

He seemed startled then pleased. "Naomi."

***

The hall leading back to the dressing rooms was narrow and not as well lighted as she would have liked. Naomi made a mental note to speak to the electricians. Rehearsal would start in about an hour. If Charmaine wasn't already in the dressing room, she'd leave a note to be paged when the choreographer came in. She'd worry about what to say then.

Just as she'd worry about what to say to Gabriel when confronted by the problem. Until then she'd focus on her new mantra: Action not reaction. She couldn't continue to live her life waiting for others to make the first move on her behalf.

There were no lights on in the dressing room. When Naomi

threw the switch by the door the mega-bright vanity bulbs at the makeup table blazed to momentarily blind her. A flutter of movement breezed past her, and she found herself catching at a long white veil.

At first she thought the thin gossamer was a wedding veil, but upon closer examination, she saw that it was old, very old, like the long tails of fabric that fluttered from a medieval lady's horned headdress. What it was doing in with the Jane of the Jungle attire designed for the show?

Then she heard the music.

With the crash of a troubadour's tambourine, the laughter began, softly then with increasing volume. Conversation sprang up all about her, loud and boisterous. Almost clear enough for her to make out the words. Almost. Her ears told her she stood in the center of a large, animated gathering. Her eyes argued that she was alone. Which to believe, what she heard or what she didn't see? Someone called out her name, but when she looked about, she saw only the empty room.

Not real. Not real.

Putting her hands to her ears to shut out what she knew wasn't there, couldn't be there, Naomi turned in a tight circle, seeking, praying for any explanation for what could not be explained. Except as madness.

The sound crowded in, intensifying until it thundered within her skull, beating against her brain, thudding against the backs of her eyelids. She slid to her knees with a whimper.

Make it stop.

The pain in her head grew agonizing. Blackness seeped up to steal away her awareness of the time and place and even of self. In a void of all but darkness and the insistent sounds, she drifted upon a sea of distress. Even as she struggled to stay afloat, she wondered how much easier it might be to just relax and go under.

"Naomi?"

She glanced up. For a moment, the light dazzled, then became the gleaming pale gold of Gabriel McGraw's head. Gabriel, yes, but not McGraw. He stood in an awkward hesitancy before her, clad in a hip-length linen tunic with brightly colored borders over snug-fitting breeches. A cloak hung negligently off his shoulders. And on him, the odd garment seemed strangely suited.

She sat on a stool, hand folded upon a velvet draped lap. Her hair was down, spinning in loose waves about her, forming her own cloak as it trailed nearly to the floor. She'd been nervously twining several locks of it about her fingers while waiting. Waiting for…him. For Gabriel.

"Did you think I would leave on the morrow without bidding you fare-thee-well?"

His image glistened against the torchlight. She'd been crying.

"'Tis not words of parting I wish to hear. I have spent my years sending men off to war. Too many have not returned to hear my welcome home. 'Tis not an occasion to celebrate."

"You mourn me before I've gone."

He said it lightly, making sport of her concern. His smile, usually so charming, mocked the heaviness in her heart. Yet when she tucked her head so he couldn't view her pain, his fingertips skimmed beneath her chin, lifting her teary gaze to meet his. The laughter was gone.

"I will return to you. Then we shall have reason to celebrate, my love."

My love…

A hand touched her arm. She screamed, not because the contact frightened but because she wasn't sure the source of that contact was real.

"Miss Bright? Naomi?"

She opened her eyes, looking up through a glaze of tears into the alarmed face of Charmaine Johnson.

"Do you hear it?" she whispered.

"Hear what?"

Naomi paused then laughed weakly. "It doesn't matter. It's gone now."

"Lordy, girl, you're pale as a ghost. Sit yourself down, and I'll go fetch somebody."

Naomi gripped her forearm and uttered a forceful, "No." She couldn't let news of her instability spread. It couldn't get back to Zanlos. "I'll be all right. Just a little dizzy spell."

"That was some sort of spell all right, but lightheadedness it wasn't. You were talking to folks who weren't there. And from what you were saying, they haven't been there for a lot of years."

"W-what do you mean?"

Charmaine lifted her to her feet and guided her back onto one of the vanity table stools. She kept Naomi's cold hands clutched in her own. "Honey, something's put a terrible fright into you. Maybe if you tell me what it is, I can help. I know all about being scared and alone, and it's an ugly place to be, believe me. You're not alone, baby. You can trust me. We have a mutual friend."

And at that moment, what Naomi needed more than anything was someone to believe her. And to believe in her.

"I think I'm losing my mind."

"Oh, I doubt that. From all that I've heard tell of you, you're the sanest one of all of us. The girls call you the Rock. Did you know that?"

She shook her head, provoking the dampness gathered on her lashes to track down her chalk-white face in gleaming rivulets. "No, I didn't." The knowledge warmed through her like a smooth shot of bourbon. The tears kept coming. She tried to wipe them away with the back of one trembling hand, but they only came faster. "They don't know me very well, do they?"

"I think they know you better than you think. They know you well enough to depend on you."

"I would never let them down," she sniffled.

"I know that, honey."

"But I am, Charmaine. Look at me, hiding from things that aren't there. Seeing things that haven't existed since the Thirteenth Century. And recognizing them, Charmaine. I recognize them. I know the names of the songs. I know I've worn the clothing. I swear most of the voices are familiar to me. How is that possible?"

"Maybe they are familiar to you, sugar. Maybe these are places you've been and people you've seen."

"What? What are you saying?"

"I'm saying what do you know about past lives?"

"You mean like from the late show? Or from the Nut House where people claim to have been Napoleon?"

"No, baby. Like Shirley McLaine and we have lived before. It sounds like one of the lives you've lived before doesn't want to let go."

"The things I dream are terrible things," Naomi confessed. "There's such pain and loss and confusion."

"These are things you experienced as another person in another lifetime." She made it sound so reasonable, so commonplace. So acceptable.

"Charmaine, I think I—she—whoever—killed herself."

Charmaine sat back on her heels and nodded. "Well, that would explain it. Violent events, especially that bring death, leave a soul restless."

"Where did you hear that?"

Charmaine smiled, but her expression was secretive and wreathed in caution. "The late show."

Naomi returned the smile shakily. "How do I find out more? And how do I get it to stop?"

"Find out what it wants and finish whatever it's left unresolved."

"How do I do that?" She couldn't believe she was actually believing this.

"I'll check around for you, honey. I know some folks who dabble in the spirit world, not those phonies who take the tourists for money, but folks with a real gift." Charmaine stopped abruptly and turned toward the door. There, Rita stood just within a cloak of shadows. Listening.

How long had she been there?

"Don't let me interrupt your little girl talk."

Charmaine stood and regarded the icy-demeanored Rita with an easy smile. "We were just talking about superstitions and silly stuff like that. Miss Bright got a little scare coming back here by herself after getting spooked by that temple. Have you seen it now that it's finished?"

"It's magnificent," Rita proclaimed. "You can almost hear the drums and the shrieks of the human sacrifices."

"Sacrifices?"

That squeak came from Grace, who'd just stepped in, followed by Molly and Candice. Rita turned to them with a razor-sharp smile.

"Oh yes. Didn't you hear the story, since we're into storytelling this evening. That temple isn't something built by Nevada architects to look like the real thing. It is the real thing, moved stone by stone up from Peru. Legend has it that the people there worshiped some god called the Fanged Deity. They'd appease it with gold, but occasionally it would call for a sacrifice of blood. Preferably a virgin."

A nervous giggle, then Candice said, "That let's us off the hook, girls."

"That's what our routine will lead up to. Who wants to be the first victim?" Rita pinned Grace with a penetrating stare. "How about you, Grace?"

While the girl paled and retreated a few involuntary steps, Charmaine scowled at the instigator of her fear. It was Naomi who spoke up to quiet the agitated mood.

"None of that's been worked out yet. From what Kitty Parsons left in her notes, it's going to be a revolving honor. But no one has to do it if it makes them uncomfortable." And she smiled reassuringly at the anxious dancer.

"That's right," Rita purred. "Heaven forbid that we try something challenging when we can stay safe and unnoticed. Isn't that right, Naomi?"

Naomi fought not to wince at the cruel barb. Her voice relayed a confidence she didn't feel. "Not always. Sometimes the risk makes it worth the while."

Rita's smile twisted thinly. How had she ever thought this woman was her friend? "Spoken with experience. Dress rehearsal in a half hour. I've got a call to make. Ladies, get busy."

After she'd gone, Candice grumbled, "She's getting almost as bad as the Kitty Bitch. And I thought she was one of us."

Nods and mumbles of agreement from the other girls couldn't take the sting of truth from Rita's words. Safe and unnoticed. Yes, that was Naomi's motto, all right.

But that could change.

"Charmaine, we need to talk some more after rehearsal."

"You got it, honey."

But as the rehearsal got started without Rita, who never returned to the stage, Charmaine took control of the routine, turning it into a sultry seduction of the stone idol standing watch at the foot of the tomb. From the way Marcus's stare followed the willowy dancer, Naomi had to restrain her smile and a pang of regret. Something told her their stoic bouncer was going to find the courage to approach the lovely choreographer before the night was over.

Seeking her past could wait a bit longer while Charmaine and Marcus explored a potential future.

Charmaine's daughters arrived toward the end of rehearsal. Marcus lifted the little one high so she could see her mother perform from a more unrestricted view. When Charmaine saw them, her concentration faltered for just an instant, and in her expression Naomi saw the envied purity of a mother's love. Something she would never experience with the damaged womb she held inside herself.

What man would desire a woman who could bear him no fruit of their union? A child gave a man his immortality, and that gift was one she couldn't offer. She was as barren as she was bewildered by its cause. The doctor she'd seen for her mood swings and depression had confirmed it, though he had no answer either. He'd suggested gently that it appeared to be damage done by a violent sexual assault.

Was that the secret her memory was trying to hide? Had a vicious rape stolen her fertility as well as her past?

Was that what delving into her psyche would awaken, memories so cruel and brutal that her mind had blocked them from surfacing? If that was all that was there, would she be wiser to leave that door locked and the pain safely inside?

The girls rushed to their mother after she'd climbed down from the stage. Charmaine was moving slowly, limping as if suffering from some terrible physical pain. But her smile bloomed big enough to shadow the hurt, whatever its cause, and her shy yet speculative welcome of Marcus's advance submerged it further.

Could emotions like blossoming attraction and possibly even love overcome the anguish her scarred memories concealed? Confront your pain then move on. Find your center. Find your strength. Rita had given her those truths. If they were to be believed, her only hope lay with Gabriel McGraw.

But what could she give him in return for unlocking her past?

As she watched Charmaine and Marcus together, an idea began to form.

***

"So, our new friend thinks to interfere, does she? We can't let that happen."

In the private room overlooking the stage a single figure stood staring down at the dancers as they warmed up. In the dark body of the room, a limp and dazed Rita lounged in one of the chairs. Her expression was euphoric even as blood dribbled down her throat to slowly slide down the curve of her bosom. She didn't answer. She wasn't able to. In his agitation over the news, her lover had been a tad too greedy, and now she lay chilled and nearly drained.

"Meddlers," he continued, growing worked up again and beginning to pace. "Why must we be beset by meddlers?" He whirled toward Rita. "The past must stay hidden, at least until that knowledge serves our purpose."

Shivering now, Rita's sluggish brain processed the painfully obvious. "Our" was an empirical term, and it didn't include her. She was a pawn, a tool—and she'd betrayed those who'd trusted her. The reward he'd offered her, that of unlimited power and a freedom from pain and loneliness, seemed hollow. What good was an eternity when it was shared by regret and dishonor?

She would tell Naomi. She would warn her of the plot against her and Gabriel.

After several uncoordinated attempts, she managed to get her feet aligned and tried to order her legs to support her. It didn't matter, though, for the moment she began to stand, his hand pressed down on her shoulder. Hard.

"Stay, my dear. I insist. You need your rest. Don't complicate your mind with thoughts of morality. It doesn't apply in our case. We are beyond the needs and desires of these puny mortals, as you will understand soon. I will see to our little meddler, don't you fear. Until then, think of nothing."

His warmed fingertips touched to her eyelids, drawing them down like shades over her soul. To darkness.

Nineteen

Stars spread across the dark map of the heavens like precious dreams. To Naomi, they glittered with promise but remained tauntingly out of reach. Like her dreams of family and love and belonging.

She sat out in her little oasis garden with the constellations for company. She had left the slider open to the house so strains of Mozart could trickle out. Something brushed beneath the calf of her leg but before she could react, the wind was nearly driven from her as Mel jumped up into her lap. The big cat plopped like a sack of cement and commenced a rattling purr. Hesitantly, expecting the unfriendly creature to run away, Naomi stroked the plush coat. The rumbling of pleasure intensified, until it felt like she had a belt sander across her knees.

"What's the matter, big guy? You lonesome, too?" Abandonment made for strange bedfellows, she thought as she rumpled the thick fur. There was always food in the animal's bowl, but Rita was ever absent, forcing the arrogant feline to seek out second best for attention. Naomi was a little more choosy, preferring to hold out for her first choice.

Apparently, Mel agreed, for suddenly his throaty purrs turned into a menacing growl. He leapt from her lap and waddled into the house, leaving her to brush at the trail of residual hair left on her lap.

"Beautiful evening."

She gasped and jumped to her feet.

"I'm sorry. I didn't mean to startle you." Gabriel separated from shadow. Suddenly, the stars were no longer the brightest thing upon her private heaven. "Charmaine said you wanted to talk to me."

Feeling foolish with her heart racing and her dress decorated with pet fur, Naomi stalled to give her brain time to catch up. She'd spent extra time on her appearance, wanting for once to hold a man's attention. The dress was new. She'd spent more time looking for it than she had when buying her car. Its plum color and gentle folds of clingy knit flattered her pale skin and willowy form. She'd even purchased a pallet of soft pastels to accentuate her eyes, cheeks and lips. She wore her hair down and swinging about her shoulders. The only thing she hadn't changed was her perfume. The delicate yet tenacious scent of violets never failed to please her. Had the time and effort been worth it? Gabriel's lingering stare said yes. A tingle of awareness brushed across her skin.

"Charmaine is a godsend. Have you known her long?" Instead of casual small talk, the question smacked of accusation, but Gabriel didn't seem to mind.

"We met shortly after I came to Las Vegas. She's an admirable woman forced into a tragic situation. I helped get her back on her feet."

"Why, with her talent, I'd think she could find work anywhere." Secretly, she didn't want to think of Gabriel extending a special helping hand.

"Perhaps before an auto accident left her nearly crippled."

Of course. The limp, the pinch of pain that always pulled about her features. Her pettiness dissolved into a guilty concern. "Should she be working so hard?"

"No, but she has something to prove to herself and her children. I've given her what I can to get her through the worst of it."

"And what would that be?" Her tone thinned. She was thinking of Marcus's insinuations about narcotics. Trust me, Gabriel had once said. Why did she find that so difficult a proposition?

"Encouragement. She needed someone to believe that she could do it."

"Oh." Could he see she was blushing in the half-light escaping from her living room? "And she's passed some of that on to me. She's offered to help me get the better of some problems that have been holding me back, too."

"Anything I can help with?"

"No. Not just yet anyway." A lie. Why else had she asked him here other than to experiment with the power of love? Was it love? Or would infatuation be a better term for what stirred inside her whenever he was near? Could one love a stranger?

Her head said no. Her heart had made up its own mind the first time she'd seen him. And just when was that, she wondered? Certainly not that night on the Strip when she'd thought he was an angel.

He'd never felt like a stranger and, from what she'd been told, they shared a segment of her missing past. A good piece? She wondered. Or were the memories concerning him the tip of another nightmare? She didn't think so. She felt uncertain around him but not afraid, never in danger.

He was watching her closely, as if he could read the complexity of thoughts tumbling through her head and heart. He remained silent and still, giving her time to sort them out. Finally she plunged right in over her head and hoped he wouldn't let her sink.

"Are the memories we share good ones?"

He nodded. "For the most part, I'd say yes. But I let you down, Naomi. I disappointed you when you were depending on me. I let my responsibilities get in the way of your happiness. That won't happen again."

"A promise?"

"A pledge."

Okay, so far so good. She began to pace, plucking an exotic night bloom from one of her bushes and twirling it between her fingers. The petals fluttered like the fragile state of her emotions.

"Tell me about my life in D.C. Was I happy there?"

"You were busy."

"Did I like my job?"

"You were afraid, Naomi. You helped Zanlos' partner Nick Flynn get information to expose an illegal extortion ring he was involved in."

"I did?" She stopped, stunned. She couldn't imagine herself embroiled in intrigue. Where had she found the courage? Then she continued walking, her step quickening apace with her thoughts. "If I betrayed Mr. Zanlos, why did he bring me with him to Las Vegas?"

"As insurance. For when I came after him."

She wanted to deny it, but it felt right and reasonable. And so very Kaz Zanlos. It hurt to think that her boss, whom she revered, had used her as a shield to hide behind. It hurt, but that didn't make it any less true. She'd always assumed that theirs was a relationship of professional respect and mutual need. He needed her quiet, behind-the-scenes capability and she needed the security she always felt when in his service. If he'd held her in such regard, why had he let her go on existing in an emotional limbo? Why had he hinted at her mental weaknesses as the cause for her memory lapse? To make her feel more dependant and afraid of the world beyond his employment? To keep her fragile and uncertain and unable to make choices on her own?

What kind of man manipulated those in his care to such a cruel degree?

He let her think he'd brought her with him to protect her, when all the time he was protecting his own interests at her expense.

Waiting for the threat Gabriel represented to surface.

"And here you are," she stated quietly. "For him or for me?"

"Both."

She'd wanted him to claim it was for her. Selfishly, she wanted to believe she was the only reason, the motivating force behind his cross-country quest. But knowing Gabriel as she did from their limited new acquaintance to the deep abiding truths held in her heart, she knew that duty was much of the man he was. Duty tempered by but never ruled by desires.

"And which would you sacrifice for the other, Gabriel?"

Her softly asked question brought a sudden fleeting change to his expression. Guilt. But his words denied the conclusion she drew. "I already answered that. I won't put my job before your safety." Now, he paced the small garden area, building up to something she was sure she wasn't going to like.

She didn't.

"I've been asked to go to California."

Leave? He couldn't leave. Panic rattled through her like window glass after a sonic boom. "By whom?"

"My boss."

"I thought you were a policeman."

"I am. Of sorts. What I do is very specialized."

"And dangerous."

"Yes."

"And you'll go alone?"

"Yes." A pause. Here was where he should end it. It was the right and honorable thing to do. What he always did when he came to this kind of difficult crossroad. One road read "work" the other "want." Rolland's early words nagged at him, warning him of the futility of those wants, but looking at her bathed in moonlight, he couldn't find the necessary character to walk away. Even if it might be best for her. "Unless you would go with me."

The suggestion startled her into a long silence. "With you? As what?"

"Whatever you want to be." He took a step toward her, then, thinking better of it, retreated two. "I have searched for you, Naomi. Now that I've found you, I don't know that I can let you go. I don't know that I have the will to go on without the reward of you to encourage me."

The simplicity of his statement nearly knocked the knees out from under her. They went weak in a sudden quake of humility.

"I've never been anyone's reward before." Her tone tightened with the sharp edge of despair. "What if it's a reward of less value than you anticipate?"

"Naomi, you could never disappoint me."

"I can't have children." There. Though gracelessly blurted out, she'd said it. Now he knew. She waited in agony for disdain and rejection to surface, for him to realize she was damaged goods.

But miraculously, the only thing shining in his gaze was tenderness. Questions, yes, but not disgust. Not dismay. Not rejection. His fingertips touched to her face, drawing a gentle line through the tracks of dampness tracing the curve of her cheek.

"A sad circumstance that we both share, for I can't father children either. It would have to be just the two of us."

She placed her hand over his. His was surprisingly cool in the balmy evening, almost as if he'd been holding an icy beverage.

"Two who have been so alone becoming one. How could that be a disappointment?" She turned her head slightly to press her lips to his palm. He went so still she could swear he stopped breathing. At that moment, he looked almost as afraid as she felt. "I'm not very good at this," she said at last.

"At what?" His voice rasped softly.

"At this seduction thing. I've never been good at games. I prefer things to be direct."

"Then be direct."

"I want you to kiss me again, Gabriel."

He complied without a moment's hesitation. It's what he'd been waiting for for centuries, for her to ask him to cross the barriers of polite restraint. Though modern women required no such delicacy, he considered in his heart and soul Naomi to be the shining epitome of courtly love. And that involved an entirely different set of rules.

He'd courted. He'd waited. He'd shown infinite patience.

And now she'd asked him to toss all that aside to let passion reign.

Who was he to argue?

He found her mouth softly parted. There was no rush. He took his time reacquainting them both with the sensations they'd discovered earlier. Sweet. They were so sweet. He used his hand to tilt her head this way and that. She was pliant and wonderfully receptive to his touch, responding with a shy eagerness that made restraint a saintly virtue. He wasn't that saintly or virtuous when her tongue slipped in to tempt his. He was hungry, starving, for this taste of her. Hungry for the reality of dreams that had sustained him through decades of loneliness. Hungry for the completion of a promise, that she would be his, not in the way of the savage creature he'd become, but in the gentile fashion of the man he'd once been when he was deserving of her love.

He knew he couldn't be that man again but, lost in this tender exchange, he felt as though he was, as if it were truly possible. So, with dark urges carefully suppressed, he became that man for the moment, to lavish Naomi with what might have been, with what he'd wanted to be for her.

Then his free hand skimmed up the dip of her slender waist

to weigh her small breast with the side of his thumb. Her compliance ended. She went stiff and still. When she stepped back from him, death couldn't have been more cruel an ending to what he'd envisioned for so long. But even though it might nearly kill him, he would respect her wishes.

"Can we continue this inside?"

Her tiny question shattered his tension into sharp shards of expectation.

"If that's what you want." His tone growled with anticipation.

She took his hand and led him, as if he'd need to be guided, into her small, neat little home, through the lighted living room to the promising mystery of her darkened bedroom.

In that shadowed bower where long held fantasies would finally know fruition, Gabriel hesitated. The man who'd show the ways of love to Naomi Bright should be a man. Not a creature of perpetual night. Was it fair to let her believe he was something he was not? So many had used her, lied to her. This was a time for honesty. Or was he afraid that without this extra tie of intimacy between them, that he wouldn't be able to keep her once she discovered what he truly was? The truth needed to be shared before anything else passed between them.

"Naomi," he began in a voice rough with regret and reluctance.

"You don't need to say anything," she insisted. She started unbuttoning his shirt, focusing there because she was unable to meet the intensity of his gaze. Afraid she would see a truth there she didn't want to recognize. Not at this moment.

"I have to. There are things you should know."

He put his hands over hers to still them, but she shook off his staying touch. "I don't want to know them now, Gabriel."

"Yes, you do. Or I can't continue this in good conscience."

"Damn your conscience. Do you think I need to know that you're using me to get to my boss? Do you think I have to hear that there's something special between you and Charmaine? I can see that with my own eyes. Do you think this room is a confessional where you have to bare your sins? I don't want to know about your sins, Gabriel. What you've done isn't as important as what we're about to do. So don't keep me waiting."

She was nearly in tears. And she was right. They'd both waited long enough.

He tilted her chin up so he could take her mouth in a long, languid kiss. When he leaned back, her eyes were still closed, and her breathing hurried along in excited little puffs. That rapid movement of her chest created a delightful friction between the soft fabric of her dress and the tightening pucker of her nipples. They stood out in bold relief against the clingy knit.

"That was some speech," he murmured, lips brushing over the curve of her cheekbone.

"You liked it?"

"You really think I'm a cad, out to bed you and betray you?"

"I think you're the sexiest man I've ever seen, and I've wanted us to be naked together since the first time I laid eyes on you. How's that for a speech?"

"Works for me."

"Then why are we still dressed and talking?"

Her speech was a bluff. Hopefully, he'd have her clothes off before he realized it. Oh, she wanted him. That wasn't the problem. The problem was the niggling fear that once they reached a certain point in their passionate exchange, she'd freeze up and deny them both the pleasure of completion. She didn't tell him her suspicions about past abuse. She wanted him to erase those doubts, those fears, to soothe them away with his touch and his kisses.

She couldn't have that if she let him know she was shaking right down to her recently painted toenails.

In the darkness, his bare chest gleamed like polished marble. Pale. She hadn't expected his skin to be so fair, but given the midnight hours he inhabited, she shouldn't have been surprised. Cool, so cool to the touch, like that unyielding stone. Nothing else about him was cold or resistant.

He combed his fingers back from temple to nape, his hands fisting gently to tilt her face up to his.

"I like your hair down like this. Free. Like silk."

The rough purr of his voice chafed a quivering deep down inside her where her body had a vague recall of pain rather than pleasure. On this night, he would give her something else to remember.

"And I like this dress. Did you wear it just for me?"

Before she could nod, he'd found the floating hem to gather the soft fabric as his hands traveled upward until the garment slipped over her head. Beneath it, she wore a pink slip and matching wisp of panties. She'd never felt so naked in her life, but as he gazed at her, never had she felt so adored.

She gasped as his mouth touched to the lacy bodice. Her aureola puckered as the fabric dampened beneath the insistent tug of his lips. Sensation pooled and became a tight, tremulous ache there at the tip of her small breast and more embarrassingly against the cotton crotch of her panties. She arched into the heel of his hand as it cupped her suddenly hot and eager sex. He let her movements encourage his until her hips pushed and ground against his palm. Her wet heat told him she was ready, at least to go one step further.

One step at a time, he told himself with a rigid self-control.

He leaned back long enough to skim the slip and the scrap of now hot silk from her body. And though he wished to look his fill, the way her arms crossed protectively over her bosom and her hands sought to shield the nested curls between her thighs, he knew this was an awkward moment for her. He couldn't bear to think she was ashamed of anything they might do together.

"You are so lovely, you take my breath away. You are a goddess, Naomi. Let me worship you."

He'd chosen the right words.

With just a slight hesitation, her guarded gestures relaxed, and her beauty was revealed to him fully as her arms lifted to ride the hard swell of his shoulders. Her gaze offered him everything he desired.

His arm curved beneath her rounded bottom, lifting her up off her feet so he could carry her to the bed. He laid her down upon the coverlet, where she glowed like precious pearls within a satin jewel box.

His hands shook as he stripped off his clothing.

As he came down toward her, one knee on the mattress, his

palms on either side of her head, her gaze slipped from his, and her shift in focus brought a furrow to her brow. His skin jumped where her fingertips rested upon his rib cage. Her touch was light, curious.

"You have no wound, not even a scar from where Marcus shot you."

"It was just a scratch. I'm a fast healer."

"I wish my scars would disappear as easily."

He took her tiny hand, bringing it up so he could press a kiss upon its palm.

"That's why I'm here," he told her just before his mouth came down to capture hers for a tender, thorough plundering. Her tension defused into a series of liquid tremors.

He sought her breasts, making her moan and twist from the way his lips tugged and tasted. Threads of fire burned from those achy pinnacles, streaking through her system to form a lake of molten longing at the juncture of her thighs. His kisses trailed down along the sweeping line of her torso to the jut of one hip. Her breath came in expectant shivers as his tongue traced over that rise to delve into the sacred hollow and soft mound below. She gasped as he shared a kiss so intimate her body wept with joy.

And then he was lifting up, challenging her tenderly with his burning stare. Did she want to continue? Was she ready to go on?

She reached up, burying her fingers in his mane of blond hair, clutching so she could drag him down to discover the answer within her wanton, open-mouthed kiss.

She tried not to stiffen as he moved above her, as the velvety tip of his engorged phallus trailed across her thigh and belly in its search of its reward. She was his reward. She would remember that now when older, darker memories threatened to crowd the pleasure of this moment aside. His reward.

He claimed it with a sudden strong push, spreading pressure not pain up to the very valley of her scarred womb. And there he remained, huge, unmoving, letting her adjust to his size and shape. Letting her brief alarm lessen to an awareness of how beautifully they pulsed together, like a single, reverent heartbeat.

A pulse that increased to a heavy, impatient throbbing.

Her acceptance sighed into his mouth then was followed by the encouraging lift of her hips asking, more please.

She welcomed his first acquainting thrust with a soft cry of wonder, opening to him, body and soul. What was damaged knew a miraculous healing in spirit as he woke her body to the joy nature had intended between a man and a woman. He found in her no passive lover waiting for him to supply her with a release. She pursued each sensation with unabashed urgency, chasing the pleasure he'd promised with an undulating rhythm, until it ran through her in strong, hot pulsations. Her fingertips bit into his shoulders. The bottoms of her feet pushed up and down his legs. Her lips parted with a breathless desire he was helpless to ignore. He fed from her soft, willing mouth as his own passions heated from aggressive rumble to raging howl.

And when she gripped him with the first of her body's completing tremors, the sensation of hot silk rippling about him urged him to take his own explosive release, emptying into her in scalding wave after wave that which would never take seed except in the needy, fertile ground of her heart and soul.

As she lay beneath him and he within her, one thought pulsed in time to the exhausted exhilaration he'd felt before only at the end of a glorious battle.

Finally. Finally. Finally.

She was his. They were one.

***

He could scent the dawn. The danger of it edged out the heavy luxury of emotion weighting down his strength and ambition to ever move from the warm curl of Naomi's arms and legs.

Just another minute.

And then she muttered softly and rolled away from him to burrow into her pillow, freeing him to leave.

But he didn't want to go. This would be the hell of it if they were going to have a life together.

He came up on his elbow and gently brushed the hair back from her face. As he bent close to press a kiss upon her brow, his attention caught on something that made his tender mood plummet.

Zanlos' mark scarred the smooth line of her throat.

The bite was old, but the significance hadn't lessened. She belonged to Zanlos. She was his to call at any instant. She would do whatever he asked, even if it meant betrayal. Gabriel could take her away, but no matter how far they went, how long they waited, there was no escape from the shackles binding her will to another.

Unless Zanlos was dead. Or Naomi was.

No dreams, no hopes, no exchanged vows could change that. She bore the brand of another. She could never be his. How had he conveniently forgotten that bit of knowledge?

Zanlos would have to die. But in killing him to free Naomi, he would be dooming himself to a life as a fugitive for breaking the laws he protected. He knew Marchand LaValois. He would hunt down a rogue with more determination because he would see it as a betrayal of his trust and of the integrity of his organization. There would be no escape. If Naomi ran with him, she would live every moment in danger because his pursuers would get at him through her. That was the way it was done. How could he take her from one nightmare to another?

There was no way out. No way for them to have their happily-ever-after.

The charm of the moment gone, Gabriel slipped from the bed and from the dream Naomi represented. He stood for a long moment, simply absorbing the sight of her so blissfully oblivious upon the bed they'd shared. He should never have touched her, but he could not regret that he'd done so. He would have their night together as another token to wear, this time within his heart. He could make her forget. Perhaps that would be easier for her, but part of him wanted her to have those memories after so many had been stripped unfairly from her. He wanted her to remember him even if for a short time those memories brought her an unhappy pain after he was gone.

So tangled up in the confusion of his thoughts, he left the little bungalow through the back, his caution at an ebb.

Until the round circle of a .38 touched behind his ear.

Twenty

In one fluid shift of substance, Gabriel reversed himself so he was facing his assailant. Marcus Sinclair stood, gun in hand, so startled by the preternatural movement, he made no attempt to stop Gabriel from taking the pistol from his hand. He didn't seem as alarmed by the barrel pressed to his temple as he was by what he'd just witnessed.

"What the hell are you?"

Gabriel chose to ignore the question by asking one of his own. "What are you doing here? Isn't this a little after hours and above and beyond the call?"

"I shot you," Marcus continued in a daze. "Where's the bullet wound?"

"I mend fast. And you'd better be a fast talker if you want to get out of this alive. What are you doing here?"

"Following you."

"Why?"

"I'm not off duty. I'm a Las Vegas detective."

"And I'm the Pope."

"I've been working the Zanlos case ever since our D.C. office contacted me. I though it was drugs at first, but it's not. I thought you were involved at first, but you're not. At least not with Zanlos. So, what's your story?"

"I believe the man with the gun doesn't have to answer the questions."

Gabriel winced as the big bore of a .44 poked his ribs.

"How about now?" Marcus asked.

"Still not a standoff." With a feint to the side, Gabriel was no longer in the line of fire. And the .44 was just as quickly in his possession.

"Son of a—"

Marcus stared, flabbergasted, as Gabriel reversed both guns and handed them back butts first.

"Just so you know I don't have to be cooperative here."

"I believe you, brother, even though I don't believe for a minute what I just saw. Who and what the hell are you?"

"I'm a D.C. cop. Or I was. I came out here after Zanlos. And Naomi."

"Why didn't they tell me you were coming? Professional courtesy and all."

"Because I didn't tell them. I'm not a cop right now. I'm policing for a different kind of enforcement organization. And we want to know what Zanlos is up to, too."

"Zanlos isn't the big fish here. He's just the front man. The one we need to go after is the money man, an Alex Cross."

"And just who is Alex Cross?"

"Nobody knows. He's a shadow, a question mark. No past. No present. Just a crap load of gold and a real fetish for privacy. Hey, where do you think you're going? We're not done here."

But the sun was rimming the far mountains, and Gabriel's skin was beginning to feel a size too small.

"We're done for now." He nodded toward the side yard. "There's my ride."

Marcus glanced that way, and when he looked back Gabriel was gone. He stood, a gun in each hand, staring at vacant space.

"Sonuvabitch."

***

Step, clunk. Step, clunk. Step, clunk.

Closer and closer.

She drew herself up into a small, tight knot in the bottom of the cupboard, beneath the heavy pile of furs and velvets.

"No matter what happens. No matter what you hear, do not make a sound. Promise me."

The urgent tension in her mother's voice prompted her own whispered reply.

"I won't. My word on it."

Darkness. Hot, dank and nearly airless. Each breath tasted stale, like the musty odor of her father's hunting hounds after a run in the rain. Despite the smothering heat, she trembled ceaselessly. Until the crash of the chamber door flying open. Then she was cold, cold and silent as death.

"Where is your daughter, Lady Magdeleen?"

"She has flown far to where you will never find her. Think that I would allow the likes of you to have her? Not while I yet breathe."

How strong and unafraid her mother sounded, until the thud of his fist reduced her to a soft moaning.

She huddled beneath the cloaks, biting back her own cry of protest until her lips bled. Pressing her fists to her ears, she refused to hear any more. If she did, she could not complete her promise. If caught, she could not slip away and ride for assistance from their neighbors. They would believe the truth from no other but the daughter of a slain servant to the king. Only she could see this treachery repaid.

But she had to be strong for her mother's sake. And she had to remain still. And she had to endure the awful grunting sounds of the beast taking his pleasure upon her mother's form. The beast who had once been her uncle and supposed protector, until greed exposed his true intentions—to take what would not be offered or easily surrendered. By force, if necessary.

Then the silence. The silence was the worst and the longest she could ever remember as she hid in the dark, her mind conjuring pictures her eyes could not see.

Until finally she felt it safe to ease open the door...

Naomi sat up with a gasp. Daylight flooded her bedroom. Still she shivered in the thrall of terror, yet blinded by the shadows in that blackened room, hearing the tiny rasps of her breathing and feeling the tears of anger and helplessness on her face.

So real. As if she'd experienced these things herself.

Perhaps in another life.

Charmine. She would see Charmine and ask her help in discovering the mystery of this ancient past.

But first the mystery of her missing clothes. She was naked beneath the sheet she clutched to her chin.

Then remembrance returned along with a wild exultation.

She and Gabriel had made love. And it had been...fabulous.

She sank back down into her pillows where the scent of him remained. She breathed it in and reveled in the achy overuse of her body. He'd made her feel loved, like a whole woman, not an imperfect fragment with nothing to offer.

His reward.

Just as quickly her mood dissolved into chaotic panic. He was leaving. How could she let him go? How could she return to her impersonal routine, where joy and anticipation never touched her? Where nothing touched her.

Gabriel gave her the courage to go forward instead of fretting about what she'd left behind.

He'd asked her to go with him.

Could she? Could she leave her job and the security it provided? Could she take a chance and trust in the feelings that glittered like sunshine all through her?

Would Zanlos let her go?

A sudden dip in the mattress forced her from her reverie. Mel sat on the foot of the bed regarding her through eyes aglow with annoyance. Her daydreams could wait until he was fed, that unblinking look told her.

"Oh don't be such a killjoy," she grumbled then patted the sheet beside her. The huge hairball considered the offer for a long haughty moment, then waddled up to drop beside her, allowing her the privilege of adoring him.

And as Naomi stroked the arrogant creature, the frightening clarity of the dream ebbed before the splendid reality of her and Gabriel together.

She had her answer. Love could overcome fear.

She was ready to face the truth.

                    ***

From the start of the corridor the sound of the drums created an irresistible lure. Echoing the beat of a loud, lusty heart, the increasing tempo hinted at excitement and thrills to come.

Naomi and Marcus watched the guests for the special preview streaming in. The wealthy and influential of Las Vegas. Some Naomi recognized from the closed door meets upstairs. Most Marcus recognized from their mug shots. The press was conspicuously absent. Under Marcus' direction, security was tighter, he boasted, than a twelve-year-old girl. Figuratively speaking, he added in anticipation of Naomi's blushes.

But she wasn't blushing. She was flushed with expectation. This was what she'd worked for and, tonight, she'd know its success or failure. The set was frightening, the girls were luscious. What could go wrong?

"I'm going to take my seat, Marcus," she said a bit nervously once the steady parade of invitees slowed down to a trickle of late comers.

Marcus showed her crossed fingers.

The interior of the theater was dark and misty. Only the front rows of tables were filled. She waved off the help of an usher dressed in a scanty jungle loincloth and gleaming oil and took a side aisle toward the middle of the auditorium. The touch of a hand to her elbow caused her to flinch. Then she heard a familiar voice.

"Mind if I watch the show with you?"

She smiled shyly up at Gabriel. "Of course not. We couldn't have done it without you, after all."

"No, Naomi. You're the drive and the power behind this event. Any laurels should be on your head."

Ordinarily her cynical side would have added, *"Uneasy is the head that wears the crown."* But this wasn't an ordinary night. Nothing could dampen her spirits.

She smiled, but inside she glowed with pleasure. "It was more like a family effort." Yes. That notion warmed her. Family. That's what it felt like between her, the girls, Gabriel, Marcus and even the quarrelsome Rita. Each had contributed in his or her own way, even the unlikable Kitty Parsons. And tonight was the payoff.

It was like sitting down to watch her children perform. Pride bubbled up like the champagne being served up on silver trays to their appreciative guests. They took their seats, and when Gabriel's hand slipped over hers, she hung on gratefully.

Not even in dress rehearsal had she seen all the elements of the show put together. She was as anxious as the other audience members by the time the first dance number began. The girls looked sexy and strong yet spicy, too. Perfect. Grace's kicks would have done a Rockette proud. The percussion band brought up from Brazil for background beat created its own smoky fire around Marty's sinuous solo. The *a cappella* singer's bell-like tones hung in the air like an exotic bird in flight, soaring, hovering, diving, fluttering to capture the imagination and soul of another civilization.

Naomi lost herself in the colorful spectacle, forgetting her own woes and worries as she was absorbed in the tableau of choosing a comely sacrifice. As the dancers quivered on the steps of the temple, one strode forward from among them to face her dramatic fate. Naomi recognized Charmaine with some surprise. She hadn't known their choreographer was going to be part of the show. She glanced at Gabriel, but his attention was on Charmaine, his furrowed brow displaying an equal degree of confusion.

But Charmaine mesmerized. She climbed the stairs with such regal grace and steady purpose one would believe her to be an ancient queen. Naomi hoped her daughters were here somewhere to see her. They would be so proud.

"Something's wrong," Gabriel whispered. His tense tone broke the spell being woven on the stage as the dancers began to sway and slither to the undulating tempo.

"What do you mean?" Instantly alert to some unforseen danger to the production, Naomi scanned the set and tried to see to the wings beyond. Everything seemed to be progressing seamlessly. "I don't see any problems."

But Gabriel didn't look convinced. His handsome face sharpened into strong angles of concentration. Now Naomi was truly alarmed as Charmaine continued her doomed ascension.

"What is it? Shall I go check backstage?"

His hand tightened until she winced. "No. Stay with me."

Something in his voice made her go rigid with fright and caution. *What was it?*

Tension brought a familiar ache to pound between her temples. The image of the dancers crawling up the steps after a serenely focused Charmaine blurred and altered colors. Naomi blinked, trying to restore focus, struggling to stay on guard for the danger Gabriel intuited.

A thickening mist billowed from the top of the tomb. A figure stood in its midst, cloaked in secrecy and suspense. He wore a cape and mask of quill-like feathers. Only the line of his jaw and the glitter of his eyes was visible, but Naomi went suddenly cold with recognition. Over the drums and moaning chants, she heard the familiar *step clunk, step clunk*. Something in the cruel thinning of his mouth, in the raw fury blazing in his eyes. Nausea churned. A sweat broke on her brow.

The beat of the drums reached a frenzied tempo. The dancers writhed on the steps with arms stretched upward. Now at the top, Charmaine stood placidly, her expression a beautiful blank.

"We have to stop this."

Gabriel stood and signaled to Marcus at the door. The big bouncer also appeared disturbed by the scenario playing out on the stage. He started down the center aisle.

The masked man gathered Charmaine in an embrace. She swooned into it, and for a moment their bodies rocked and swayed in an erotic harmony. The drums thundered wildly as expectation thickened like the rising fog. He bent Charmaine back over his arm, his back blocking their view. Her cry was sudden and terrible. Her arms stiffened and flailed briefly, too briefly.

Then the ancient god raised his head and turned to face the entranced audience. A unified gasp arose, for he was no man but a monster. A monster with glaring red eyes and almost human features beneath a spiny crown of spikes that were no longer part of a costumed mask. The creature's mouth and chin were stained bright red. Hideous fangs were exposed in an obscene caricature of a triumphant grin before it buried its horrible face against the slack curve of Charmaine's throat. She made no sound, no movement as the mists enveloped the two of them.

And they were gone.

Marcus skidded to a stop, looking to Gabriel for direction. He gestured to the wings on the left side of the stage while he hurried right.

Silence shrouded the auditorium. The mists slowly cleared, revealing the motionless dancers sprawled face down on the steps, steps that darkened ominously as a spill of crimson poured down from the top, covering the supine bodies of the women. A dazzling brightness bloomed from behind the temple, like a purifying sun. The drums began to pulse softly, a delicate flute melody playing about that beat. Then the room plunged into darkness.

Hesitation, then the applause was deafening.

Naomi took no time to revel in the show's success. Despite Gabriel's final order for her to stay put, she ran after him, stumbling around the tables until her eyes adjusted and the house lights began to rise.

Backstage was a bustle of activity, but none of it out of the ordinary. Naomi beelined for the dressing room. The dancers were there, stripping out of their feathered headpieces and discolored costumes. They looked like the aftermath of a massacre with their red-splattered skin and hair. Half of them were giddy and noisy with the adrenalin rush, the others sat quietly washing their faces before the mirror, their stares oddly emotionless.

"Wow, what an ending," Candice was gushing. "Who came up with that at the last minute? It was awesome."

"Did you hear that crowd?" Molly crowed. "They loved us. They really loved us. I think I'm going to go out and shop for an expensive little sports car. I'm going to be famous. What did you think of it, Miss Bright?"

"Have any of you seen Charmaine?"

Candice and Molly exchanged puzzled looks. Marty and Grace continued to stare blankly at their own bloodied reflections.

"Not since her grand finale," Molly said at last. "Maybe she's meeting admirers back stage. She was fabulous. I'm going to ask her if I can be the sacrifice on opening night."

A chill shuddered through Naomi as she backed from the room then raced toward the emptied stage. The guests had been efficiently ushered to a private reception in another room. Marcus and Gabriel were at the base of the temple, but no Charmaine.

"How do you get into this thing?" Marcus demanded of the stage hands. None of them seemed to know.

"Is there a trap door? How do they get in and out?"

One of the workers shrugged. "I don't know. A special crew set it up like it was some big secret. They never let us near it."

They spent the next few hours searching above and below the monolithic structure to no avail. The rock sides were seamless, and on top, there was only a small slit through which ancient tribes poured their golden offerings. And the blood splashed liberally on the stones looked frightfully real. None of the backstage crew knew anything. None of them had seen Charmaine.

Naomi had an awful feeling that none of them would ever see her again.

And with her went Naomi's only link to her past.

***

"What have you done? This is madness!"

Alex Cross regarded his partner with a calm, unblinking gaze. "Just taking care of business."

"Is that what you call it? Making a spectacle in front of a human audience? In front of Gabriel McGraw?"

Cross shrugged, unconcerned. "Perhaps it's time he knew what he was facing. Perhaps he needs to know that he isn't dealing with a run-of-the-mill night crawler. Perhaps then he'll show some respect and well deserved caution and give us space to maneuver."

"You don't know him like I do. He'll be all over us. He has no fear. There isn't a cautious bone in his body. You're mad, Cross. You're mad, and you're going to destroy us both."

"Mad, am I?" He turned on Zanlos, eyes blazing with an unnatural cold fire, breath seething through extended fangs and movements becoming jerky with agitation when he finally began to pace the room. His image flickered, becoming one thing then another as if unable to fix on either.

It was more than simple madness fermenting behind that blazing glare. It was a fatal flaw that Zanlos was just now beginning to recognize. A flaw that might well get him killed. Again.

"It's not madness, fool, it's brilliance. Brilliance like mine is rarely recognized by the simple masses. But in time, you will understand how what I've done tonight has set the stage for the ultimate production. You have no insight into a man like Gabriel McGraw. You are a creature of this century, and his is an old, noble soul. You have to understand where he comes from to realize how to finally devastate him. You have no clue. You think your security teams and your pretty little secretary are going to keep you safe from him. He will crush you like a bug, Zanlos, if I were to let him. Perhaps I will. Perhaps you are not the type of man I need to stand by my side. I had not thought you would be squeamish."

"Not squeamish, Alex. Cautious. Perhaps if you told me what you had planned—"

"I've told you all you need to know. The rest is my business. My pleasure."

Cross faced his wary partner, all smooth charm once more. But having been once burned, Zanlos wasn't deceived.

"Kaz, you have fulfilled your end of our arrangement beyond my hopes and expectations. For that, I thank you. You deserve the success this hotel will reap as long as you allow me the latitude I need to conclude my plans."

"Which you refuse to share."

Cross smiled. "Exactly. They do not involve you. Not directly."

"Do they involve Miss Bright?"

"Oh, you might say they do. Oh yes, you might." His chuckle burbled with manic genius, then his stare grew hard and fierce. "Don't interfere, my friend, unless you'd like the lovely ladies of the Amazon to come looking for you."

***

Gabriel wouldn't let her remain at the Amazon. He didn't give reasons. She didn't ask. She knew he thought it was too dangerous. She agreed.

He and Marcus would remain in hopes that Charmaine turned up. His tight expression said he didn't think that was going to happen. She was too heartsick to let him know she saw right through him.

She drove home, her emotions on autopilot.

What had she witnessed? A murder? A sacrifice? Right in front of a room full of people? How could that be?

But Charmaine was gone. And deep in her soul, she knew she'd seen and recognized evil in the eyes behind the mask.

Chilled to the bone on the balmy night, she locked her house up tight and headed for the shower. If Rita came home, it wouldn't be until dawn. Tonight she was glad for the solitude. She didn't want to speak. She didn't want to think about what she had or hadn't seen.

And as the steamy water beat down upon her shoulders, she wept where no one could hear her, until the spray grew cool and her throat ached too much to draw another sobbing breath.

Her hair toweled dry and her shivering form wrapped in a plush terry robe, she made herself a cup of strong tea. Some of Rita's herbal brew without caffeine, taste or any harmful additives. All she wanted was the heat to restore what had seeped out of her.

She sat curled on the couch with a single low-wattage bulb burning. The tea helped calm her nerves and so did the blob of motor-revving fur stretched across her lap. But nothing could erase the sight of that face, of that remembered horror. Remembered from where?

Mel's contented purrs lowered to a more menacing rumble. He jumped down from her lap and went to stuff himself under her end table. Before she could puzzle over his behavior, there was a knock at the door. She glanced at the numbers on the VCR she rarely used. 4:55.

Gabriel McGraw stood on her front step looking woeful and yet wonderful to her. What she couldn't see through the peep hole that was revealed by the opening of her door, was that he wasn't alone.

Charmaine Johnson's three daughters were with him.

Twenty-one

Gabriel's somber expression belied her question.

Naomi opened the door and gestured them inside. "I was just sitting here by myself thinking how nice it would be to have visitors." She forced a cheerful tone as her heart swelled for the three children.

Janeece, the six-year old, spotted Mel's fat tail twitching underneath the end table and forgot her shyness. "You have a kitty!" She raced across the living room and began to drag the fat feline from his lair by the hind legs.

"Careful, honey. He's not too friendly."

But the child had Mel wrapped in her arms, cooing about the creature's beauty and softness. Mel, though he looked displeased hanging like a sack of suet from the strangle hold the little girl had under his front legs, began what sounded suspiciously like a purr.

Holding the dozing Tonya in her arms, Roxanne regarded Naomi through swimming eyes, though her features were composed in grim lines. She either knew or guessed the truth. "Gabriel said we might be able to stay with you for a while. If it's all right."

"I'd love the company. Come in."

The couch pulled out into a bed. Naomi supplied sheets and pillows. The younger girls curled up and were asleep in minutes with Mel snoring between them. The eldest watched Naomi with a look way too serious for her years.

"We won't be any trouble, Miss Bright."

"I don't expect you will be. If Mel says you're all right, I'm sure you are. Sorry the couch isn't more comfortable."

A wry smile shaped her pretty face. "We've slept on worse." How much she looked like her mother at that moment.

"I want you girls to make yourselves at home until we find out something…definite."

The girl's expression grew weary and resigned, as if that truth was already apparent to her.

"I know I'm just a stranger to you," Naomi continued, "but

you'll be safe here."

"We trust Gabriel, so if he says it's all right, we're not worried."

She slipped under the covers with her sisters and turned off the nearby light, but sleep was most likely hours away for her.

Naomi stared at the three unmoving shapes. Tears returned to burn her eyes. Poor little things. Alone and afraid, despite Roxanne's brave words. She joined Gabriel in the kitchen area.

"Are you sure you don't mind?"

She waved off his hesitation. "Don't be silly. What did you find out? Anything?"

His gaze fixed upon the silent trio. "Nothing encouraging." He turned away, his tone growing harsh with self-castigation. "I let her go in. I knew it was dangerous. I seem to have a talent for getting those around me killed."

"We don't know that she's—"

His stare cut through her hopeful naivete. "Don't we?"

Naomi lowered her gaze, anguish ripping through her.

Gabriel sighed and reached out to gather her up against his chest. Her instinctive stiffening yielded to the comfort he offered. She looped her arms about his middle, leaning in while he struggled to come to terms with what he considered his failure to protect one of his own.

"I just don't know why they killed her," he concluded in quiet misery.

A sheet of icy knowledge spread through Naomi's belly. She knew. It was because of her. Because of what Rita had overheard.

What was in her past that would threaten Kaz Zanlos enough to have an innocent woman murdered so brutally and publically? Was it a warning to her? Just to let her know that he knew she was thinking about abandoning him? Just to let her know the type of consequences that might be in store for her or anyone she cared for?

Gabriel stepped back suddenly. "I have to go. You'll be all right, Naomi." Then he said something strange. "Zanlos isn't a danger to you or the girls."

She saw the concern in his gaze and pounced upon it. "But

someone is. Who? Do you know who?"

"Not yet. But I will. I let those girls become orphans. I won't let their future come to a sudden end."

"You're not going to do anything foolish, are you?"

He grinned at her alarm. He looked so young and handsome, it was hard for her to view him as a seasoned warrior. "Probably, but you don't need to worry. I have a habit of surviving my mistakes." Then his expression altered subtly until he appeared positively ancient. "If only those around me were so lucky." His fingertips traced Naomi's jawline. "Don't look so distressed. I won't let anything happen to you."

"I wasn't worried about me."

Boldly, she reached up to bracket his face between her hands, drawing him down into her urgent kiss. She dove in without shyness. There wasn't time for tact or diplomacy. When Gabriel backed away, it was with obvious difficulty.

"I have to go," he repeated. Reluctance steeped in his expression.

"I'll take care of them. I'll enjoy it. The older one, Roxanne, reminds me of someone."

Gabriel smiled as she puzzled over it. "She reminds me of you."

He pressed a quick kiss upon her willing lips and was out the door, locking it behind him. She touched her dampened mouth wistfully.

"He likes you."

Naomi glanced toward the couch to find Janeese smiling at her. "You think so?"

"Sure. He'd stay if he could."

"I'm sure he had other places to go."

"He can't stay past the dawn, Mama said."

"And why is that?"

"Because he's a vampire."

And with that incredible conclusion, the child rolled over and went back to sleep.

                    ***

"Don't let anyone go in."

Marcus Sinclair nodded.

"I'm trusting you to keep them safe."

Sinclair leaned on the window frame of the big classic car to peer chidingly at the man behind the wheel. "Even if it wasn't my job, I would."

"If Rita Davies shows up, you might want to suggest she find another place to stay, at least until we know who she's with, Zanlos or his unseen partner."

Marcus's features tightened. "You think it was the partner who put on the show tonight?"

"Maybe," was all Gabriel would volunteer. "He must be someone with a lot of power behind him for me not to have sensed him."

"You and him…you're the same?"

Gabriel flinched at Marcus's awkwardly put question. "No. We're not the same. Not at all."

"Do you think we'll ever find her?" The undercover cop asked in an abrupt change of topic, not that the new subject was any more pleasant.

"Not alive," Gabriel finally admitted aloud. "And if you do happen to see her, she won't be the same. She'll be—"

"Like him," Marcus supplied. He caught on quickly and didn't waste time demanding explanations.

"Yes." He glanced in his rearview to see the pastel approach of daylight. His eyes narrowed and watered. "I've got to go."

"Because of the dawn?"

"Yes. And I've got miles to go before I sleep. I'll rest easier knowing you're here."

Marcus pressed a big hand down on his forearm. "Then rest easier. And tomorrow, we're going to have us a conversation."

Gabriel smiled thinly. "I look forward to it."

Vampire.

Naomi wanted to laugh off the idea as the product of a child's imagination.

But as she lay in her bed, atop the covers and still fully dressed, she could see the beast drenched in Charmaine's blood. That image was quickly followed by Jeannie's burning stare.

Vampires.

Her hand had gone subconsciously to the faded marks on her throat. She'd explained them away to her own satisfaction as some sort of insect bite.

Or inhuman bite?

Would that explain her memory losses, her odd weak spells, her compulsive behavior?

Strange that it would be more palatable to blame a mythical creature of the night for her quixotic moods than ascribe it to mental illness. She blindly accepted Zanlos' claims without questioning, without asking for proof. Why? Why couldn't she bring up the subject or demand an accounting? Why was she always so grateful and subservient around her boss, when her usual type-A manner required an analytical approach and substantiated cause.

Was that because Kaz Zanlos had mesmerized her with a vampire's bite?

A laugh burbled up at the absurdity of it. But when the nagging suspicion should have gone away, it continued to linger, to fester in the back of her mind.

What was really going on at the Amazon?

And if such things as vampires were real, and her boss was one, was Gabriel McGraw one as well? If so, how could she possibly love him? Wouldn't that make him a monster? A beast preying upon the life blood of others to sustain his own self-gratifying existence?

She recalled the coolness of his touch and his ability to seemingly disappear at will.

Her breathing shivered slightly.

Gabriel was not a vampire. Kaz Zanlos was a lawyer and a businessman and if he was a blood sucker, it was only in the figurative sense. Jeannie was drug crazed and impervious to pain.

But what about Charmaine? Who…or what had killed her?

Naomi closed her eyes as the familiar throbbing began to build at the base of her skull. Was it her own psychological flaws that made the impossible seem plausible? Was she making Gabriel into some kind of unnatural being because it would be easier to reject his attention and potential affection if he was other than a man?

There had to be records. Some paper trail that would lead her to the truth. She'd depended upon numbers and facts to guide her whole life. They couldn't let her down now.

Records. Paper. Documents. Facts would protect her and provide her with answers.

And those facts were in Kaz Zanlos' private files.

But just in case, she would search them before the sun set.

***

She awoke with a scream on her lips, and another nearly followed when she saw an unfamiliar figure seated on the foot of her bed. Naomi released a ragged breath when she recognized Roxanne Johnson. The young woman sat, still and silent, her eyes fixed unblinkingly ahead.

"I'm sorry," Naomi managed in a semi-calm voice. "I didn't mean to frighten you. I was having a bad dream."

Roxanne's stare never wavered. "It wasn't a dream. It was memory. You're the one my mother said was caught between two lives. She'd asked if I could help you but never had time to arrange a meeting. It was you, wasn't it?"

"She said she knew someone with a gift."

Roxanne's mouth warped in a bitter smile. "Gift. Curse. Call it what you like."

"You're a psychic?"

"I prefer to think of it as being sensitive to other worlds. I just know things about people, whether they're good or bad. I recognized the good in Gabriel right away, despite whatever else he might be. And you, too. I had a feeling about you."

"Tell me about Gabriel. What did you mean by whatever else he might be?"

"That's for him to explain to you. But you have another question for me."

Naomi gathered her courage and convictions to ask, "Whose memories and why me?"

"It's hard to explain. It's like a layering of your life over another." She spoke these things so matter-of-factly while sitting there wearing one of Naomi's tee shirts, like a teenager at a slumber party instead of a mystic about to unveil the secrets of a hidden universe. Her tone was old, so old. "In spots, the one bleeds through the other and you see with each others' eyes, hear with each others' ears, feel with each others' hearts. What do you know about reincarnation?"

Naomi shook her head. "Nothing really. Is that what this is?"

"It's stronger than a past life because the memories, the desires, the needs are very real to you here in the present. The soul of this other person has somehow mingled with yours. That other spirit can't find peace, that's why it won't leave you alone. There's something you need to do first."

"What?"

Roxanne jumped up suddenly, her mood tense, her reply evasive. "I don't know for sure."

A lie. Why the sudden lie after she'd revealed so much? What had she seen? What did she know?

"Roxanne, what am I supposed to do?"

"I can't see it clearly." Still lying, and the girl was a bad liar. The truth was imprinted upon her furrowed brow.

"Roxanne, please."

Unable to avoid answering, the girl sought to diffuse the power her reply would carry. "I must be reading it wrong."

"What do you see?"

Then Roxanne fixed her with a still, unwavering stare, as if she were looking right through her and seeing another. "For her to find peace, you have to die so she can live through you."

Before Naomi could recover from that startling revelation, a cry arose from the other room. Tonya, waking up in a strange place, began wailing for her mother. As Roxanne wearily went to calm her baby sister's anxieties, Naomi was left to wonder how to quiet her own on this strange night of impossibilities.

Twenty-two

A knock on the window of Marcus Sinclair's Bonneville jolted him awake. He rolled down the window to sheepishly take the cup of coffee Naomi Bright offered.

"What are you doing here, Marcus? Guard duty?"

A moth pinned to a mounting board, he saw no reason to flail his wings. "Gabriel asked me to keep an eye on you and the girls."

"Since when are you and Gabriel such close compatriots?"

Hoping to forestall her grilling with vagueness, he replied, "We're sort of in the same line of work."

Naomi blinked. "You're a cop?" Then her expression took on a speculative gleam that made Marcus squirm. Justifiably, when she asked, "How are you at picking locks?"

"My personal specialty. Why? Did you lock yourself out?"

"In a manner of speaking."

And before he knew it, she'd talked him into giving her a ride to the Amazon. The girls were told to lock the doors and stay inside. Roxanne, who appreciated the gravity of the situation, nodded. As long as it was daylight, Naomi figured they'd be safe.

Look at me. Believing in fairytales about the undead.

As they drove into the parking garage, Naomi finally asked, "Marcus, what else is Gabriel?"

Without missing a beat, he said, "I'm not sure, but I'm glad he's on our side."

It was Sunday and even though that meant next to nothing in Las Vegas, the crew had been given the day off with orders to finish the final touches the next day for the Monday night grand opening. Only a few security guards were in the building, and Marcus knew their pattern of surveillance. It was ridiculously easy to slip inside unnoticed, dodging both guards and cameras. Using her security card, Naomi and Marcus started up in the private elevator.

"What exactly am I breaking into?" Marcus whispered lest the elevator was monitored.

"Files. Mr. Zanlos' files. If he's not guilty of anything, he should have nothing to hide, should he?"

Marcus raised a brow but said nothing.

The executive floor was empty, with only the dim security lights burning. Office staff would come in at eight. Until then, they had the place to themselves.

She headed straight for Zanlos' suite.

"Can you get us inside?"

Marcus slipped a thin case from his jacket pocket and selected a pair of delicate picks. With a few expert jimmies and a quiet curse or two, the door came open.

Naomi had expected guilt to settle in at some point, but what she experienced when she crossed the threshold into the office was an apprehensive distress. Reluctance and dread seeped in to drag upon her determination. Agitation stirred into a seething foment in her belly. Each forward step increased the level of anxiety until she was sure she was going to be sick.

But then she saw the files. Then she was able to push aside her misgivings.

"I need access to what's in there."

Marcus went to work and soon was sliding out the file drawer.

Hesitantly, Naomi peered at the tabs, unwilling as of yet to touch them.

He'll know. He'll find out that you betrayed him.

It wouldn't be the first time if what Gabriel said was true. She'd helped Zanlos' former partner gather information in D.C. If her treachery was discovered then, why was she still in a position of power within Zanlos' business?

Because he's aware of everything you do.

She knew it. She could feel him as clearly as if he were standing behind her, looking over her shoulder as she prepared to break his trust.

After all he's done for you.

What exactly had he done? That was what she needed to know.

Put up a wall using your will. She could hear the voice of a woman she could almost see. *You can keep him out if you stay strong.* Nicole. Her name had been Nicole. She remembered an attractive, dark-haired woman with eyes like freshly cut emeralds. She was in the woman's house, a guest but also a prisoner. She'd been weak, ill, wild with fear that she'd betray...whom? Whom would she betray if she didn't remain strong?

Gabriel.

It had been Gabriel.

"Miss Bright and I are leaving now. I wouldn't suggest that you think to follow immediately. But I will be disappointed if we don't meet again."

"Yes, we will. And when we do, I will kill you for putting your hands on her."

When had these words been spoken about her between her boss and her lover? The answers were close, prickling just beneath the surface, just waiting to be uncovered.

Her fingers skipped along the tabs until she came to one listing her own name. She pulled out the jacket and took a breath before looking inside.

Nothing. There was nothing of any help to her. A fact sheet listing her home address and her medical coverage. Nothing prior to her position here. No records, no medical or mental evaluations. No resume listing next of kin or previous employment. It was as if her life started with this job in Las Vegas. Disappointment overcame the sour taste of betrayal. If her boss had footed the bill for her psychological breakdown, why wasn't there any kind of paper trail, at least for tax purposes?

"Find what you need?"

Replacing her woefully incomplete folder, Naomi shook her head.

"Then do you mind if I poke around a little to find out what I need to know?"

Her attention sharpened. "And what's that?"

"More about Zanlos' silent partner. We, Gabriel and I, think he's calling the shots. Not that your boss is a Snow White, but Zanlos is a doer not a dreamer. He's the one who figures out how to make things happen once someone else sets him on it. I want to know who that someone else is."

"You've got about a half hour tops."

So Marcus made the most of it.

He rifled the files and had her make copies of whatever he felt might lead to something important.

"Alexander Cross," he mused then looked to Naomi. "Does that name ring a bell with you?"

Naomi shrugged. "I've heard it." But when she mulled it over, her mind went maddingly blank. As if her thoughts were concealing the information from her. She shivered as the image of the man in the mask flashed through her head like heat lightning.

Put up the wall.

She took a breath and made her thoughts clear, shoving back the thick mists of confusion until an image took form. A man with fair hair and pale eyes and a smile both filled with charm and menace. Alex Cross. She'd seen him once, had stumbled in inadvertently upon a private meeting. She hadn't recognized him. But then again, she had. Not the face, not the voice, but what lay beneath both those things. Beneath the mask.

Her voice was small but sure. "He's the one you want."

With a nod of affirmation, Marcus went back to his digging. "Bingo," he cried after long minutes ticked by. He jerked out a fat file. "Banking transactions. Converting Peruvian gold into working capital for the hotel. Who the hell is this guy?"

The overhead fluorescents snapped on, blinding them like deer in headlights.

"You can ask him yourself."

They turned like guilty children caught taking change from their father's pants pockets. Rita stood in the doorway, one hand on the light switch and the other holding gun metal not quite as cold as her glare. Seeing she meant business, Naomi decided to go for the bluff. There was a chance, at least, to keep Marcus out of it.

"Rita, you scared me. I was looking for some of my medical records. Those headaches are back, and Marcus was going to run me to the clinic before work."

"Then what are you doing in those files?"

"Mine's empty." She held up the folder to demonstrate. "I figured that they'd been misfiled. Mr. Zanlos' secretary isn't exactly a nuclear physicist."

"And you're no rocket scientist either if you expected me to buy that." She gestured with the barrel. "Both of you take a seat."

"I'm really not feeling well. Mr. Zanlos won't be pleased if you keep me here against my will."

"Surprise, Little Miss Sunshine. I don't work for Zanlos. And I don't take orders from your buddy McGraw, either. Though if I were you, I'd rethink that relationship. What kind of man has a stranger come cross country to spy on a woman he supposedly cares about? He called in a favor from one of my former cop buddies and had me come out here to babysit for you. That's right, I'm a cop. Used to be a cop." She paused to assimilate that difference but quickly toughened up to that new reality. "Guess I'll earn my keep tonight, because you're not getting into any more mischief."

Seeing Naomi's stricken expression, Marcus sought to deflect the hurtful attack. "And what's this Cross paying you to betray someone who took you in?"

"Not money, but someone like you wouldn't understand that, would you? You've never had an original thought of your own that didn't get you into trouble. Cross appreciates me."

"He's using you, doll, just like he's been using up the other girls. And when you get in his way, you'll end up just like Charmaine Johnson."

"And what happened to that pushy bitch? She get fired?"

"She got dead," Marcus corrected bluntly.

For a instant, something flickered behind Rita's inanimate stare. Naomi was quick to take advantage.

"But you didn't know that, did you? You couldn't have known that and just let it happen. Not to one of our girls. Not the way it did to Jeannie."

A sweat broke out on Rita's brow. "Sit down and shut up. You're just trying to confuse me."

"Rita, Cross is killing our girls or worse. We can't let that happen. We can't let him hurt them."

More shadows scuttled through her glazed eyes. "He's not hurting them. He's rewarding them for their loyalty. Something you'd know nothing about."

"You're wrong, Rita. I'm loyal to the girls. I'm loyal to my friends. I'm loyal to my boss, even though I'm very afraid he doesn't deserve it. And I'm loyal to you."

Agitation increasing at that impassioned plea, Rita argued, "You're a bleeding heart, Nomi. You only see the good in people. They'll disappoint you every time. Every time."

"It's not too late, Rita. Come home with me. We can get this straightened out. No one else has to get hurt."

There was a glint of ruthless steel as Rita swung the pistol. The butt of it struck Naomi in the temple, and she went down without a sound.

"I guess you're wrong there, sweetie. Dead wrong."

***

Pain came and went in shivery waves. Naomi was vaguely aware of the couch's fabric beneath her cheek. When she dared slit open her eyes against the pin dots of sickness, she saw Marcus's big hands braced upon his knees, flexing in frustration and helplessness. She ventured a look farther to see Rita's pacing interrupted when someone else joined them.

"A party? How lovely."

Jeannie.

Panic closed about her heart. Naomi no longer believed that the former dancer was human.

"Caught them snooping around and figured I'd better see what Cross wants done with them."

Jeannie's laugh rippled low and menacing. "One guess."

"Enlighten me."

"The same thing he does with anyone else who gets in his way." *You moron*, her tone said.

"Like Charmaine Johnson?"

"And our old friend Kitty Parsons. It's good to have powerful friends."

Naomi sat up slowly, drawing the attention of the two women. Scenting the blood on her temple, Jeannie's gaze flared red and hot.

"Good evening, Miss Bright. Nice to see you again."

Naomi regarded her with pity and regret instead of fear. "I'm so sorry, Jeannie. I should have known something was wrong. I should have protected you and all the girls better. I had no idea of the danger you were in."

"And if you had, what would you have done?" Jeannie sneered. "Issued a memo? Hidden under your desk? Lucky for you, you're Zanlos' puppet, or you'd be like Kitty and Charmaine."

"They're dead." Naomi clarified flatly.

"Duh."

"Like Jack?"

At the mention of her boyfriend, Jeannie's expression crumpled slightly in confusion and pain. But her cockiness returned too quickly. "That was a mistake. I was still learning what I was." She shrugged. "It's for the best, I guess. He would never have accepted what I'd become."

A vampire. Naomi finally admitted that truth to herself. Jeannie was a vampire. Kaz Zanlos and his unseen partner, too. And Gabriel.

And Gabriel.

"Good evening," Kaz Zanlos drawled in his honeyed-accented voice, and for a moment Naomi fought the urge to laugh hysterically as she cast him in Bella Lugosi's role. He gave her a perplexed look then his expression hardened. He took his displeasure out on the other two women.

"What's going on here?"

"Rita caught them going through your office."

"And you thought that presented a prime opportunity to share all our secrets with them?"

Jeannie gave him a sulky glare. "What does it matter? Cross's is going to kill them anyway."

"This isn't his affair."

Her laugh was sharp enough to cut glass. "You think you're in charge here? You're just his front man, his lackey, his stooge. You don't have a say in anything he does. This is his show."

Naomi was surprised by the sudden sense of invasion within her thoughts and mind, like fingers hooking about the edges of an orange in an attempt to tear back the peel.

What have you done? Whom have you told?

The questions speared through her already aching head with such force she barely had time to fling up a defense. Then there was just the insistent pounding, tolling out with each painful beat her betrayal at the hands of a supposed friend.

Frustration briefly touched Zanlos' expression at his failure to reach her. It did little for his mood. He turned upon Cross's creation.

"Leave."

Jeannie opened her mouth to protest, but Zanlos shut it with a slicing stare. She gave an elegant shrug. "We'll see what Cross has to say."

"Run tell him, why don't you."

"Oh, I will."

He gestured at Rita. "You go with her. And take him. Don't let him out of your sight." To Marcus, he said, "A shame to lose you. Good help is hard to keep."

Marcus flipped him a finger gesture and preceded Rita out of the room. Zanlos was chuckling at his bravado as he turned back toward Naomi. Turning right into her surprisingly forceful slap.

"You lied," she accused, her voice shaky with hurt and anger but amazingly not with fear. "I never had a mental breakdown, did I? There was nothing in my past you were trying to protect me from, was there?"

"Alas, your past was painfully uneventful. It was only the recent developments I had to block from your memory. Like the fact that you betrayed me to McGraw and my associate, Mr. Flynn. You can't know how badly that hurt my feelings."

"So you stripped me of my thoughts and of my identity so I could work for you as your slave." She spat that at him, too irate to show proper caution.

"It was for your protection, my dear. I couldn't risk your disaffection a second time, especially not while doing business with Cross. He isn't as…forgiving as I am. If he saw you as a liability, he would have disposed of you. I've tried to keep you safe from his agenda."

"Why? Because good help is so hard to find?" Tears glistened in her eyes. How naive she'd been, so puffed up with pride about her position, so blinded by the notion of his faith in her.

"Because I enjoy you, Miss Bright. You are efficient, hard working, witty when you allow yourself to be, intelligent—"

"And a pawn for you to hide behind to keep Gabriel at bay."

He inclined his head. "There's that, too. He and his friends stripped me of one very lucrative venture. I have no plans to lose another."

"And silencing me will keep your secrets safe."

"Oh, my dear, you have no idea how deep my secrets run. You were the one bright light in my grim existence. I'd look at you and see that, yes, there was good in this world. A shallow and selfish interpretation, perhaps, but you never failed to lift my spirits. And though you would never credit yourself, you have an amazing courage and resilience. You are the only one who has ever been able to block out my commands. You say you were my slave? No. You are a treasure, Miss Bright. And I shall miss you."

He was going to kill her. Or allow Cross to do the deed for him. She pinched her lips together so he wouldn't see them quiver. He'd commended her for her courage. She couldn't let it fail her now.

When she continued to face him with her shaky show of bravery and resignation, Zanlos smiled sadly. "I'm giving you your severance, Miss Bright. Go. I don't know what Cross had planned for you, but I vow it wouldn't be pleasant. It was never my intention to let him...abuse you after all your years of dedication and loyalty, however misplaced it might have been. But I fear after Jeannie tells him of this little incident, he will break his vow not to harm you. I can't have that on my conscience. And I am a bit surprised to discover I have one left. You brought out the decency in me, Miss Bright. Allow me to make this gesture of thanks. Run. Run far away and hide. He'll come after you, and I won't be able to stop him. I know I should do more to protect you but, admittedly, I am not that decent nor is my conscience that troublesome."

She started for the door, weak with relief. All she had to do was go and say nothing. To just walk away. She wasn't responsible, after all. She'd never been more than an easily manipulated pawn.

But with one hand on the door and her escape eminent, she turned back toward him.

"They already know about you and Cross. They'll never allow the hotel to open so Cross can carry out his plans. Perhaps you should take your own advice and run. While you can."

He reacted with genuine surprise then with an odd emotion. Gratitude. Then he simply smiled in his usual bland and inscrutable manner. "Thank you for the heads up, my dear. Perhaps I will."

***

Rita and Marcus stood uncomfortably watching Jeannie pace the conference room in increasing agitation and hunger. She no longer bothered to maintain the mask of humanity, and her image fluttered like bad reception on the television. Her movements quickened and blurred, running together as if controlled by a time and space different than theirs.

And the sound…soft hissing breaths ending on a feral rumble.

"What's keeping Cross?" she growled. Her focus darted from the door to their captive. Finally, that burning stare fixed upon Marcus, and her restless travels ceased. Danger and death pulsed from her as she studied the beat at the base of his thick throat. Her gaze narrowed, glittering behind the fierce slits. Her nostrils flared and thinned as she sucked in his vital scent.

"Perhaps we won't wait," she purred at last. Her tongue ran slowly across elongated teeth.

Then her head whipped around as her preternatural hearing picked up a sound they couldn't hear.

"The elevator," she muttered to herself.

The frenetic energy returned, she went to a wall cabinet and opened the doors. Several monitors flickered to life, displaying different areas of the first floor hotel. Just normal activity with a few select craftsmen laying down the finishing touches and service staff running vacuums.

Until the door to the private elevator slid open and Naomi Bright slipped out.

Jeannie howled, the sound raising hairs on the necks of the other two. She pointed a now taloned finger at Rita.

"You keep him here for Cross. I'll take care of our little defector. Zanlos is a fool if he thinks I'd let her escape."

Her form faded and thinned, becoming wisps of smoke that dispersed beneath the silent breath of the ventilation fans.

For a moment, the two simply stared at the monitors.

"She's going to kill her," Marcus stated at last, hammering that fact home like a stake to the heart. "You know that. Maybe you didn't know about Kitty and Charmaine, but you know if that monster catches up to Naomi, she intends to kill her."

"You can't stop her. You can't prevent it from happening." Rita's tone was hallow and fatalistic.

"But I know who can." He took a chance and gripped her arm. "You're a cop, for God's sake. This isn't how we do things."

He wasn't reaching her. Her expression was remote stone. He tried again with a ruthless appeal.

"Rita, she was your friend."

She stared at him, and he could see the dark swirls of indecision clouding her gaze. Finally, she lowered the gun. And she extended the papers that would damn Cross's scheme.

"Then get him. Save her. It may be the last good deed I'm ever able to do."

Twenty-three

She ran.

Her only thought was to find Gabriel. Gabriel was the only one who'd stand a chance against Cross and the ghouls at the Amazon.

Because Gabriel wasn't human, either.

The sidewalks were filled with tourists spilling out of the various casinos and shops. Easily identifiable by their expensive cameras and tee shirts emblazoned with the names of their hotels in flagrant billboardesque advertising, they gawked at the sights, at the pirate ship launching in front of Treasure Island, at the graceful water ballet fountains of the Ballagio, at the erupting volcanos and light shows and dazzling neon displays, all blissfully unaware that she was racing for her life and possibly for theirs. For whatever Cross had planned for the naive visitors to Las Vegas, she was certain they wouldn't leave well entertained.

As she continued her hurried pace, blessing her sensible shoes, she pulled out her cell phone and began punching in Gabriel's pager number. Before it had a chance to ring through, her elbow took a hard knock from an Hoosier fan wearing a John Deare cap. He obliviously jockeyed for the best shot of his family posing stiffly in front of The Mirage and the huge statue of its founders, Seigfrid and Roy, and seemed unaware of the collision. To her dismay, the phone went flying. It landed on the crowded walk with a damning crack then was puck-handled by indifferent feet until it skidded out into the street and under the crushing weight of one of the trolleys.

Uttering an uncharacteristic curse, she happened to glance up and there, on the curving paths playing about the edge of fountains with Caesar's Palace rising up behind her, stood Jeannie Baker, one time Miss Cornhusker from Nebraska, now newly made vampire.

Jeannie slowly turned her head, not scanning the crowd but rather, like the predator she was, scenting the air.

Naomi had no doubt in her mind who she was looking for.

She faded back through the throng of senior citizen tourists
rushing from their bus to catch Steve and Eydie's next show.
Careful not to draw attention to herself and grateful for the fact
that she blended with such anonymity, Naomi crossed with other
foot traffic and headed into the palatial casino at the Venetian.
There, she'd find the first available phone and send out an S.O.S.

It was impossible not to glance about, seeing the players
popping tokens and pumping arms, hearing the bing, bing, bing
and the occasional clatter of payback, and not to imagine what
the Amazon might have achieved upon its opening. A sadness
sank deep into her soul at all that had been hoped for and now
would never be realized. At least, by her. She wouldn't be there
to reap the kudos, to experience the pride, to bask in the
satisfaction of a job well done.

But, if all went well, she'd be alive. And that's what she
needed to concentrate on.

That and getting the rest of the girls out of there before
they fell under Cross's foul influence. It was too late for Jeannie
and for Charmaine, perhaps for Rita, Marcus and Grace, too.
But the others, she could save. It was her duty to try.

Sinking back into shadow next to the phone banks, she
dialed Gabriel's pager number and stated a brief message.

"I'm at the Venetian. Jeannie's after me. Zanlos and Cross
know everything."

She punched in the number and waited. Seconds passed.
Then a minute. She jumped when the phone rang, snatching it
up before the second tone.

His voice was a soothing balm of sanity.

"Wait for me at St. Mark's Square."

"Hurry."

***

Grandly dressed opera singers and costumed entertainers
quoted the plays of the day. Domed ceilings painted to resemble
Renaissance works of art created a fantasy world Naomi wished
she could enjoy. She drifted along the shop fronts, pretending
to daydream about the extravagant displays of millefiori beaded
necklaces, Venetian glassware, casino apparel and feathered
ceramic masks. All the while, she searched out of the corners of

her eyes for signs of discovery or salvation. Who would find
her first? She couldn't burrow in too deeply for fear that Gabriel
would pass her by, and she had to effect a rescue for those at the
Amazon.

How could she think to rescue them when she couldn't even
save herself?

She ducked into one of the expensive gift shops and picked
out an elaborate half mask on a stick. Hiding behind the painted
lion's face and lush golden plumage that resembled a mane,
she stepped back into the square to continue her search through
the slanted eye holes.

Not immune to the romance of the setting, Naomi was drawn
to the stone balconies overlooking the marvel of the Venetian—
the Grand Canal flowing through the shop area on the hotel's
second floor in a basin of concrete. Gondolas toured sleekly
along that waterway with polemen in their black- and white-
striped shirts steering cuddling lovebirds and occasionally
breaking into song. She watched curiously as one of the boats
bumped the wall beneath her and the gondolier held up a hand.
She gasped to see Gabriel's features revealed beneath a floppy
hat.

"Jump down. I'll catch you."

Naomi hesitated. Suddenly, all she could see was water,
black and cold, surging toward her, seeking to suck her under.
She stepped back.

"I can't."

"Naomi, trust me," he called up to her. "Trust me."

Blinking against the visions her mind thrust up as barriers,
she focused on Gabriel, on the steady intensity of his gaze and
the surety of the hands spread wide and extended toward her.
She could barely breathe. She slipped one leg, then the other
over the rail while those around her paused to watch, wondering
if this was part of some pre-staged show.

Closing her eyes against the images of a dark surf racing
up to engulf her, she stepped out on faith.

A brief rush of wind and the solid feel of Gabriel's hands
upon her waist. Her eyes flew open then shut again as she
wrapped her arms tightly about his neck. The shoppers above

politely applauded and went on about their business.

He eased her down to the bottom of the boat and poled them quickly out onto the waterway. She leaned back against the spraddle of his legs and let herself relax. She was safe now.

"Marcus told me what happened. Rita let him escape. Fill me in on your meeting with Zanlos," he asked without looking down. The tenderness in his voice conveyed his concern without further embellishments.

So she told him, sparing no details, not even those surrounding his true dark nature. He said nothing until she was finished. And then, he wasn't sure he knew where to begin. The moment was crucial. Her regard of him meant everything. If she looked up and he saw horror in her gaze, he didn't think he'd be able to go on.

Her head tipped back and turned. His stomach clenched. His breath suspended for that instant it took for her eyes to lift, for her stare to connect with his.

And in her sweet face, he saw acceptance, and he wanted to weep.

The gondola slipped past cafes, under balconies and along lush streetscapes. As they crossed through the shadow of a bridge, they were too engrossed in one another to notice that one of the scantily clad living statues followed them with a marble-cold glare. Passers-by gasped as a sleek woman in the fluid wrap of a toga hopped down from her pedestal and lithely vaulted over the side of the bridge.

The gondola scarcely rocked as Jeannie landed in the bow.

"Oh, how melodramatic," she sneered. "A lover's rendezvous comes to tragic consequence on the pseudo-streets of Venice. I'd cry if I could shed tears of regret."

Though Naomi drew back in alarm, Gabriel issued a low, threatening growl of his own.

"Zanlos won't like it if she comes to any harm," Gabriel warned. "And I'll like it even less. Catch the next boat."

"If three's a crowd, I'm not the one who's going to be leaving."

She lunged toward Naomi, lips curled back, fangs hideously exposed.

Without thinking, Naomi reacted.

For a moment, Jeannie's features showed complete surprise. She glanced down and seemed even more amazed to find the stick from Naomi's mask thrust into her chest. She started to laugh at the absurdity of it, of a wimp like Naomi Bright striking her down in all her glorious power. Then the laugh became a gurgle and her body thrashed wildly.

Leaning over a dazed Naomi, Gabriel shoved the rapidly decomposing Jeannie over the side of the boat. She hit the water without a splash and sank out of sight. Where she'd gone under, the surface boiled for a moment then grew still again. Only then did Gabriel pole them out from the bridge's shadow and back into the light.

Recovering from the magnitude of what she'd done, Naomi looked up with a renewed strength.

"Charmaine's girls. They won't be safe if Cross is coming after me."

"Then let's go get them."

***

They drove to Naomi's house in silence. Conversation was beyond Naomi at this point.

She'd killed someone.

The shock of it pulsed through her in a jerking arrhythmia. But what frightened her more, what created more agitation than that final realization she'd seen in the other's eyes, was the fierce sense of justice even now taking seed inside her.

She'd made a stand. She'd destroyed something evil, something that would have ultimately harmed those she cared about. Pride blossomed where courage had taken root and she didn't recognize the woman who embraced that emotion.

She needed to have a discussion with Gabriel about how her perception of everything had changed. But that would have to wait. They needed to get the girls to safety. A moment of playing the hunter didn't erase the fact that they were now the hunted.

The lights blazed inside her bungalow. A strange vehicle sat out front with the motor running. Panic shifted from neutral into overdrive.

The moment Gabriel stopped in the driveway, Naomi was out the door, heedless of his call for her to wait. The front door was ajar. The first thing she saw was Charmaine's three girls sitting on her sofa. Janeece held Mel. Relief was short-lived as Rita emerged from the bedroom area. She carried a suitcase and dragged several heavy plastic trash bags behind her. She stopped to regard her roommate stoically.

"Where are you going?" was the only thing Naomi could think to say.

"Far away and as fast as possible. Marcus is taking some pretty damning stuff to the LVPD and the Feds. Unless I miss my guess, my welcome has worn out. I don't want to wait around to see who comes after me first, the cops or Cross."

Naomi didn't have to ask. Rita had let Marcus go the same way Zanlos had released her. Now they were both in danger.

"You could come with us."

Rita chuckled wryly at the offer, but her gaze softened. "Don't be silly. Cross could track you through me. I'm outta here…as soon as I meet Marcus to make a statement."

"We can protect you," Gabriel insisted with a quiet conviction. By *we* he didn't mean him and Naomi.

"Maybe. Maybe later." She regarded Gabriel for a long moment, then said, "Zanlos wants to meet with you. He said he has a parting gift for you."

"He's leaving?" Naomi couldn't help the slight note of uneasiness in her voice. She was still linked to him no matter how faded the connection. The thought of an unspecified distance alarmed some subconscious part of her.

"If he's smart. His whole gig is coming apart. He's about to become a liability to Cross."

"The girls…Candice, Marty, Molly, the others. We have to get them away from there." Naomi looked from Rita to Gabriel with a somber determination, ready to walk back into the jaws of the beast herself if necessary.

"Marcus is having them picked up. They'll be placed in safe houses until this thing is finished. And he knows how to keep them safe from even the unexpected. Even from themselves."

"How can it be finished?" Naomi asked. "How do you defeat something like Cross?"

"That's my job," Gabriel stated grimly.

"I've gotta go." Rita dropped the garbage bags filled with her belongings and impulsively embraced Naomi. "You take care of him and yourself. It's better I not hear what you've got planned." She leaned back and touched her fingertips to the goose egg above Naomi's ear. "Sorry about that. And about the things I said to you, Nomi. That wasn't really me talking."

Naomi covered her hand for a quick squeeze. "I know. You be careful, Rita."

"I'll be in touch...if I can shake this thing."

When Cross was dead. That's the only way she'd be free. Naomi understood that just as she realized she'd always be part of Zanlos, his to command should he try to call her. Knowledge of her lack of control unsettled her.

"Good-bye kids," Rita called to the girls. "Take good care of Mel for me." Sudden moisture welled up in her eyes as she turned away then nodded once to Gabriel. "Give Rae my best and tell her I'm sorry I wasn't more help. I guess I didn't settle my debt to her after all."

"I think you did." He smiled briefly and stepped aside so she could hurry out. Then to Naomi and the girls he said, "Grab whatever you need. You can't stay here."

Naomi balked. "I don't want to leave my things, my house."

"We'll be coming back to them. I promise. Take just what you need."

Less than fifteen minutes later, bags were tossed into Gabriel's big trunk. With the three girls and Mel seated solemnly in the back and Naomi at shotgun, Gabriel drove away from the life Naomi realized with some sadness that she'd never be returning to. A life she had barely lived and could only partially regret leaving behind. Her future was linked to the man behind the wheel, and wherever her would take her, she would gladly go.

***

They took the diagonal ride upward in the Luxor's elevator, following the slant of the outer pyramid. The girls might have been impressed, but they were too weary to express it. Gabriel held little Tonya in his arms. Hers looped trustingly over his shoulders. Janeece sagged against Naomi's side, an uncomplaining Mel crushed to her chest. Naomi wasn't sure how Gabriel had convinced the night clerk to let them bring the cat in at all, let alone without a carrier, but the big animal's kitty box and sand rode on the bellhop's cart. Roxanne remained aloof, her dark-eyed stare shifting between the two adults as if she was trying to puzzle something out.

Gabriel had paid for one of the $800 a night suites without blinking an eye. The girls mustered up enough energy to murmur over the angled wall of glass that overlooked the lights of the strip while Gabriel paid the bellman to unload their scant belongings and, more gingerly, the cat box. Roxanne herded her sisters into one of the bedrooms where they climbed up onto the big king size bed and instantly, with the innocence of the young, were asleep. Naomi got Mel situated in one of the spacious bathrooms, placed him in his clean sand so he'd be acclimated, and poured some food into a sparkling, crystal mint tray. After sniffing about with a haughty discrimination, Mel decided to accept the situation and trotted in to leap up onto the girls' bed. He gave Gabriel a wide birth but was no longer growling.

"This is lovely," Naomi exclaimed, trying hard to sound normal as she looked out over the dazzle of lights. Under other circumstances, she would have felt charmed.

"You're lovely," Gabriel corrected. "And brave and resourceful and compassionate."

She smiled faintly. "Stop."

"Naomi, you are all those things. You always have been. And that's why I—" He broke off awkwardly and pretended to develop an intense interest in the traffic passing far below them.

"Good night," Roxanne called, interrupting the tense interchange.

"Sleep well, honey," Naomi responded with all the warmth of a mother to her child. And those feelings surprised and delighted her.

Roxanne hesitated, looking uncomfortable.

"Was there something else, Roxanne?"

"The two of you need to talk. You've got shared centuries to untangle." With that curious pronouncement, she returned to the bedroom and shut the door, leaving a little crack so that Mel could find his way out if he needed to.

"Shared centuries," Naomi mused, then looked to Gabriel for an answer. For all the answers. "Pick one."

"I lived in the Thirteenth Century," he began without preamble. "I was a knight, a man of honor and duty and a determination never to tarnish either of those ideals. I was a man of pride. I wasn't aware of what a sin that could be until it cost me the only woman I ever loved.

"Her name was Naomi Beorhthilde. Her family lived in a neighboring shire. Her father was killed in the wars, and when a cruel relative tried to take the property by force, her mother sent her to us for assistance then took poison so she couldn't be forced into marriage. Naomi became a ward of my family and everyone loved her. I loved her. There was such kindness and light about her. Her name suited even though many frowned upon the Old Testament reference. Not a popular name choice for the times. It meant bright counselor, and soon everyone went to her with their troubles for her advice and wisdom. Her intelligent reserve and air of mystery mesmerized me from the first. I knew I would wed no other."

"And did she feel the same?" Naomi asked, wondering why it felt as though he was discussing the two of them rather than a woman who might have been some distant relative.

"I was called to protect our borders against the man who'd tried to steal your heritage. It was my duty, my pleasure. How could I not go? But Naomi, who had lost all who'd sworn to protect and cherish her, begged me to stay, to honor my vow of love to her."

"But you went anyway." Of course, he would. Knowing this Gabriel, she could imagine him no less compelled by honor centuries ago. *Centuries ago...*

She could see him perched upon his huge charger, fair hair surrounding his face like a halo, his armor gleaming in the sun, a piece of embroidery work stitched by his lady love tied about the hilt of his sword and the token that would seal their troth on a cord about his neck. *She could see him...*

"We took the day, but I fell in battle, gravely wounded. In the chaos and confusion, news of my death was prematurely taken back to the castle where Naomi awaited my return. In her despair at having sent me to my supposed death, she threw herself from the high window of the rooms we would have shared as lord and lady and was broken on the rocks below then swept out to sea. Her...body was never recovered. Her soul never found rest. And my pride was to blame. I had to be the one to avenge the wrong done to her family, even though it was her wish that I remain by her side. I never had the chance to tell her that none of the fault was hers."

"But that's what she died believing." Naomi experienced the other woman's sadness and guilt as if those things weighed upon her own heart.

"But I couldn't let her soul wander between heaven and earth never knowing that I forgave her, never having the opportunity to beg it from her as well. And when the means to seize that chance arose, I took it, never once considering the consequences of what I would become."

"You became a vampire. Why?"

"Because her soul still roamed, and I knew I could find it if I but had the time to search. I knew I would recognize her again, no matter what form she took, no matter what age she lived in. Our spirits would cry out to one another were we to meet again. Or at least, that was what I was led to believe. That was the fiction I followed as centuries passed."

"And you found her in me."

His smile was so sorrowful, it broke her heart. "I thought I did. I saw in you the same qualities I so admired in her. I wanted to believe that the sacrifice of my life and that of my best friend had come to this reward. But you weren't the woman I'd loved and lost, and for time, I was angry at you for not being her."

Naomi fell silent. Now she understood his tension and his purposeful distancing. How devastated he must have been to discover she had failed to live up to the legend of his tragic love. Then she truly heard his words.

"For a time? But not now?"

"How could I not love you, Naomi? Not for the woman I'd lost but for the woman you are. But how could I ask you to love what I am? What my pride and false purpose allowed me to become?"

"Don't ask."

She rose up to kiss away all the regrets, all the disillusionments, all the heartache they both had suffered. She sighed into his mouth as his hands captured her small waist to pull her nearer still. She went liquid with longing, melting down his sturdy frame until nothing separated them but a barrier of fabric and the distance it took to cross the room. Both were barriers easily breached.

They fell together on the big bed. By the end of the first bounce, he was inside her, claiming all that she was and bidding farewell to that she would never be. She would never be his fragile noble bride. She would never restore his innocent beliefs or return them to an ancient time. But she could and did renew his faith in goodness and in the strength of that purity. She completed him with her total surrender in a way the Naomi of his dreams could never have achieved. This was no ideal, no paragon, no subject for verse or jousts. This was a woman who could only be claimed by virtue of winning her heart. And by some lucky miracle, he'd managed that feat.

Now, to be worthy of it.

***

They lay entwined the way lovers did, with a complete abandonment of self and absorption of the other. With passion sated and answers given, Naomi found she had more questions.

"This being that you are now," she broached carefully. "Are you alive? Does your heart beat?"

"The life I live is not the same as the one I led or the one you live. I exist in darkness, but when I'm with you, my heart takes wings."

She couldn't restrain her pleased smile. "The ladies at court must have adored you."

"But I only saw you." He caught himself and glanced away, chagrined. "I meant her."

"It's all right, Gabriel. I'm not envious of the love you had for her as long as I have you now."

"For as long as you live," he promised.

"As I live. But you'll go beyond that, won't you?"

He put his forefinger to her pursed lips. "Don't speak of that now. There'll be plenty of time for us to come to terms with our...differences."

"You take blood to survive."

"Yes. But only enough to survive and never from the unwilling. That's what makes me different from Zanlos and Cross and others like them. That's why I've devoted my life to seeing that those who are evil don't thrive on the deaths of the unsuspecting. I bring them to justice, the justice of my kind for the crimes against mankind."

"And that's why you're here. To punish Zanlos. Because he abused the powers of what he is?"

"No. Because he took you from me. I couldn't forgive him that. I'll never forgive him for that."

She touched the side of her neck, feeling the slight scars that enslaved her to another man. "But if you take my blood, won't I belong to you and not him?"

He smiled wistfully. "The claim of the first is always the strongest, and it can only be broken by his death or..."

"By mine?"

"No. Not even death can free you."

"What could, Gabriel? There is a way, isn't there?"

"Not one I'm willing to discuss." He looked toward the ceiling, his jaw set in a stubborn denying angle. Naomi took his chin and turned him to face her and her question.

"What is that way?"

He was reluctant, but he didn't deny her an answer. "If you were to become like me, like us. Then you would be equally powerful and independent of all other claims."

"Like you," she repeated.

"But I won't allow it, Naomi." The firmness of his tone spoke of his determination. A man used to giving orders, he didn't expect to be disobeyed. Or questioned. But he softened his tone so she would understand. "You are light next to the darkness within me. I wouldn't condemn you to my existence. I love you too much to see you give part of your soul away."

But part of her soul was already missing.

Even as he made sweet love to her a second time, making her moan and sob in the throes of blissful release, a part of her was absent.

The part of her that was Naomi Beorhthilde.

The part of her that still sought justice.

Twenty-four

She slept soundly and without dreams. To awake to the glare of late afternoon and feel refreshed was so unusual she had to lie in bed for long moments just marveling at her splendid mood of contentment.

Of course, Gabriel was gone. Understanding the reason didn't lessen the desire for him to still be beside her. As her hand stroked over the pillow where he had laid his head, her fingertips encountered something wrapped in small leather pouch. Curiosity overcame her brief melancholy. What had he left for her?

She tugged open the sides of the pouch and upended it. Out fell a heavy piece of ornate silver in the shape of a T. Lifting it in her palm to study it more closely, she could see that it was a valuable antique. Or maybe it once had been when it was whole. It wasn't meant to be T-shaped. The top had been shorn off. What she held was half of a cross and the end of a phrase. *Binds Us.*

Naomi slipped into a baggy tee shirt that Gabriel had left behind. Though it might never hold his heat, his scent was warm upon it. Reaching for her purse on the empty dresser top, she unzipped one of its compartments. On a silken cord was the other half. She read its inscription and smiled when she put the two halves together.

Gabriel de Magnor had given her this token. Through a fuzzy remembering, she saw Gabriel McGraw handing Naomi Bright another, more modern crucifix. But this one, this one she'd always worn close to her heart until she went to work for Zanlos. He'd said he didn't like jewelry, so she'd put it away in safe keeping. Something about it, though its origin had been unknown, was precious enough for her to risk her life battling with a purse snatcher. And now she knew what it was.

It was a symbol of Gabriel's love.

Using a coated hair tie as a temporary fix, she joined the halves together and slipped the cord over her head. She would never take it off again.

The main room held the delicious smell of fresh brewed coffee. Roxanne sat on the couch stroking Mel as he groomed himself post-breakfast. When the girl saw Naomi, she looked uncertain then said, "Mama always liked a cup of coffee to get herself going. I thought you might, too."

An unfamiliar sentiment speared through Naomi's heart. "Thank you. That was very kind."

Roxanne continued to fidget and watch her until Naomi realized it was because the girl didn't know where she fit in now that her mother was gone.

"Roxanne, do you girls have any other relatives? Anyone who'd take you in?"

She shook her head, the wary caution increasing in her dark eyes.

"Well, you'll stay with me then, if that's all right with the three of you."

"You'd take us in?"

"Why not? I think we'd complete each others' lives quite nicely."

"Yours and Gabriel's?"

Sly girl. Naomi smiled. "That remains to be seen."

Roxanne tucked long, dancer's legs underneath her. "You didn't tell him that you are her, the woman he dreams of."

Naomi blushed. "I'm not, Roxanne. I couldn't be. That Naomi threw herself out a tower window in the thirteenth century."

Roxanne frowned and cocked her head as if searching for something that was obscured from sight. "Did she?"

"Yes." The cold sensation of falling, of the water closing over her head made her gasp slightly and turn away. Roxanne misunderstood her distress.

"Are you afraid of me? Of the things I see? Do you wish I'd just go away?"

The girl sounded so scared and insecure that all Naomi's concerns disappeared in a rush of maternal instinct. "Of course not. What gave you such a silly idea?"

"Mama's second husband. He used to look at me strange, and I could hear them whispering at night. He said the devil was moving in me."

Naomi came to sit beside her, wrapping her up in a snug embrace. "Nonsense. You're no more damned than—"

Than Namoi Beorhthilde?

"It wasn't suicide, was it, Roxanne?"

The girl glanced up, hopeful yet still uncertain. "I don't think so. I don't see an unhappy soul. I see an angry one."

Angry.

"What does she want me to do?"

"She wants you to set them free with the truth."

"She and Gabriel?"

"You and Gabriel."

And there was only one place she could do that.

***

The Amazon felt like a tomb. All the bustle and energy of a grand hotel and casino were gone, abandoned like the workers and hired help over the course of the past twenty-four hours. Marcus filled him in during a brief phone conference. Cross was gone. With the evidence Rita had supplied, he could never surface in Las Vegas again. Only his criminal activities were known to the police. The contracted hits. The murder of Kitty Parsons and Charmaine Johnson, both of whose remains had been found when a hole had been knocked through the temple by demolition experts. A trace was being done on the monies brought in illegally in the form of ancient Peruvian gold. All accounts had been seized, and the opening of the Amazon was in limbo.

Gabriel rode up in the elevator. The top floor was dark, and Zanlos' office door stood open, illuminated faintly by the Strip's lights below.

"You came. I wasn't sure you would."

Zanlos stood unconcerned with his back to his guest while he stared out into the night.

"Why did you ask me here? I'd think you'd be running for your life."

"Oh, I am, dear boy, running that is. I have little faith in human nature and even less in the integrity of our kind. I put away a small fund for a rainy day, and I plan to live quite comfortably and quietly on some tropical island. That is, if your people will let me go."

"I see. You did me a favor by releasing Naomi. And now, I'm supposed to turn my back and let you slip away."

Zanlos revolved to face him. "No, no quite. What I did for Naomi has nothing to do with anything but Naomi. She is a good, decent girl, and she deserves better than what Cross had planned for her."

"What is she to Cross?"

"I guess to understand that, you'd have to know Cross's secret."

"And why would you tell me that?"

"Because if something isn't done about Cross, I'll be looking over my shoulder for the rest of my days…or rather, nights. You will do something about him, won't you?"

"Count on it."

                              ***

Pennants waved against an inky sky. In the darkness, the towers of Excaliber glowed. A fairytale kingdom.

As Naomi crossed the drawbridge, she didn't try to block out the sensations rushing over her. Instead, she allowed them in so she might better understand the woman whose soul called to her from a watery grave.

The answer was here. It had always been here. She just had to recognize it.

After crossing through the casino, she took the elevator down. The music bubbled up to meet her. She knew the tune. It had been playing the first time…the first time she had danced with Gabriel. A smile curved her lips as she listened and began to remember.

De Magnor. The fighter. Yes, a warrior, a hunter, a conqueror. With the tousled blond mane inherited somewhere down his lineage from ravagers from the North, the fierce dark stare of his mother's prideful Anglo-Saxon stock and the unaffected arrogance from the royal houses of France, he was the best with a sword, the most fearless on horse, and more at home in a sea of mud and blood than in the velvets and hose demanded at court. So handsome yet unaware of his charm, so shy with the ladies who flocked for his favor. Then their gazes had met as this tune played, and all the confusion of the world around them fell away.

Because of the violence of her past, she'd been drawn to his strength and enchanted by his awkward innocence. From him, she had no flowery verses meant to lure her into dropping her reserve and her resolve. He spoke passionately...about battle, about honor, about the home he would hold and protect and the woman he would cherish. And his gaze slid to her when he said that last, and she knew she was destined to be that woman. And all the stars were right in heaven again. She'd found a man who would value her for what she could offer, not from a pedestal or for political purpose. She would keep his house in order while he was at war, tending his people like they were her family, and when he returned, when he returned, she would greet him as lover and partner not merely as wife.

That was how it was supposed to have been.

What had happened? What had knocked that treasured destiny askew and sent her to the grave and him into an eternal hell?

What...or who?

The first show wouldn't start for an hour. Several of Excaliber's knights took advantage of the empty arena to practice sword play. One, the Green Knight, guided his big horse through a series of figure eights. She came down the steps of the vacant gallery to pause at the rail. Her gaze followed the mounted knight as a sense of déjà vu crept up on a cold mist of apprehension. The same sense of the familiar clung to him, just as it did to Gabriel.

He saw her then and directed his horse to the side of the arena. With his visor down, she could only see his eyes, eyes that seemed to alter in color and shape even as she watched. Then he reached up to lift his helm, and she gasped to see Alex Cross seated in the saddle in regal battle attire.

Wrong. It was all wrong.

"Ah, Miss Bright. Come to enjoy a good show and cheer me on? I do hope you've brought your troublesome friend with you. There's much I need to settle before circumstances force me to flee."

"Who are you?"

"Why I am Legion, for I am many. But there's only one you should recognize. Or are there more, my dear?"

She continued to stare at him, into the features she knew from the Amazon, past them to what lay beneath. To the man behind the mask.

Step-clunk-step-clunk-step-clunk.

Yes, she knew him. But not as entrepreneur Alex Cross, vampire murderer. He was more. But what? What? The truth was there, just out of reach. If she stretched, if she reached out to the very limit, she could just brush it with her fingertips. The truth behind the mask.

She knew. Some part of her knew.

Her breathing increased in tempo. A rigid tension seeped up her limbs, as if she'd been plunged into ice water. Or an icy sea.

"I know you."

"Do you? Tell me."

"I know what you are."

"Excellent. No more surprises except perhaps one."

It wasn't a surprise to her after all. Somehow she'd known. She'd seen the dangerous undertow beneath the invitingly serene surface. She hadn't recognized him until it was too late, but now, she saw the madness and the nightmare.

And then she saw behind the mask.

She screamed as he reached for her.

Twenty-five

"Gabriel de Magnor, come on down."

Gabriel descended the steps to the rail of the arena where Rollie stood practicing his sword thrusts. Gabriel watched his friend for a long moment, heart shredded by the knowledge he carried. When at last he could bear the pain no more, he cried out, "Why?"

"You still don't know? I could never beat you, Gabriel, and I could never be you."

"Why would you want to?"

Rolland, the plain and the poetic, stared at his friend and stated with bland simplicity, "Because my father loved you. And she loved you."

As Gabriel continued to look at him through tragic eyes, Rollie spun away, his movement with the sword growing more vicious.

"You had everything, Gabriel. You were everything I wasn't. Handsome, brave, strong, all the things my father wanted me to be, but I was ever the disappointment. He wanted a hero and he got a poet. I was smart and sensitive and skilled in diplomacy, but he didn't admire those qualities. He wanted a brutal thug for a son, someone with a sword arm and a mindless love of violence. He loathed me, did you know that, Gabriel? He'd often say, 'Why can't you be more like your friend Gabriel?'"

"I'm sorry."

Rolland turned on him with an angry, "You will be. But not yet. That comes later." He went back to twirling his blade through the exercises they'd learned as boys. "My father believed the measure of a man was in the length of his sword, if you get my meaning. Because I hadn't ravished half the shire by the time I was thirteen, he called my manhood into question. He didn't understand. I didn't want just any peasant slut, any warm body ready and/or unwilling to be bedded. I wanted perfection in a woman. And I saw it when she came. But she saw only you.

"What did you know of romance or courtship? You were a

strutting brute fresh from the battlefield. And the minute she saw you, she forgot all that we had in common, all that we'd shared in your absence. I was her friend; you were her dream come true. I hated you as a man as much as I loved you as a brother."

"I didn't know," Gabriel repeated lamely.

"Of course you didn't. You were too stupid, too caught up in your own pride and purpose." His tone grew darker. "When I saw you fall in battle, I was hiding behind the bodies of the dead. I was only there because my father insisted that I accompany you in your folly. I saw you fall, and I saw my chance to have everything that was denied me."

And he told how he raced back with news of Gabriel's death, raced back to break the news to Naomi, to comfort her in her despair, to quickly offer his support and his protection, his love.

"But do you know what she said to me after I laid my soul at her feet? 'Where is his body? How could you have been so cowardly as to have left him behind?'"

Coward. Her words echoed.

He hadn't checked. He'd been too afraid to approach the fray, too eager to leap at the chance to lay claim to what Gabriel had left behind.

Coward. Her accusation burned.

He hadn't meant to hit her, but suddenly he'd seen red then black in his frustration. He hadn't planned to drag her to her bed to brutally vent his lust and anger upon her fragile virgin's frame. But when it was over and her sobs finally quieted, he knew she could never shake his claim. He would wed her as soon as it could be arranged, Gabriel's memory be damned. And she would accept him and learn to love him. Gabriel would be forgotten.

But when he'd awakened while darkness still shrouded the room, he saw she was up and about and already dressed. When he demanded to know where she thought she was going, she tore out his heart with her reply. To find Gabriel. To search for his body on the field of battle because she couldn't believe he was gone.

"I tried to talk to her, to tell her how it was. I'd bedded her.

She belonged to me. Her beloved was lost to her, whether she liked it or not, whether he lived or not. Do you know what she said?"

Gabriel shook his head, too numb in heart and mind to imagine.

"She told me she'd rather be dead alongside you."

Gabriel squeezed his eyes shut, his thoughts too active now as he pictured her leaping to her death, not out of grief but in desperation.

Because he had valued honor more than her love.

"Because of you," Rolland continued bitterly, "I lost the only woman I could have loved. And then you killed me with your foolishness. You changed my destiny, Gabriel, so I made you the focus of my future. I wanted you to know the horror I felt when she went out that window. It was so easy to poison your soul with guilt. You never suspected my part in her demise. You saw me only as your devoted friend. You believed everything I told you once you were carried back with your shield instead of on it. Killing you then would have been too easy, too merciful. You were so fragile, so dramatic in your grief. What did you know of grief, you who'd had everything? She was everything to me, Gabriel. The only thing. I decided in that cold, black room you dragged us to where we awoke to face our new existance, that I would devote the centuries I would now have to making you pay for my pain. You will know that horror. I couldn't save her, couldn't keep her then, but now I can hold her forever. Now, she will never leave my side. I've beaten you at last."

Icy terror gripped his chest.

"Where is she, Rollie?"

He gestured to the end of the arena where the king's and queen's thrones would hold pseudo-royalty during the show. A figure slumped in the queen's chair. With a flash of preternatural speed, Gabriel was beside her, despair taking him to his knees.

Her head was at an odd angle. Her throat had been ripped open, and her crumpled medieval costume was black with blood. Gabriel's hand shook as he reached beneath the spill of her hair in search of a pulse.

"What do you say, Sir Gabriel? Would you give up your honor now to save her? Would you walk away and let me go free to have her? Turn your back on your notions of justice just to have her die in your arms?"

His words croaked from a throat closed tight with awful sorrow. "Yes. I will."

"You'd turn down the adoration and acclaim that comes with being a hero, a defender of justice? I don't believe you."

"For her."

"Even though she's not the woman you pledged to love for an eternity?"

"Even so."

Amazingly, Naomi's eyes flickered open. The slight movement was a struggle, and speech even more demanding upon what little life remained. He leaned close to hear her whispered words.

"He pushed me, Gabriel. When I said I'd rather have your memory than his shallow devotion, he pushed me out the window. I didn't jump. I wouldn't have damned my soul by suicide at the risk of not spending the hereafter with you. That was my mother's way, not mine. I love you, Gabriel, then as now. Don't let him escape his fate. I would see justice done."

Her eyes slipped shut even as he called out her name.

"Would you hear the rest of the story now, Gabriel?" Rollie taunted from the arena. "Would you like to know why you will not win?"

Slowly, he rose to his feet and turned to confront his tormentor. "Tell me with your last breath."

The cold fury in his friend's glare set Rolland back, but the hesitation was brief.

"While you were chasing about the globe trying to reunite with your lost love, I was busy getting stronger. Instead of making war and dreaming of days past, I was seeking out sources of power to one day defeat you. You bastard. In your arrogance, you killed me. You made me this beast that I am."

"No." Gabriel shook his head. "What you are is not my doing. You've been shaped by hate and madness and jealousy. I no longer see the man I once called friend."

"Oh he's here inside somewhere, the poet, the gentle dreamer. But that man was never good enough, never brave enough to best you. I had to become more.

"While you honed your skills at killing and doing the right things, I continued to learn, to search, to gather knowledge. Knowledge is power, friend, not brute strength. And then in the early 1600s, when I was pursuing that thirst for enrichment by following the Catholic campaign to stamp out native religion in South America, I came across a legend, the story of one of our kind, an ancient creature trapped in the jungles, worshipped by ignorant savages. The priests, of course, in their narrow-minded piety, were horrified, but I was fascinated. I thought if I set it free, perhaps in its gratitude, it would share its wisdom with me."

"And what did you learn from this beast?"

He chuckled, a low nasty sound. "It had nothing to say. It sucked up my soul and ripped my body to pieces. But it was a revelation in disguise. This creature, this Fanged Diety, had been fed on weak, human natives. When it drank my vampiric blood, it evolved. It became a thinking, higher being capable of so much more, and I became with it. But just like that beast, whom I now inhabited, I was a prisoner within that tomb. The essence of my soul had no body to return to. The creature was bound by some ancient magic to the stones of that tomb, and I was held there with it. But the power, we shared the same power in that prison until another luckless soul stumbled in to set us free."

"Cross."

"That's one name he might have used. Quinton Alexander is who he was as a man. A scheming lunatic, a serial killer with a shrewd mind and a talent for survival. We shared what we were with him, not that he appreciated it. We used his knowledge of this century. Here's where the story gets interesting. Knowledge is power, but money means control."

He'd used his resources well. He had tons of ancient gold, but no way to bring it into the country. Until he met a fellow entrepreneur named Zanlos who just happened to have the things he desired most: Naomi Bright and a way to move his stone prison out of the jungle. He needed another schemer and he needed his revenge. He found both in one.

"I found her for you, Gabriel. Through Alexander, I found her and used Zanlos' greed to bring her here, to set a trap you could not resist. In the same body, I used Alexander's face to build my temple here in Las Vegas and this one you remembered so well to play upon your foolish sympathies. No one, not even Zanlos, knew we were one in the same. Now you know, so you might as well know everything. How I planned, how I manipulated, how I longed for the moment when my revenge would know fruition." He smiled dreamily as his gaze fell on the motionless figure slumped upon her mock throne.

"It was so difficult seeing her every day and not taking her then. But that pain was part of this ultimate pleasure. She didn't know who she was. I didn't believe it myself until my little thrall Rita made me privy to her nightmares. Imagine my shock to find out you'd been right all along. Her spirit had survived the centuries. But I couldn't have her ruining my surprise too soon. She was my means to finally acquit myself. She had rejected me and for that, she will suffer. I let you believe you were the cause of her death, and how your torment delighted me. And now you will die while she watches, and I will have her. For an eternity, I will have her. I'll be the better man."

"You will get what you deserve."

They were distracted for a brief moment as two of the Excaliber's pseudo-knights entered the arena thinking to get in a little pre-show practice.

With a fierce mental push, Gabriel knocked Rollie off his feet. While he rolled back and forth, his armor making him a turtle in a shell, Gabriel vaulted down into the arena floor to snatch the sword from one of the mock combatants. When the 'knight' began to protest, Gabriel looked at them, his eyes blazing red and horrible, and growled, "Go!"

Stumbling back in shock and terror, the two men fled.

Rollie got the momentum to flip over and scrambled to his feet. He pushed back the visor that had fallen over his face, and what it revealed was a seething mass of changing images. Rolland then Cross then the beast from the tomb in Peru and on to whatever souls it had devoured over the centuries. All a part of the creature Gabriel confronted with sword in hand.

"You will not become what I am," it snarled, fangs exposed and dripping. "I will not share what I am with you. What you are ends here and now. I will crush your bones and scatter the ashes."

"Only if Rolland defeats me. And that's never happened. Never. Come on, Rollie. Don't be a coward hiding behind your new friends. Face me, man-to-man. Or was your father right all along?"

Roaring with centuries of rage and frustration, what had once been Rolland Tearlach charged him. Gabriel managed to throw up his blade in time to avert the shattering blow as it descended. He went down to one knee under the force but used his other leg to sweep Rollie's footing out from under him. Trapped on the arena floor a second time, Rollie struggled with the straps and buckles to his breastplate, flinging the protective gear aside, along with his gleaming helmet. Then he was up and looking for first blood.

They circled and feinted, searching for weaknesses. Those failings were well known to each other. Rolland's was fear and hesitation, Gabriel's the rashness of pride.

Now Rolland would try to goad him into a reckless move so he could defeat him with his own vanity. Gabriel drew upon his mental training to flush away the passions of the young man he'd once been. He wasn't Gabriel the Fighter who sought out battles to avoid the dreaded complaisance of peace. He wouldn't think about the sense of betrayal and bitter regret Rolland's actions stirred. He wouldn't fixate on the fact that even now Naomi's life was ebbing away a second time because he hadn't protected her properly. Or of the orphaned girls in a suite at the Luxor. The fight he fought was no longer personal. It was a matter of justice. Justice was cold and indifferent to emotion. It couldn't be swayed by past friendships and present losses. It went beyond him and what he wanted or needed. It wasn't about settling scores or righting past wrongs. And that justice would be served.

He advanced steadily, sword singing through the air, sparks sizzling off Rolland's blade as he parried each swing. This wasn't the Rollie he'd sparred with in his youth. He was stronger, more cunning, more aggressive in his attitude. And he wasn't going down easily.

With a sudden lunge to the left followed by a quick spear of his sword, Rolland managed to lure Gabriel just far enough off balance to slip in a piercing jab. Pain scalded through Gabriel's shoulder, forcing him to scuffle backwards in momentary retreat. Lifting his sword instigated agonies, making him clench his teeth and struggle against the spreading flames numbing his arm. Blocking the next hacking blow sent shattering waves of misery through him.

"You're finished, Gabriel," Rolland gloated as he observed his wounded friend through dispassionate eyes. "In your final moments, I want you to think about Naomi and me together, about the things I plan to have her do for me, to me. Or perhaps I'll just let her die and return as a drooling, decaying corpse who'll howl at the moon in mindless hunger. Then I will have the satisfaction I've craved since your shadow spread over me."

Panting to control the pain, Gabriel saw not the companion of his youth—the poetic, pensive Rolland Tearlach who shared his joys and sorrows. He saw instead a man warped by inferiority and rage, shaped by circumstances beyond him and groomed by the madness of the spirit now merged with his own. He wasn't the Rollie who had written him steamy sonnets to pass to the Lady Erlina, who was years older and wiser and the first to teach him the ways of love. This wasn't the friend who'd sat with him while he mourned the death of his two younger sisters from a fever caught in a sudden rainstorm. This wasn't the companion who'd listened to his longings and his grumblings and his fears with a compassionate ear and a comforting heart. This was a monster who needed to be stopped before he inflicted more horror upon the world. And more unforgivable retribution upon the woman he loved.

He would be stopped.

"I am not to blame for your failings," Gabriel told him. "If you fell short in the comparison, it was because of the measuring not the man. I was never the better man, and it was our differences that made me love you so as my friend. I begged for your forgiveness once, and I do so again. Forgive me, Rolland."

And he swung with both hands firm on the hilt, swinging through with unerring accuracy just above Rolland's shoulder line. Momentum had him spinning about on wobbly legs, spiraling down to one knee. And from that submissive position, Gabriel looked up into the eyes of the man who had been like his brother. And there, he saw for a fleeting second the forgiveness that would allow him peace.

Rolland's head rolled back, dropping to the arena floor, followed a second later by his crumpled body. A sudden blue silver flame engulfed the figure, burning fierce and hot until nothing remained but ash upon the sand.

Gabriel closed his eyes, his mouth moving in a remembered prayer, his injured arm screaming in protest as he made the sign of the cross over his chest. He walked away from the remains of his past, from the tools of his profession, hurrying now back to the future he coveted with the woman he loved.

She was dying.

He could see it in the translucent pallor of her skin, in the waxen color of her lips, in the faint bluing of her eyelids. But her life was not yet gone.

He gathered her into his arms, turning to sit on one of the steps with her frightfully light and limp body in his lap.

"Naomi," he called urgently, hoping to reach her. "Your soul is now free. Justice has been done for you. You can go to your rest and be at peace." His voice shook. Tears streamed down his face, unnoticed.

And then her eyes flickered open. Such love, such contentment in that tender gaze. His throat closed up tight around a sob. God, how could he let her go?

But hadn't her soul been punished for long enough? Didn't she deserve this chance to sleep undisturbed?

One frail hand lifted, touching his damp cheek then lowering to the bodice of her gown. There was a cord about her neck. She gathered it in the twist of her fingers until the cross hanging from it was revealed.

"Remember what it says," was her faint and failing whisper.

He didn't. He bent to read the ancient inscription.

Eternity binds us.

"I love you. Bind me, Gabriel, so eternity will be ours."

Understanding took hold of him in a sudden jolt to the heart.

Eternity.

Gently, so gently, he lifted her hand, fitting its palm to his face then turning his head so his lips could caress the blue veins at her wrist. Such a slow, fading beat. She gasped softly at his bite, then the breath left her in a wondrous sigh.

Too late? Was he too late?

Her vitality came zinging through him, hot, bold, as passionate as she'd been in his bed. So little left. Would it be enough?

While she lolled back against the bolster of his arm, he tore a gash in his other wrist and pressed it to her still lips.

"Drink, my love, and eternity will be ours."

She lay motionless, lifeless.

"Naomi! Don't let fate cheat us from this chance."

Her mouth stirred slightly. He felt her fragile swallow, and then her hands came up to grip his forearm, holding him with surprising and increasing strength while she fed from the wellspring of rebirth that he offered. And when he was faint and close to losing consciousness, he broke the connection and held her tightly in his arms as she awoke to a new existence, to a second chance to grasp the destiny they deserved.

And when her jewel-like eyes opened upon her new world, her gaze shone with an unchanged love for him. She made one simple claim that made all the pain and sacrifice worthwhile.

"Eternity is ours."

***

The big car idled at the junction of the highway, its blinker pointing east.

"You and the girls can stay with Rae," Gabriel was saying as he waited for traffic to clear along the long dark ribbon of roadway. "She had a son last night. For some reason, she came up with the name Rolland." He was silent until the huge wad of emotion could be swallowed down. "The girls will love spoiling the baby, and Rae will enjoy having you spoil her."

Naomi considered this. She remembered Rae and that she'd

liked her very much. She remembered everything, even the bad things that had happened to Naomi Beorhthilde and to Naomi Bright, but she embraced them all, for it was better than having nothing. Even now she wasn't sure how their souls had mingled, how the damage done to Lady Naomi by Rolland Tearlach's savage possession had scarred her own psyche and reproductive system. Roxanne tried to explain it away with talk of astral bodies and such, but the reason and the result didn't matter so much any more. Not now that they were a family. Accepting a pain-filled past spanning two lifetimes was better than not knowing. And knowing all made her love Gabriel all the more.

"And you'll go to California."

Naomi tried not to let her reluctance weight her words. It was going to be hard enough to let him go so he could do his job. But she would. And she would be waiting for his return.

"We're almost to California now," Roxanne piped up from the back seat. "It seems stupid to go all the way to D.C. when we're right here."

"It's dangerous where I'm going," Gabriel reminded sternly, but his gaze was soft with affection when he gazed at the girls and their lazy pet in the rearview mirror.

"And it wasn't where we've been? Naomi, you talk to him. I don't want to go to D.C. until we can all go together."

Naomi silently agreed. She didn't want to be left behind, either. "We might be able to help, you know."

Gabriel turned to her, ready to argue how ridiculous that was. But then he took in the firm set of her lips, lips he'd tasted and been taunted by long into the night the night before. Her gaze was steady and filled with cool logic.

"The sooner you finish what you have to do in California, the sooner we can set up house on the other coast."

How could he disagree with that?

"I must be crazy thinking I could ever win an argument against four women."

"And we're crazy about you," Janeece stated for all of them.

He grinned, a wide flash of white teeth in the car's dim interior. Hell. The hotel rooms were closer heading to California anyway. Did it matter which way they went as long as they went that way together? He flicked the blinker to the opposite direction.

The big car made a left turn toward their future.

ABOUT THE AUTHOR

With 43 sales to her credit since her first publication in 1987, Nancy Gideon's writing career is as versatile as the romance genre, itself.

Under Nancy Gideon, her own name, this Southwestern Michigan author is a Top Ten Waldenbooks' best seller for Silhouette, has written an award-winning vampire romance series for Pinnacle earning a "Best Historical Fantasy" nomination from Romantic Times, and will have her first two original horror screen plays made into motion pictures in a collaboration with local independent film company, Katharsys Pictures.

Writing western historical romance for Zebra as Dana Ransom, she received a "Career Achievement award for Historical Adventure" and is a K.I.S.S. Hero Award winner. Best known for her family saga series; the Prescott family set in the Dakotas and the Bass family in Texas, her books have been published overseas in Romanian, Italian, Russian, Portuguese, Danish, Dutch, German, Icelandic and Chinese.

As Rosalyn West for Avon Books, her novels have been nominated for "Best North American Historical Romance" and "Best Historical Book in a Series. Her "Men of Pride County" series earned an Ingram Paperback Buyer's Choice Selection, a Barnes & Noble Top Romance Pick and won a HOLT Medallion.

Gideon attributes her love of history, a gift for storytelling, and a background in journalism for keeping her focused in the discipline of writing since her youngest was in diapers. She begins her day at 5 a.m. while the rest of the family is still sleeping. While the pace is often hectic, Gideon enjoys working on diverse projects—probably because she's a Gemini. One month, it's researching the gritty existence of 1880s Texas Rangers only to jump to 1990s themes of intrigue and child abuse. Then it's back to the shadowy netherworlds of vampires and movie serial killers. In between, she's the award-winning newsletter editor and former vice president of the Mid-Michigan chapter of Romance Writers of America and is widely published in industry trade magazines.

A mother of two teenage sons, she recently discovered the Internet and has her own web pages at: http://www.tlt.com/authors/ngideon.htm and http://www.theromanceclub.com/nancygideon.htm.

She spends her 'spare time' taking care of a menagerie consisting of an ugly dog, a lazy cat, a tankful of pampered fish and three African clawed frogs (adopted after a Scouting badge!), plotting under the stars in her hot tub, cheering on her guys' hobbies of radio control airplanes and trucks, bowling and Explorer Scouting or indulging in her favorite vice—afternoon movies.